ISOLATED MATTERS

ISOLATED MATTERS

John Ruggiero

Copyright © 2014 by John Ruggiero.

Library of Congress Control Number: 2013923637
ISBN: Hardcover   978-1-4931-5899-7
           Softcover   978-1-4931-5898-0
           eBook   978-1-4931-5900-0

All rights reserved. No part of this book may be reproduced or transmitted in any form or by any means, electronic or mechanical, including photocopying, recording, or by any information storage and retrieval system, without permission in writing from the copyright owner.

This is a work of fiction. Names, characters, places and incidents either are the product of the author's imagination or are used fictitiously, and any resemblance to any actual persons, living or dead, events, or locales is entirely coincidental.

This book was printed in the United States of America.

Rev. date: 01/23/2014

To order additional copies of this book, contact:
Xlibris LLC
1-888-795-4274
www.Xlibris.com
Orders@Xlibris.com
144645

INTRODUCTION

There were times, insular, confused and anticipating triviality when she wished she were dead. Yet at that very moment, more than any other, caged within the confines of her bedroom closet, MJ Matters genuinely bemoaned having those prior cravings. She now knew the probability of her downfall was no longer a pipedream but absolutely certain, and her first thought was the pain she would likely endure at the hands of the woman who trapped her from the other side of the closet door. MJ's second thought focused on Bernard. Grief thundered inside her as she imagined the shock her husband would have when finding her lifeless, tortured body later that evening. There would be no mistaking it, or any command that would reverse his horrible find. She would be dead.

More than anything else, MJ was now enraged. She already experienced terror, which was in fact the fuel that forced her to find ephemeral protection hidden within the fetid surroundings of that closet. She was lucky enough to have locked herself inside before that evil thing tortured her one last time. MJ also already experienced a profound gloom after imagining her demise. Now though, no matter how much she didn't want to be, she was angry—angry that Bernard and Alby hadn't believed her about the haunting. She felt more alone than she had before, left to defend herself against the cackling specter pounding on the door, determined to capture and harm her.

Hideous sounds continued to ricochet around her. MJ screamed to outdo them as much as she could, but the tempestuous demand for her to "come out", followed by "you're dead" would not be drowned. The atmosphere bled a pure malevolence, and MJ knew she had failed herself in every attempt to ensure her welfare. There was no longer anything she could do. MJ was isolated.

PART ONE

MJ Matters

"I think it's dangerous to be optimistic. Things could go terribly wrong virtually overnight."—*Nicholas D Kristof*

MJ'S ACCOUNT:

University of California-San Francisco Medical Center, *After*

To those who read or hear this account, it should be noted that my physician, Dr. Armstrong, is the one who wanted you to read it, not me. He says that, "*beyond the corporeal pain I regularly endure, the persisting emotional stain I now have because of this disease is enough to have traumatized me for life.*" In short, I think he believes me recording this account will help me cope with that *stain*. While I still would prefer to first focus on stopping my physical discomfort, I begrudgingly agreed to start logging this story.

Additionally, you should note that it took me a long time to realize *the fortune bestowed upon me*. Dr. Armstrong helped me realize that too (*fortune bestowed*—that's his phrase actually, not mine). A staunchly committed husband? Yes, I had that fortune. A dedicated routine? I guess I had that too—if you could call being nearly paralyzed in bed all day, every day, *routine*. An unexpected and horrifying haunting from some deranged female specter? So it seemed, but that will be discussed in due time. Regardless of it all, Dr. Armstrong's point—I was fortunate because before this shocking experience, as terrifying as it was and as implausible as it may be perceived, I was wasting away. I had no reason for living. I was a lump of unused clay in an isolated city. But when the fog surrounding me finally settled, Dr. Armstrong helped me realize that it was the character of my city itself that just may have saved my life.

I wasn't naturally born in Pacifica, California. For those who do not know it, the city is beautiful and remote. It is barely a few miles from some major cities, San Francisco to the north, San Jose and Santa Cruz to the south, and kind of near Silicon Valley. With so much surrounding this coastal town, you would think it is bustling with incredible traffic. You would be completely wrong. In its pure shoreline beauty, houses in the hills, and lush, adoringly dense vegetation, Pacifica is a retreat of sorts from everything that surrounds it. A serene town, isolated, and surrounded by more than bustle, it is caged by its beauty—the ocean to the west, the mountains to the east, and blanketed by a thick layer of mist that comes and goes as it pleases.

The town seems to have two moods, both pleasant, at least in the eye of the beholder. One mood, a sunny disposition that shines through a good portion of the year, this is when Pacifica presents itself as an amazing beach town. The rays are enough to warm the coldest of surfers, and their reflection on the always crystal blue-green water surrounds the city in diamond-like moments of clarity and perfection. The other mood, the prior's foggy companion, seems to enter as she pleases as if telling the sun, "enough already, my turn now." When the fog takes over, Pacifica greys, but the people do not. For those of you who are not accustomed to the Pacific coast of the Bay Area, fog may seem odd. And it is. That is what is so beautiful about it. It is calming, yet authoritative. You may not always want the fog around, but Madam Fog always commands presence and a beauty of her own. And it is for this reason alone that every year the town celebrates Fog Fest, an annual event that rejoices in the magnitude of her beauty and importance, as much as the town celebrates the warm days sunbathing. You know, it's funny. I once heard a quote by Patrick O'Neill, from whom I heard it, I cannot remember. *Fog is a mystery, not a problem to be solved.*

I live close to the coast by Mori Point, an area of wildlife, cliffs, and seaside, protected by the government, filled with natural habitat and yes, predators, who are more concerned with being left alone than finding prey. I often dream of it and try to remember what it was like when, before being paralyzed, I used to wander, as free as the seaside birds, and exist by the powers of something as simple as my own strength. Sometimes when I think this way, I am grateful for the memories. Other times, my mood changes as quickly as Pacifica's, and I remember how pure was the fear I felt when Bernard wasn't home, and I knew I would soon see the specter again. And I trembled from what she was planning to do to me each day.

A few days before . . .

CHAPTER ONE

Seagulls are rather demure creatures, she thought while reminiscing about the ones she saw in her recent dream. MJ Matters envisioned the unmistakably large white, black-wing-tipped birds, gracefully colonized in front of her walking path, inquisitive and surely coherent of her presence. To her, the gulls in her dream were highly developed and social birds that announced themselves in a way that was commanding, yet strangely beautiful. She had noticed that the birds seemed to be nestled together rather compactly, almost laying claim to their territory, and each were quite attentive in caring for their three or four young. Within her dream, as MJ continued to saunter past them, she had easily noticed that these gulls had a highly developed communal configuration.

How peaceful they seem, she thought. *How proud and satisfied they are to claim this property as their own.* Yet, within the same tranquility that MJ detected, she also sensed their seriousness, and therefore appreciated that if pushed, this society of gulls would be ready to defend one another. She couldn't help but feel a connection with this. Although the later events of her dream proved themselves to eventually be horrifying, causing her to defend herself as she imagined the gulls would do for each other, the presence of the peaceful yet authoritative gulls centered her and made her feel aided. She was thankful that they seemed to have been watching over her, ready to protect her if necessary; and this thought comforted her enough to have the strength to face another realistic day.

"I am relieved you are here, Alby." MJ, barely able to turn her body toward her visitor motioned toward her chest as if, albeit momentarily, she fought to grasp even the slightest bit of air to breathe. Bernard, her near-to-perfect but unfortunately absent husband, was still out laboring over his research for her cure. His office, approximately twenty miles from their home, was becoming his new place to escape the realities of their marriage. MJ was now bedbound, incapacitated, or as MJ liked to consider it, a burden. Either way described, her condition was simply dissuading him from living to his full potential. And slowly, but unquestionably, she realized it.

"My day yesterday was quite . . . interesting," she claimed, stroking the sides of her mouth with her tongue. "But it's last night that I want to talk about right now."

Her body, slumped and numb, could shift only marginally, and her visitor—a friend and brother-in-law, Alby—appreciated the amount of exertion it took for her to adjust herself into a relaxed position. As such, Alby took the initiative to grasp the straw-fit plastic mug of flat Ginger Ale. Gently, he moved it toward her face, with one hand steadying her head toward the straw, and the other hand firmly surrounding the mug. After a minute, MJ seemed to immediately be hydrated, and her strength slightly improved.

"Last night I dreamt I was drowning directly off Mori Point. And the gulls that once were peaceful to watch laid there staring at me suffer," MJ continued.

MJ knew that Alby was purposely staying silent, observing her as she closed her eyes, reliving the dream as if she was just recently rescued. He seemed to continue to visibly notice the pain she was feeling, and she knew he continued to have sympathy for her. Yet, MJ was comforted by the thought that he dare not reveal it out of gentle concern for her feelings. She rationed in her mind that for him to do so would be counterproductive, and he was there to provide her support, not feed into her self-deprecation.

The truth of the matter was that MJ, though very close to it, was not fully paralyzed. She remembered that, at one point over the course of the year, she could indeed walk when she forced herself to do so. But it was much easier on the stress of her muscles for her to remain bedridden. And while, within the past year, only three times had she encouraged herself to rise from bed, most of the time, she did everything in her room—eat, sponge bathe, read, relieve herself, sleep—all because of the help of Bernard. She did not like living like this, but she understood she was unfairly stricken ill. And she knew, despite all of the poor fortune that hit her, she was the luckiest woman alive to have a husband like Bernard. Not every man would serve her food, dispose of her waste, bathe her, and love her—a woman in this condition. Among these thoughts, was the wish she was telling this dream of drowning off Mori Point to Bernard, not Alby. However, MJ was also a compassionate and realistic woman. She knew Bernard needed to focus on his work as well.

"It has been at least a year since I was at Mori Point, and yet I still remember everything about it—the way the Pacific smells right by the coastal line, fresh, just where it meets the protected area—do you know that smell, Alby?"

"I do."

"And the wild flowers that grow, just beyond the warning signs," MJ continued, "the ones that alert wayward hikers to beware the mountain lions and coyotes."

"Those flowers are quite beautiful. But those signs unfortunately somewhat ruin the peaceful hiking moment, don't they?" Alby, a realist was someone who, as MJ often mandated, must be her honest stronghold. To the contrary, Bernard approached topics dexterously, often saying what he thought as being diplomatically needed, as to not distress her in her condition. Alby's sense of practicality and scrupulousness was refreshing to her. Yet, despite her appreciation for truth, MJ certainly did prize her husband's vigilant endeavors to always pacify her.

"Alby, the details of the dream seemed so real, even the details of those flowers, those signs, and the smells. I simply meant, well, it has been a long time since I have been there, and yet I feel as if the sand was truly right under my feet, and the colors of the flowers were speaking directly to my soul. I even think I felt the breeze from the flight of the seagulls and crows that surrounded me."

"Well unless you walked down to the beach in your sleep, you know it's your senses regurgitating their memories, MJ, correct?" Alby interjected softly and diplomatically.

"I do. I know my condition is worsening, and I know I've been stuck in this bed for a year. It just seemed so lifelike to me."

Alby motioned to the flat Ginger Ale again, but MJ declined with a very slight shake of her head.

"You said you were drowning?" Alby asked, intending to get her speaking about it.

"Yes."

Suddenly MJ was overcome by trepidation, and Alby felt guilty for pushing the subject's continuation.

"I'm not quite sure why, but something intrinsically urged me to investigate the water," she said, slowly piecing the images together in her head. "So I walked toward the coast. The sun was shining, the fog had dissipated, and it felt natural to relax and swim."

MJ could tell that Alby thought her gaze was being governed by the optimism and desire to someday experience life outside again. She was sure he almost suggested that he rent a wheelchair and start helping her take strolls outside, but if he suggested as much, she would reject it immediately. She simply hated being viewed as a burden.

"The water was tranquil. It felt so calm and refreshing, and I wanted to get naked and swim in it."

"Do you think it's wise to talk about your nudity to your husband's brother?" Alby jokingly interrupted. "I'm sure he wouldn't be too comfortable with it. I am not too comfortable with it either," he laughed.

"Alby, this was my dream, and it was liberating to be in the ocean instead of being cooped inside this bedroom. It felt natural."

"Of course. Understood. Please continue," Alby said apologetically.

With the minute mobility she had, MJ buried her chin into her duvet, readying to relive the danger that was ahead, certain that recreating the experience would cause her shock.

"The Pacific's under-toe violently and suddenly came from nowhere. One moment the ocean was still, and I was in peace. The water, although cool, felt natural and free. And without warning, I was caught in its rough and disturbing clutch. There was nothing for me to grasp in order to fight this unbelievable force. It felt as if someone seized my legs and without any clemency, jauntily continued to pull me under the surface."

Her voice, just a moment ago cheerful and liberated, became cold and shocked with identifiable pause. Alby did what he could to express his support, yet he clearly knew it was a dream and must have questioned whether to truly feed into the worried state in which she already seemed to be.

"MJ, you're back at home. You're not in danger. You're safe, and soon Bernard will be home as well."

MJ, again desperate to breathe, gained enough composure to slightly, ever so slightly, turn her head toward Alby and calmly protest.

"I understand that, Alby. I know the difference between reality and dreams. It was the nature of the dream that freaked me out. But it wasn't the drowning itself. It wasn't the pressure from the water filling my lungs," she paused and then continued. "It was the unwavering force of being controlled. And I could do nothing about it. I was trapped," she cried, "and I couldn't escape."

MJ began to equate her dream with her being unable to do much of anything these days, including escape, if necessary. This thought became more and more relevant due to her recent frightful experience just the other day with what she thought might be a haunting. But for the moment she believed that experience was best left private.

"MJ, honey," Alby delicately said, similar to Bernard's way of handling a situation, "have you told Bernard that you're being ill and bedridden is making you feel trapped?"

MJ regained composure. Asking Alby to wipe her tears from her left cheek, she then thought of her husband's kindness toward her and suddenly her visions of him calmed the storm of emotions inside her.

"What would I do without him, Alby? He is my rock. Bernard dotes on me left and right, to the point where he simply doesn't rest until he's found a way to eradicate this fucking disease. And when he comes home, he sits with me all night, caressing me until I am able to sleep, promising me that he'll go to the ends of the Earth to provide me comfort. No, telling him I feel 'trapped' would only make him feel worse for me. It would make him feel worse about his own situation."

MJ knew that Alby recognized the pain she was feeling. It was obvious she was intent on keeping together the little life she had left to give to Bernard. Her spirit was dampened from being sick, but her resolve was strong; and she was determined to alleviate the demons life dealt them. Life could certainly, at times, prove itself unfair.

As such, MJ took a moment to collect her memories. She pardoned herself, which Alby understood to mean 'time for a quick, silent break' to which he respectfully submitted. MJ thought about her time, not too distant from now, when she had soared as a beautiful ballerina. She and her family were so proud of her artistic abilities as a dancer, her graceful presence in the world that once was, and the souls she touched when working at the Churchill Theater in San Francisco, a mere sixteen miles from where she lived now, yet so distant to her new reality, formed in the past year. Now at thirty years of age, MJ felt decrepit, misplaced, confused, and a slave to an all too rare disease which took hold of her life just like a vice's cruel and unforgiving grip. Who was she? What purpose did she have now? Those were the questions she often asked herself. And she hated these decaying thoughts that viciously infringed upon her days lately. She knew that, for all intents and purposes, there was much for which she should be grateful.

MJ had a prince for a husband—a common West Coast town's man who adored her and stopped at nothing to make her feel royal and appreciated. She had a wonderful friend in Alby, the younger brother of Bernard. He was a local botanist, never too busy or distant to visit her each day, as he promised both MJ and Bernard he would do. And her home was a peaceful, beautiful coastal home in the Bay Area in northern California—Pacifica, to be exact, where the crystalized, smooth, cool fog was a magnificent departure from the standard heat once thought to be the stronghold on the state. But when the sun shined in Pacifica, it was a brilliant and equally superb spectacle. These thoughts comforted her; and she realized that all would be fine soon.

"I think it is time for me to make you some of that hot green tea that you enjoy so much," Alby mentioned as he rose to exit her bedroom, the makeshift health center, complete with adjustable hospital bed, medicine desk, and soothing flowers to the left.

MJ did not respond, but simply smiled and nodded. She was in agreement that something, beyond her thoughts, was necessary to bring her some peace; and thus she gladly accepted Alby's gesture.

After a few quiet minutes, MJ felt the need to speak.

"I wish you would stay a bit later today, just to greet Bernard when he comes home," MJ called out, projecting her voice toward the kitchen.

Silence.

MJ wondered why Bernard and Alby couldn't put some of their differences aside—differences for which she still couldn't fully comprehend. Yet, she was not intent on testing waters that she had no business diving into. *No more drowning for MJ*, she thought. *I have simply had enough of that*. No, she would focus more on saving herself and her marriage. And when she thought this, it somewhat frustrated her that Bernard didn't think anything needed to be fixed. To him, MJ was just fine, ill or not. She was the perfect wife.

"I must stop thinking this way. It's time to be more positive!" She said aloud. "Bernard is always reminding me of this."

"Talking to yourself again?" Alby interjected, carrying two cups of tea toward her. She could smell the sweetness of the liquid, and the caffeine almost jumped at her like an animal urging to find prey. It was a better scent than the stuffiness of her room, filled with the stench of an ailing woman, which was now pungently obvious after her recent memories of the Pacific Ocean's dainty smell.

"Fire in the water," she claimed.

"Come again?" Alby asked.

"I was just thinking . . . I don't understand why I often dream about swimming, and drowning," MJ retorted. "I simply hate the water. I don't belong in it. It douses me, always has. So it makes no sense to me that I would dream about it."

"Maybe," Alby said after an awkward moment of silence, "maybe it is simply a way for you to reconnect to the life outside that you seem to be missing?"

What a conscious life reaction, MJ thought. A beautiful explanation for yearning for what she once had, before the illness took hold. She agreed it was a definitive motive for the purpose of the dreams that left her feeling even more powerless than she was in reality. With that thought, she couldn't possibly imagine how anyone could revel being in her sick chamber. She thought of Alby, and his botanical responsibilities; and she was regretful for taking him from them.

"Let me ask you, if I can, Alby," MJ wondered, peering into her tea, "do you enjoy your time here?"

"Why ask such a silly question? You know I visit you, not out of requirement, but because I enjoy our time together."

"Yes, but you have your own life," she quickly answered. "You've been such a wonderful friend, such a wonderful brother-in-law, you visit me almost daily now. You must continue to be missing your own life opportunities while you focus on babysitting me. When was the last time you went on a date, for example?"

"Oh dear me," Alby laughed. "The love-life conversation arises. I was waiting for this. It's been nearly a week since you asked about my relationships." Alby continued to smile; and he gracefully indulged MJ's question.

"Has it ever occurred to you that perhaps meeting you as often as I do helps to keep me focused? I enjoy our conversations, and I know you enjoy them as well. If I had a better place to be, I'd be there. And trust me, I would let you know. So you needn't worry about whether or not I am missing any of my gay parties or easy hook-ups."

"Well, the last escapade you had," she continued, with strong emphasis on the word 'escapade', "was with that six foot runner, Michael, correct?"

"Ah, Michael. Great ass. Thanks for the reminder," Alby retorted as he held his head and laughed. MJ laughed as well. It was true that, as manly as Alby was, the time she spent with him was easily used talking about her 'girl-things' since she simply knew that a gay man just had to understand these yearnings. She valued this relationship with Alby, for MJ never felt she had close girl friends in the first place, before meeting Bernard, nor now.

"Michael was a flash in the pan, hon. He and I are over each other and I do not have any recent juicy information to share with you. But how's this?" Alby offered. "Next visit, I'll tell you all about some of the men I have seen over the past year."

"That's a deal," agreed MJ. "And then you can be sure not to leave one dirty detail out."

"Drink your tea, you bitch," Alby responded.

"Dirty details . . ." he laughed. "As if I have any dirty details to offer."

MJ reclined, sipping her tea with Alby's assistance. The tea was now lukewarm at best. She moved her eyes and glanced out the window, beyond the Mori Point cliffs that were clearly visible from her home, yet at times seemed a thousand years away. Alby's company was a sufficient escape from her recent destructive thoughts. She almost forgot about the remarkable panic she experienced just the day before. The sheer thought of it continued to chill her insides. She knew that, at some point, she'd mention it to Alby, but unlike the dream, this was an experience she was not willing to currently relive. She would have to wait to relay that story.

Fatigue now set in. She was starting to feel the weight of the day wearing on her, and she was sure that Alby could notice. And he did.

"MJ, it's been a rough day for you. You've been focused on some negativity today. Once in a while I believe it is ok to be sad. We have permission to be so. But you simply must get back on the positive train."

MJ agreed. Another sip of tea, another sleepy nod, she was reluctant to sleep in front of her guest, but she was eager to rush away the turbulent day and be greeted by Bernard when he returned. She closed her eyes, this time longer than before. She thanked God that Alby was there. Had he not been, she was sure that the ghost would be back to harm her.

CHAPTER TWO

"Hello, my darling," Bernard Matters said, just as soothing as always. As MJ woke, she felt one of Bernard's warm hands caressing her hair while the other held a cool towel that he used to gently wipe her forehead. "You're quite warm, darling. Did you have a fever today?"

MJ was momentarily confused. She wasn't sure if Alby was still there, or if he had already departed for the evening. She wasn't even sure if she was dreaming at the moment. Bit by bit though, she began to gain clarity on the present, and standing before her, caring for her as usual was the man she revered.

"Bernard," MJ said beaming like a child who had just opened a birthday present she'd been waiting to receive. "What time is it? I must have slept longer than I thought."

"It's later than before, apparently" he retorted.

At times, as much as MJ loved him, she couldn't help but think that Bernard's attempts at humor were unmistakable bombs. But, as with many other things about this man, she enjoyed his attempts to please her.

"It's curious," she said, "I slept really well just now. I don't remember having any dreams, certainly nothing like I had earlier."

In an instant, MJ sensed a sheltered environment, more so than she had experienced in the past few days. She remembered the dream she'd described to Alby. Now it didn't seem as realistic to her. She was somewhat thankful to be jokingly sharing it with Bernard who, of course, would be most delicate in helping her to understand she was safe.

"I dreamt I was drowning again."

"Mori Point again?" Bernard assumed.

MJ methodically nodded, knowing full well he'd make that supposition. Of course it was the Mori Point dream.

"My dear, you simply could not drown out there," Bernard answered. Before MJ had time to protest by elucidating the details of the dream, Bernard continued.

"There are too many surfers in those waters," he said. "One would save you and try to steal you from me, you beautiful girl."

There he goes again, MJ thought. Treating me like the ballerina princess I am. "If only people could have seen what I once was," she said.

"I must say that I am quite surprised you have so many repeat near-drowning experiences," Bernard added. "You *are* afraid of the water, aren't you?"

"You understand me so well, Bernard." MJ smiled. "This is one of the reasons I feel so safe around you."

With that statement, MJ knew that Bernard was happy to see her beaming once again. It had been far too long of a period that MJ was not hopeful and constructive, for she typically remained optimistic about her situation. She believed he could recognize something was changing though, and though not drastically yet, maybe it began to make him nervous, she thought. But then MJ also knew that Bernard likely assured himself that he would not display his true feelings of worry, at least not yet, unless it got serious enough for him to do so.

"Alby was here to keep me company," MJ said, her eyes focused hard on Bernard's hands. They were older than hers, and she imagined him working meticulously in his research 'workshop' of sorts. It was true that Bernard was almost ten years her senior, but he always remained fit as a fiddle, something for which she could no longer claim about herself unfortunately.

"I expected as much, my dear," Alby responded. "And how is my brother, the Tinkerbelle?"

"Bernard," MJ interjected strongly. "That isn't appropriate."

Although for a brief moment, the thought made her mischievously grin, MJ suggested, "You know full well that his lifestyle does not inconvenience you."

MJ believed it was now appropriate to swiftly mention her disagreement with the brothers' gradually icing relationship. At this moment, Bernard seemed to be open to discussing it a bit more than usual, and thus, she forcefully said, "I can't for the life of me fully understand why you and he do not speak more often."

For MJ, the thought of these brothers drifting apart bothered her terribly. She enjoyed Alby's company, and it goes without saying that she idolized Bernard. And her thoughts wandered back to her own relationship with her mother, Wendy—the mother who adamantly opposed her relationship with Bernard. This is the same mother who, to the complete disappointment and utter grief that was too much for MJ to bear, had not visited her once since MJ's illness took a footing.

When MJ had, from time to time, mentioned to Bernard that she felt betrayed by her mother, and would mention that she simply could not comprehend acting that way toward her own child, Bernard would kindly state, "I'm sure the thought of seeing your graceful decline from the ballerina she raised has caused Wendy to face guilt and struggles with reality, darling. Please don't be upset."

This was yet another example, despite his knowing about the horrible things her mother had said about him, how Bernard swept that knowledge to the side in order to protect MJ's feelings. If only her mother could see just how gentlemanly he truly was, unlike her mother's hopeful choice for her, Jonathan, who as it turns out was quite an ass in a man's clothes.

Bernard paused, first addressing her original claim.

"Yes, my brother's lifestyle has no bearing on me," he responded. "I would easily chalk this up to pure sibling rivalry, nothing more. You know I love my brother. And in all honesty, his visitations with you at least keep he and I in a relationship, which you know was barely existent before you . . . well . . ."

A pause.

"Before I became sick?" asked MJ.

"Dear, you'll be well soon. I can feel it in my bones. And I know you once did as well. We need you to get back to thinking that way again."

"Yes, Bernard, I feel it as well."

Bernard sat at the foot of MJ's adjustable hospital bed, stopped for a quick glance out toward Mori Point, and peacefully relocated his gaze toward her gentle stare.

"Would you," he carefully approached his words, "would you like me to lay with you this evening?"

It had been some time, a few months ago now, that Bernard moved into the guest room, to provide MJ the solace she needed to accept her state. In her mind, MJ knew he was willing to take as long as necessary in order for her to cope with her changing reality.

"Are we speaking about the same type of lay?" MJ sarcastically asked. Bernard smiled and nodded positively.

"My dear, you just made a joke. Bravo."

"Bernard," MJ responded, "I could actually use the company of my husband this evening. I think that would be fine."

Suddenly, without fully thinking it through, MJ was tempted to particularize the recent incidents that caused her anxiety—not the dream at all, but something much more disturbing that she could still not yet quite explain. She stopped herself, though, just as suddenly. She did not need her husband to start thinking she was not just physically ill, but mentally as well.

Bernard, in a somewhat surprised, but pleased state, graciously stretched his neck toward MJ's head. His lips met hers, and before rising to undress, MJ thought the gentle passion was enough to warm the coldest bitch. Soon after, Bernard proceeded toward the kitchen, surely to take his typical nightly vitamins.

MJ once again realized how fortunate she was to have someone like Bernard baked into the recipe of her life. She may no longer do ballet at the Churchill, but she felt as if she was always center stage for Bernard's affection. If she hadn't accidentally examined Bernard's hesitation in the hallway, she wouldn't have noticed his longer-than-normal, solemn pose in front of the portrait that hung on the hallway wall. The odd thing about the portrait, and most of the photographs that hung there, was that they had always been sheet-covered or turned to face the wall. She knew the person in the picture on the other side still had deep-rooted meaning for Bernard, and MJ never minded this fact, nor ever pushed Bernard to explain it. But just once, MJ wished that her husband would forget who was imprinted on those hidden photographs and come to her fully committed.

Bernard, silent and resolute, after what seemed to be a respectful, but sorrowful adoration, walked away from the portrait and promised to return to MJ in a few minutes. It was then that MJ noticed the evening fog rolling into the landscape. The sun she observed earlier when Alby was visiting was now replaced by the astonishingly, reassuring Pacifica chilly fog, and she thought this was good. She was an avid fan of a Miss Janet Spock, a creative conspirator of sorts. Miss Spock authored a continuously updated journal that tracked the wonders and mysteries of life and nature. There, she remembered the posting she read from one of her articles.

Fog is forever enigmatic, despite what it seems to be when staring straight into it. To some, fog's sheer presence is much like a lens claiming focus. To others, fog is dense and profuse. Everything looks, feels, smells and sounds different in fog. And sooner, rather than later, it is easy to lose yourself in it.—Janet Spock

Miss Spock's skillful composition helped MJ to realize that she would deal with the secrets of the portrait and other hidden pictures at another time, just as she would deal with the unspeakable and still unspoken strange events of the other day. For now, MJ would be comforted to be in Bernard's presence over night.

Bernard returned and, to MJ he seemed happier than ever. He embraced her warmly in such a protective way, and for a moment, MJ overlooked her illness and started to sleep peacefully again. But, just as the character or the town she loved alter quickly, so too did her own character. She felt a disturbing presence—just like she had the other day—that was, truthfully speaking, sinister in nature. She thought to herself, *no, not again.* If only her craving to be dreaming again was a reality, it was instead quite clear that someone eerily stood in the corner of her room, monitoring her and Bernard lounging in the bed. She could not determine the nature of the figure before her, nor make out any details, but she noticed the eyes—bloodshot, wide, confused, and angry. And as the figure remained steadfast, unwavering, eerily peering with such discontent, a voice in MJ's head said, "Go ahead and watch."

CHAPTER THREE

MJ realized that Bernard was increasingly more gentle and affectionate as time progressed. It was already slightly later than his typical office morning. Therefore, since Bernard was already running late for his appointments, he cooked MJ eggs—over easy, bacon—just as crispy as she always preferred it, and toast—slightly burned outward toward the crusts. Not one morsel of food was for him. MJ knew that he preferred to skip breakfast anyway. MJ saw Bernard's sole purpose for the savory meal he made was to provide her substance before starting her day.

The plate was a sight of perfection, a work of art at best. Bernard was simple—a researcher who, with his skill and scientific acumen, commanded the respect of his colleagues. He, however, lacked any dexterity in the arts, and to MJ he therefore seemed pleased at the chef-d'oeuvre he had just prepared.

After placing the tray of food by her side, the side of her adjustable and machine-driven bed where he had recently laid, he went to the washroom, dampened another small towel, and placed it on MJ's forehead. The coolness met her warm skin with ease and welcome; and MJ was once again grateful for the care of her husband.

"I spoke with Alby this morning," Bernard said in a subdued voice, now lightly kneading her temples, charily doing what he could to ease any existing tension. He had remembered, when waking this morning, MJ mentioned she had a slight headache that hopefully would not develop into one of her emblematic migraines.

"You were still sleeping, and he promised to return later," Bernard said completing his general statement.

MJ could not exactly remember the details before she slept. She knew she felt, and possibly saw a presence, but at this point, it seemed more like a dream. Still though, she was eager for Alby's visit. She did not want to be alone today.

"Your brother has been so kind to me, Bernard," MJ, in an incredibly grateful manner, declared. "It is obviously a testimony to the way you boys were raised. The manners you both provide me are completely and utterly . . ."

"Deserved," Bernard finished.

"Yes," MJ smiled. "I'll accept that!"

MJ took her first bite of bacon that Bernard fed her. She always seemed to like the salty items first. It was more than decent, it was nourishing with every bite. She couldn't tell if she was feeling more recovered or more content. It didn't matter. This would be a much better day than yesterday, that pathetic excuse of wasted energy feeling dreadful about her situation, as if her unpleasant condition was any worse than the abysmal terrors others in this society were facing. Maybe she was starting to absorb Bernard's positive affirmation after all.

So what? She reminded herself that she just happened to be indolent and unmovable, but with a wonderful husband and beautiful, landscaped house, with beautiful town scenery. She was alive and her senses were heightened because of her condition. She took no further moments pausing in front of her breakfast, and therefore asked Bernard to scoop some of the eggs onto her slightly burned toast. The tiniest fragment slipped over the tray and onto the duvet. MJ laughed. *Oops,* she thought. Bernard serenely placed the fragment into her mouth. She didn't mind, and she was damned if she would waste any of the sustenance. MJ once again smiled.

"Alby certainly didn't need to leave because I was asleep," MJ added, with her mouth full. "I always enjoy his company, though I don't understand why he likes to waste his time on me."

"Darling, please be positive. You seemed to be starting the day so well."

"Yes, you are right. I know he enjoys his time with me, but he has his own life to worry about."

"Oh that's right," Bernard chuckled. "He mentioned you tried to gain intelligence on his love life." Bernard continued to lightly laugh.

"For Christ's sake," MJ insisted, somewhat jokingly, somewhat perturbed. "I get concerned that he may be lonely. We have everything we need with one another. I just wish the same for him."

"I think he is quite happy where he is, MJ," Bernard reassured. "We may not be the *closest* brothers relationship-wise, but we are family nonetheless. I know him, and he is happy to be free from any commitment. I think that is why he spends time with you. You are his commitment now."

This unexpectedly made sense to MJ, or maybe she just obtained the gist—time to stop pushing the subject, and thus she digressed. Surrendering to the situation, MJ kissed her husband goodbye and wished him her usual, "go cure the world, babe." Though it was pressing her thoughts and she was tempted to do so, she knew now wasn't the time to encourage him to finally remove the hidden hallway photographs, especially that damned large portrait. She believed for so long now, Bernard bestowed his entire being to her, but in the background, pain—not physical, but emotional—continued to shroud itself inside his heart. He seems to be in a happy mood, she thought, so I am not going to disturb that. She remembered all too well the evening his pain surfaced.

MJ learned through Bernard that his colleagues not only respected him because of his proficiencies, but also because of the way he upheld himself during his personal calamity. He rarely spoke of it, but there was the one evening, over dinner, when Bernard touched the spirits a bit too much for his liking, and he opened the conversation a bit more willingly than usual. He was not a heavy drinker whatsoever, but on a rare occasion, Bernard needed an outlet for the pain; and so MJ obliged and silently listened.

She listened to Bernard wearily speak of Janice, his research colleague, who constantly expressed her condolences for his loss of Catherine, his first wife—a few years before even meeting MJ. Catherine's tragedy was a violent, accidental fall down the staircase—a stupid, random, weak ankle moment that mercilessly took her existence in a matter of seconds. Bernard's tragedy was finding her, after an evening of meeting his buddies to watch the 49ers play. The guilt he felt, for having spent Catherine's last evening on earth, watching a bunch of men toss around an undeniably, meaningless pigskin instead of being there to save her haunts his soul to this day.

Janice would tell Bernard, "you're so strong," or she'd ask, "How do you do it, Bernie?" MJ knew Bernard hated when Janice called him that, but he was too much of a gentleman to stop her.

Bernard continued to tell MJ how his other colleague, Marcus, could no longer look at him in the eye, simply out of pure sorrow and discomfort for Bernard's situation. There was also Shoshanna, the woman who shared a cubicle wall with Bernard. She, like the others, like all the others, could only articulate her sorrow by bringing Bernard coffee each day. She never owned up to that fact, but Bernard knew why she would provide him these small acts of kindness. And it tortured him to be the center of attention. MJ knew this without Bernard having to himself own up to that fact. MJ realized that life must have been very difficult for her husband. She knew that everyone's behavior and pity only intensified when news broke of MJ's debilitating illness. Bernard, the poor nice-guys-always-finish-last bastard caught a new wife but could not catch a break.

At that moment, MJ saw Bernard do something he had never done before. He threw his glass of scotch to the ground, shattering it into what seemed to be a thousand and one pieces. MJ tried to rise to the moment, ready to embrace him, though as usual she could barely move. Bernard raised his hand in the air—a sort of gentle protest and request for an apology excusing the ridiculous behavior on his part.

"No, no. Darling. Old Bernard got pissed-face drunk," he said, speaking of himself in the third person. "Bernard's feeling sorry for himself, darling. I'll clean this up. Please lay back down."

This recent memory caused MJ to depart from her morning's encouraging emotions. She unfortunately pushed them to the side for now, and instead once again focused on the hidden photographs that hung on the hallway wall. It was no secret or surprise to MJ that these pictures were of Catherine. She assumed some of them displayed happy scenes of Catherine and Bernard together. Regardless, MJ knew that Bernard could not bring himself to part with them, but he could also not look at them. She believed his guilt was too strong; his faith was too unsettled. It's not that MJ minded the pictures being there. She never had minded. She simply felt, more recently than before, that in her condition, she no longer had the vigor to endure being second-best. She needed full support now, in her condition.

With this commemoration, she even more so impatiently awaited the company of Alby. As positive as she felt today, she began to put herself back into a damaging funk. Physically, she felt rather strong today. Emotionally, she was underspent, and to be honest, quite scared. She needed to talk to Alby, for while this wasn't the time to bother Bernard with the photographs, this certainly neither was the time to mention to him that an unknown 'someone' was terrifying her to her very core.

There was something happening that she simply could not explain, and the idea of revealing it to her husband was, in and of itself, terrorizing her. No, she realized that Alby would understand. But she also knew that this was not the time to mention to Bernard that she fully believed that someone was methodically and sinisterly scouting her. MJ even thought to herself, quite often now having experienced the strange unspoken events, that possibly someone was trying to abduct her. When thinking these thoughts, MJ, although virtually paralyzed, would finally feel her muscles tighten and her nerves sting sharply. She likened the feeling to a situation that any child feels when he is taught, for the first time, to be wary of strangers with candy, and strangers in cars ready to grab him at any moment's notice.

If abduction was not the goal, MJ at least knew this someone was purposely trying to frighten her, and had observed MJ in her physically limiting and permanently immobile condition. Further, with each of the gradually intensifying experiences, MJ grasped a tremendously disturbing belief that seemed equally as disturbing when considered a reality. MJ intrinsically believed this someone had been in her house. As a matter of *clarification*, she believed the person had been in her house several times. As a matter of *fact*, MJ once again believed she was being watched at that moment.

CHAPTER FOUR

It was cool that afternoon. The fog had prematurely begun to reposition itself from ocean to coast, changing the Pacifica landscape grey once again. Just as quickly as the town experienced the change in weather, MJ was speedily transitioning from positive to worrisome, beginning to become more aware of the things she had seen. Alby sat as patient as possible, carefully listening to MJ's justifications for being apprehensive. MJ knew that he could once again sense that she had begun to spiral into a function of misfortune. And to be honest, MJ believed it sad for him to experience her decline, to which she ultimately felt responsible. MJ was aware that, according to Bernard, the two—he and Alby, had just discussed that very morning how well MJ's spirits were the very night before.

"Finished your work today then, Alby?" MJ said, taking a moment to break away from the conversation at hand.

"MJ, you know my work only just begins when I come to visit you."

MJ laughed out loud.

It had been some time since she experienced something so pleasant that it made her appreciate humor, and the laugh itself was good in one sense, but physically painful in the other. Her eyes moved toward the covered pictures in the hallway, and her laugh calmed slightly.

"Alby, please," she said, trying to move her arms—unsuccessfully—to hold her ribcage as tightly as she could. "Sarcasm is not appropriate at the moment."

"My apologies, dear lady," Alby responded, bowing gleefully at her. "Yes, I have finished my botany duties for the day, seeding the Bay Area and saving the wildlife—the world is now safe."

"I certainly wish I could believe that," MJ retorted.

"Well, enough of my small talk. You were saying you were concerned. Was it another dream? Swimming? Drowning?"

"No, nothing like that," MJ had only wished that was true. "I saw her again. I think it was her, standing on the Mori Point cliffs just staring at me."

She decided not to mention that she also thought this presence was standing within feet from her bed just last night.

MJ saw that Alby was indeed interested, but she believed that he envisaged MJ's imagination getting the best of her. How could he not be thinking this? If he were nearly paralyzed with only brief bouts of strength to sponge himself clean, or shift occasionally to avoid bedsores, he too would be swept away in fantasy and folklore.

"Surely you know that there are others in this town, MJ," Alby said.

MJ remained silent, but tried to consider what he was suggesting at that moment. She was unfortunately not making the appropriate connection, and she was eager to do so.

"And others," Alby continued, "Do walk about as they please, even on Mori Point."

"Yes," MJ responded, "the popular hiking trail. I know it."

"So, and pardon me for asking what I am sure is an obviously irritating question here," Alby quickly interjected, "but what did you actually see?"

MJ paused for a moment, carefully turning her head toward the window, gazing into the fog, and considering the consequences of what she was planning to say.

"Nothing."

"Nothing?"

"Nothing."

"Look, MJ," Alby continued, now feeling a bit culpable for having stopped MJ in her tracks, immediately casting doubt upon her before she had the prospect to provide an explanation. "I do not want you to surrender to my criticism. I'd prefer that you'd continue."

"Surrender?" MJ laughed again. "Good God, you are really helping me make up for a year without laughter today."

MJ knew that Alby was keen to understand what she meant.

"Alby, I am simply trying to imply that I saw something, or *someone*, there on the cliff, staring—no, gawking—so strangely at me, and then . . . I saw nothing."

"As in vanished?"

"As in *nothing*," MJ repeated.

"Possibly your imagination?" Alby questioned, before quickly straightening his posture so not to discourage her from continuing.

"I thought so," she agreed, "until I saw her again, seconds later. Her stare was so odd and cold, almost questioning my existence, astonished at what she was seeing, and seemingly angry, so angry. It frightened me."

"MJ . . ."

"Alby, I was so impatient for your visit today, partly because I was starting to make myself nervous, and partly because I needed to mention this to you."

"Alright, I'll continue to listen without judgment," Alby insisted.

"And this is not the first time I saw her," MJ continued. "I need your solemn promise that you will not think me irrational for what I am about to tell you."

Alby said nothing, but motioned over his heart, crossing it with his fingers, then holding them up in honor.

"I was laying here the day before my recent dream—that day I was feeling very sad about my situation; and I was thinking of my mother."

"Your mother?" Alby asked. "How long has it been?"

"Too long. I miss her terribly," MJ whispered, visibly shaking and slightly tearing.

"I'm sure you do, hon."

"I know she doesn't approve of me marrying, Bernard, and that has been a bit annoying. She had her heart set on Jonathan."

"He was your choreographer, right?" Alby, looking for clarification proudly stated.

"Yes. But obviously, I had no feelings for him, nothing except professional sentiment and respect. But still, my mother kept insisting Jonathan was 'the one' for me."

"I'm sure that was frustrating."

"Especially when," MJ continued, "I met Bernard and we obviously fell in love."

"My brother, the prince," Alby joked.

"He truly is a saint, Alby. Even in the face of utter distaste from my mother, and even when he sees that I, at times, become distraught when thinking of happy times with her, he says nothing negative about her, so as not to upset me further. He'll just simply joke and say, 'just let me know when you want to trade me in for Jonathan'."

"MJ," Alby responded. "Let's place some emphasis on you right now. I mean this with the utmost respect, but Bernard is not here. You are a strong woman—equally as strong in character as what you claim is his. I like spending my time speaking to you, getting to know you more, not really going down a path speaking about my brother."

MJ could see that Alby was sensitive to her minor depression. She knew he saw that she missed her life from before, the active life, the non-paralyzed, non-burden-on-anyone life she once had the pleasure to enjoy. She was sure that he could only imagine the strange issues that might be swimming in her thoughts, picking at her emotions. Losing a relationship with her mother, on top of this, must be impacting her ability to stay optimistic. Changing the subject at hand was probably best.

"So, back to the disappearing woman," Alby mentioned. "When does she reappear?"

"While I was thinking of my mother, I turned with my back to the window," MJ continued. "I was gazing at the reflection of the sky through the bureau mirror, wondering how long the sun would continue to shine, and then . . ."

MJ began to sweat. Her chest suddenly became tight, and her teeth automatically, without any effort, just as a new living being doesn't think to blink or breathe, began to clench on their own. Her face numb and painful from the tightening muscles surrounding her jaw, she could only describe her situation as the onset of what seemed to be a nervous breakdown about to surface in a troubling and dramatic way.

"I saw her," she whispered.

"Saw her? Again? Where exactly did she reappear?"

MJ took a moment, again beginning to tremor.

"I saw her standing directly at my window," she muttered, still shocked as the words appeared from her lips. "Her face was pressed up against the pane. I couldn't see the details of her face, but she was dressed in black, and as I usually can, I could only truly see her eyes. She looked as if she was ready to bring hell upon me, ready to beget downright terror to the situation, and I panicked."

As MJ waited for Alby's reaction, she noticed that he tried very diligently to focus on the story at hand, attempting to have very little preconceived judgment about it. It was true that his eyes got a bit wider with each passing word, his breathing a bit heavier with each scene that MJ detailed. However, MJ knew that Alby, the realist he was, was also trying just as desperately to interject science into the scenario. She imagined him thinking, *there must be some type of realistic credible and scientifically authentic explanation for this.*

"How could you not," Alby insisted, the gentleman he was. "If you think . . . if you indeed saw something like that? What did you do?"

"That's just my problem, Alby," MJ cried. "What can I do? I can't get out of this fucking bed. I can't protect myself in any way. I am useless. I am a blob of unneeded flesh just lying here getting sicker and fatter as we speak. God forbid an emergency takes place, like a fire or something. I'd be dead in two minutes. And not once during that time would I even have the ability to move. I'd die right in this same fucking spot."

Once again, MJ saw that Alby's expression presented a benevolence that only he could use to calm her nerves.

"Which," Alby confidently stated, "is one of the reasons I come to visit you so often."

"Oh, please, Alby. I'm not truly fearful of a sudden fire. It was a matter of speech. What I am considering is the possibility that something is haunting me."

"Not at all possible, MJ," Alby quickly insisted. "I just don't believe in that being possible. I think someone is seriously playing a number on you. I think someone is trying to frighten you. And you are letting them succeed!"

"Thank you," MJ responded in a drastically sarcastic tone. "Thank you, Alby, for your generous support and understanding. I chose to tell you this because I can no longer lie still with these visions in my head. It really sucks to be doubted."

"I'm willing to listen and believe you, hon," Alby corrected her just as quickly as his previous insistence. "But I simply do not believe in this haunting nonsense."

"I need a tissue, please." MJ said, for once unmoved by Alby's realism.

Grabbing the only thing close by—a paper towel—Alby wiped her face and continued. "If you say you are witnessing someone's cruel intentions toward you, I am very sure you are correct, MJ."

MJ's weeping persisted.

"I simply believe it is someone in the town, some snot-nosed kid tormenting you. Obviously. And whoever this pure bitch is, she needs to be put into her place. You need to tell Bernard."

"He's going to take me for a mental case, Alby. You know that."

Although Alby could hardly disagree, MJ recognized the he was encouraging her to make the attempt.

"MJ, if someone is, for whatever unknown reason, infringing upon your privacy—Christ, your *safety*, you need to let Bernard know about it. And forcefully. Maybe I need to tell him for you."

"I don't need you to speak for me to Bernard!" MJ responded. "I can handle having a conversation with him. I'm a big, girl, Alby."

"Well, I'm certainly exhilarated to hear this," Alby answered. "But if, for one moment, I believe you are shrinking into a meek little being, I'm coming to your defense."

With that, MJ knew her next statement was going to send Alby to a frantic state, but she simply could not hold back any further.

"Her face was pressed against the window, peering at my entire body. I could imagine her laughing, and then suddenly evil seemed to pour from her expression. And, what's worse is that I think I heard her say something."

"Well?" Alby insisted. "You're going to stop there? What the hell did she say?"

"I think she was saying . . ." MJ stopped again, turned her head slightly toward the window, and became transfixed upon it. The fog, becoming denser, began to create precipitation on the glass. She wanted to reach toward it, but frustration set in, because as usual her arms were immobile.

"What? What, MJ? What was she saying?"

"She said, 'I see you. I can see you. And I am coming soon.'"

CHAPTER FIVE

It had now been a day after telling Alby what she did. MJ still felt a bit embarrassed by suggesting that nuisance spirits were visiting her, though truth be told it was relieving to have bore the details of it from deep with inside her. By this time now, Alby had come back to visit her, and MJ had been on the receiving end of one of his fascinating stories—something about a family named after seagulls who lived on the open water, lost their parents, and did what they could to survive what was surely intended to be a tragic and epic ending. As a matter of speaking, it was likely that Alby relayed this story for the sole purpose of teaching MJ a lesson in sanity. MJ recognized its likeness to a fable, and she could easily envision Alby saying to her, *and the moral of this story, MJ—you are insane, there is no such thing as a haunting.* This must be the reason why MJ felt hollow after hearing it. She knew there was more to the tale, yet Alby, for whatever the reason might be, was not ready to dispatch the finale quite yet. Nonetheless, MJ did her best to remain composed and absorb the lessons Alby tried to teach.

"The title is sort of funny, isn't it?" She asked.

"Is it?"

"Well, this family wasn't really happy to begin with," MJ proudly stated, believing she possibly found the meaning behind the story. "I mean, I can understand why the children were now sad, but from the very start of you telling it, the family seemed at odds with one another. This unquestionably implies they were likely not at all happy with one another, right?"

MJ saw Alby examining her expressions as if trying to diagnose some sort of disease that begged to be found. The truth of the matter was that she always felt comfortable in Alby's presence. She was incredibly pleased to have him visit her during her husband's absence. But at times, his overthinking and attempts to analyze her through the stories he told were becoming a major distraction for their friendship.

"What's wrong?" MJ asked.

"Nothing," Alby responded. "I was trying to think about your statement. I thought it was interesting for you to make that suggestion."

"What suggestion? That the family was indeed not happy to begin with?"

"Yes. The story is titled *Happy House of Saddened Gulls*. I'm not exactly sure the anonymous author was intending to imply the family was joyous with one another before becoming lost at sea, but I certainly think it is quite telling that you picked up on that."

MJ paused and considered her words carefully. She meant no disrespect to her brother-in-law, and didn't want him to believe she was suggesting that their time together be cut short, but she simply wanted him to speak to her like a friend.

"Alby," she began, "I'm not your patient. I really would like you to stop scrutinizing me here. I know you like to instill meanings in the chronicles you tell me. And you are very good at it—I enjoy the times you are willing to tell me tales, or remind me of old ones that I knew when I was a child even. But can't you simply talk to me, tell me a story for the fun of it, and stop acting like a damn professor every now and then?"

Alby simply stared at her. She knew her implication was surely too strong, and likely insulting as well. At this point, MJ now felt guilty for not having swallowed her pride or having bit her tongue. *Stupid move*, she thought.

"I'm sorry, Alby. Obviously if I believe I am being haunted, I'm likely wound up way too tight right now. Please ignore me. I shouldn't have lashed out at you just now. I don't know what is wrong with me. I think I am going stir crazy because of this bed."

"On the contrary, MJ," he replied. "I like the fact that you are becoming strong and defending yourself again. Maintain this disposition, please!"

MJ smiled. It was good to receive a compliment, and further, she was sufficed to feel some satisfaction after having expressed her fear just yesterday. Telling someone that you are being hounded, no haunted, no maybe hounded by some weird woman who has her face pressed against your window is a bit difficult to bring to the surface of a conversation.

"This story—*Happy House of Saddened Gulls*—again, where did you first hear of it?"

"I didn't say," Alby responded. "But not for any particular reason other than it wasn't important. The author is anonymous. It is one of those stories that have existed over time, like a fable or a fairy tale. After all these years, I'm not sure anyone even knows who was the original author."

"It's strange," MJ continued. "The story is familiar, but I am not sure I actually ever heard it, at least in the format you told it. Maybe my mother told it to me once or twice when I was much younger."

"What is familiar to you?"

"I'm not sure," MJ responded. "Something about a family moving to the sea, and trying to live with one another in tight quarters. Loss. I remember the tale about deep loss, but the details of the story are forgotten."

"Well, they moved to the open sea because their father was a fisherman. It was his trade, and he had decided that leaving his family for four to six months at a time was too much of a loss for him, and too hard on them as well. So he moved them to a floating, traveling house on the sea."

"His children, except for the youngest daughter . . ."

". . . Piper," Alby confirmed.

"Yes," MJ responded. "Piper is the only one who seems to have been supportive of her parents throughout the entire story. The other children seem to be very negative and very selfish."

"That is the general theme of the tale so far," Alby replied. "But perceptions can often be deceiving."

"Here we go," MJ grunted. "The moral of the story. I have been waiting for this. Could it be that my perceptions are deceiving me."

Alby laughed. MJ knew that he probably tried diligently to ensure that she was not embarrassed by the information she shared with him just yesterday. All the while, he seemed to keep his poise and divulge the aphorism.

"Well, to a certain extent," Alby responded. "However, it isn't the full meaning. Misperceptions are one part of it. But there is so much that impacts our decisions, our moods, our health—so many details weaved into the fabric material of our life experiences. This often causes us to act certain ways or even see certain things."

"You mean, physically *see?*" MJ asked. "Or do you mean *perceive* certain things?"

"Both, actually," Alby retorted.

"Are you suggesting that my ghost is my perception of being caught helpless in a situation of cruel fate?"

MJ saw that Alby considered the question carefully. His hand supporting his head, he stared toward the ceiling, gently rubbing the cleft in his chin. MJ wondered what he might be thinking, how he might be cogitating the most fitting way to respond to such a sensitive topic.

"Well?" She asked impatiently.

"I think you are a very wise woman, MJ," Alby responded.

"I'm not sure if that makes me feel any better," MJ sighed, partially laughing with a small sense of sarcasm, partially expressing grief in the process as well. "You are basically confirming that I am seeing things because I feel trapped in this paralyzed state. Well, all I can tell you is that it seems very real, and it is also causing me a lot of fear and anxiety. Whatever it is, I wish it would stop immediately."

"MJ, you did not let me finish," Alby calmly specified in a manner that was both commanding and sympathetic. "I said that you were a wise woman. To me, this means that you are not only astute in interpreting my meanings here, but you are also very in tune with your surroundings. You are not foolish, nor are you incapable of appreciating the events that move around you. If you believe there is someone or something that is causing you mischievous harm, then I believe you."

Nothing can quite describe the feeling someone experiences when a weight has been elated from its stubborn clamp. This is exactly how MJ felt. She believed that Alby's simple compliment of formal belief in what she saw—no, what she experienced—as confirmation. She felt like an animal that had just been released by a trap.

"I feel like crying," MJ stated.

"For what reason?"

"Out of relief," MJ corrected. "Simply out of relief. Thank you."

Alby smiled.

"I want to remain supportive," he insisted. "But I also want us to continue to examine the situation and determine, once and for all, who is doing this to you. Like I said, you can be quite perceptive. Take some time to examine this."

"I have been so overcome with confusion and distress when thinking about this haunting," MJ responded. "I'd like a break from making sense of it. For now, it would be wonderful not to think of it at all. Would you consider humoring me by allowing me to forget that for the time being."

"MJ," Alby stated. "This is a serious issue. Let's say that you are being 'haunted', the thought itself is difficult to swallow. That is beside the point. But—and please stay open-minded for one moment—let's say that this haunting is actually some awful person trying to scare you for some reason. If that is the case, you are dealing with a somber situation that requires attention."

"I've thought of that as well, Alby."

MJ didn't mean to brush off the topic, but handling all of this was too much to bear at the moment. She was simply exhausted, at times in pain, and anxious for Bernard to come home. Instead of arguing with Alby, she decided to change the subject to focus back on the story.

"Just moments ago you said there are so many details weaved into the fabric material of our life experiences. This often causes us to act certain ways or even see certain things."

"I did," Alby replied.

"In the story, you rushed through much of it to get to the main part—the part when the family was abandoned at sea, and the parents lost overboard in a terrible storm. What happened beforehand? What experiences did the Gull children have to make in order for them to become such terrible people?"

Alby again seemed to consider the question carefully. This, to a certain extent, continued to drive MJ crazy, figuratively, though she was willing to deal with it due to his recent compliment of her.

"In the story," Alby continued, "Piper, the youngest daughter is witness to all sorts of things. She knows her parents are good people who love their children beyond words can describe, but she too is quite perceptive, much like you."

"In what ways?" MJ asked.

"I, by hook or by crook, remember parts of the start of the story, as told to me in the past, that suggest their eldest son is somewhat tortured by his parents."

"Tortured?" MJ questioned.

"Not to the extent to how you are interpreting it," Alby corrected. "I believe he is a child that, in his own right, is never seen by his father as living up to the expectations he has placed on him. It is never truly described, until close to the end of it, why it is that his father is so disappointed in his eldest son, or why it is that his father simply doesn't believe his son can be the type of breadwinner he himself always was."

"From the way you described it," MJ pursued, "the eldest son does what he can to always impress some type of authority or leadership, but never once being able to gain the respect of his siblings."

"Yes, sad, isn't it?"

"And what of the other children in the story?" MJ further asked. "There is the second boy who seems so irritated about everything, and then the other girl, Holly, who seems to be, well . . ."

"A whore?" Alby interjected.

"I was trying to be nice," MJ responded. "But yes, a bit self absorbed. She seems as if she is very angry at her parents for taking her from her home because of all of the possible male suitors she has following her."

"Perceptions, MJ," Alby said with a tone that MJ believed to intend correction. "Perceptions and misperceptions. Remember?"

"I'm not sure I am following you, Alby."

"We have not yet explored the reasons that brought Holly to what made her act this way," Alby responded. "Imagine if you will, being plucked out of your comfortable existence—an existence where you demonstrated an expertise in life—and being thrown into the unknown. In this story, Holly, the beautiful town's girl, quite in demand apparently, has been thrust into living in the open sea with no one other than her family. She is not a fisherman; she is not even close to her siblings. She knows only about being liked by boys. That is her expertise. That is from where she was taken."

MJ related to Holly in more ways than she had anticipated. She shared a depth of feeling for this character, as she too was propelled into an unexpected situation—plucked from the expertise and contentment she knew quite well. MJ hadn't expected to, once again, pity life's callous and unfair treatment toward her. Though she tried desperately not to, she could not help but focus on her previous, well-to-do ballet career and fluid life that was quickly stolen from her by an untamed and unforgiving disease-stricken joke of nature. She thought *were someone to be reading my story, like Holly's, that person would likely think I was a nasty, depressed, and pathetic excuse for a woman, when really I was very happy and beautiful before all of this.* She fully understood what Alby meant by misperceptions at that moment.

"In the beginning of this tale, we are told that Holly is *dramatic* and *bratty* when her father tells his children of his intentions to move the family to sea to be with him as he works," Alby states. "What I did not tell you was that the story also mentions that Holly does everything she can to find herself within the good graces of her parents, but is often unsuccessful in achieving this."

"How sad," MJ adds. "Why?"

"Well the storyteller, I believe, was trying to indicate that Holly was overshadowed by much in life. She was third in line to the Gull fortune, but often ignored by her brothers—shameful examples of their parents—and also ignored by the youngest sibling, Piper, who seemed to receive much of the doting that each of the other children wished they had received. This had deep effects on Holly, and therefore forced her into another reality."

"Another reality?" MJ asked.

"Instead of feeling her father's love that she so desired, she sought out worthless, empty, and distasteful lust with neighborhood boys as a result."

There was a brief moment of silence in the room until MJ broke it like shattered glass.

"This is a wonderful story," MJ interpolated mockingly. "If it was meant to cheer me up, or help me forget some of the horrors I experienced the other night, it is not doing such a great job at it."

"There is a silver lining," Alby laughed. "Though, sad it is, Holly did finally find peace with an unnamed boy in the town who intended to marry her."

"And yet she was stripped away from him as well when the family moved to the sea," MJ responded.

"True."

"This story is terrible," MJ huffed. "If they all die at the end without any peace, I am never going to forgive you for telling me this."

Alby laughed.

"I think, as you hear the rest of the story over time, you will realize that each of the Gull children had their own demons to overcome. Each of them had their own perceptions and their own realities to handle. And each of them had their own ways of adapting from what was happy—or normal—to them as something that became quite sad and tragic."

"How long is this story?" MJ questioned.

"We're getting closer to the end, but that will be told at another time."

CHAPTER SIX

MJ knew that Bernard was treading lightly. As much as he likely wanted to dive right into the conversation, she believed he knew it would be unwise to unnerve her. And so, he began communication slowly this evening.

"Well, Shoshanna did her typical 'poor you' smile after I found her coffee gift on my desk," he said. "And I know Janice motioned to others in the office that 'poor Bernie must be suffering so much'. Therefore yes, dear, my day was the same-old-same-old."

MJ, more distant than usual, asked Bernard to help her retrieve a sip of water. Without hesitation, Bernard reached for the bedside cup and assisted her. MJ readied the conversation in her head all day. She practiced every line, twice, so as to ensure Bernard would not think her clinically insane. But she knew she had to mention something. Alby was correct. If someone in the town was purposely tormenting her, her husband needed to know. Her problem though, the one she was unable to face at the current moment, was that she at no moment considered this to be the case. Deep down, within her paralyzed gut, she did not think this specter was anyone, physical at least, from Pacifica sophomorically persecuting her. She could tell she was being frequented by something purely evil, and she knew, as disturbing as the thought was to her, that eventually she would need to encounter and possibly confront it.

"Bernard, I have been rehearsing what I am about to tell you," she nervously stated, trying to find the contradicting reasons for why she actually should not proceed with providing him with the information she was about to relay.

"I think I know," he responded rather emphatically.

This caused MJ great confusion. How could he possibly know what she was about to say, unless—and strangely, it was comforting to think this—possibly he was observing this specter as well?

"You have finally decided," he continued, "to leave me for Jonathan."

MJ laughed uncontrollably.

"Christ, I needed that," she suggested. "I hadn't expected you to make that joke right at the precise moment I was looking for some relief."

Bernard smiled, sat on her bed, and said, "I think it's time for me to move back into our bedroom. Full time."

MJ replaced her laughter with a sudden and now equally uncontrollable sob.

"If I weren't a confident man," Bernard insisted, "I would take offense to that outburst."

MJ didn't know whether to continue crying or to begin laughing again. Regardless of whichever emotion won, she knew it was likely to be something over which she had very little jurisdiction.

"What is wrong with you, dear? Please tell me."

"Bernard, I honestly don't know!" crying further, MJ replied. "What is wrong with me? Am I going crazy? Am I simply stir mad because of my situation?"

"Look, MJ darling," Bernard protested. "I was careful to mention this, but after you fell asleep, I arrived home and spoke with Alby. He did not want to betray your confidence, but he asked me to ask you about your . . ."

"My what?" interrupted MJ. "My craziness? Is that what Alby asked you to ask me about?"

Bernard shook his head, negating MJ's claim.

"Please, dear, calm yourself. He said nothing of the sort. He insisted that I ask you about your situation. Mentioned you might have something you need to tell me."

MJ didn't know whether to be happy that Alby respected her wishes to say nothing to Bernard, or to be angry that she was now forced to expose the issue, meanwhile also possibly exposing herself to the asylum.

"Bernard," she started. Then paused. And then she thought she might as well risk being considered crazy. "I think Catherine does not approve of our relationship."

Bernard paused. At that moment in time, MJ undoubtedly grasped the reality that faced her. She was alone. She was certain that Bernard hadn't experienced this specter. She was completely alone and the haunting was purposely meant for her.

"You mean, Wendy, your mother? Wendy does not approve of our relationship is what you meant," Bernard gently maintained.

"Bernard, I think Catherine is haunting me."

This was one of those looks, unique and infrequent as it was, of Bernard's face turned rigid. She no longer doubted that her original intentions to keep silent should have been kept just that way. Her husband, she was sure, not only now imagined her needing mental attention, but he was now incredibly angry with her.

"Catherine is not haunting you, MJ. You are letting your imagination stir wild in here. Maybe we should move you to the parlor, just for a change of pace."

His statement seemed cold, albeit unintentional. MJ felt its callousness directed towards her.

"I've seen her, Bernard. I've seen her twice on Mori Point, staring at me, motioning toward me, aiming to get my attention."

Bernard stood unmoved, but MJ could denote a sense of concern building within him.

"I saw her at the window the other day," she continued. "And I could hear moaning—speaking to me. It was so cryptic . . . like she was watching me, or something like . . . like she was coming for me . . ."

"At the window?" Bernard abruptly asked. "Wait . . . what . . . the window? Dear, I'm confused."

"At that very freaking window, Bernard!" MJ began crying. She motioned toward the window with her eyes.

"Look, we need to calm down."

"Bernard, *we* need to do nothing of the sort. *I* am never anything but *calm*. I am so calm that I can't even move! Please don't tell me to be calm. I have been calm my entire time with you, as you sit here caring for me while I waste away and play second fiddle to Catherine, and the shrine you keep of her covered in the hallway."

While it was probably not the most polite she had been she was relieved to show her dissatisfaction with Catherine's pictures that loomed there.

Bernard looked shocked. *Alby must be encouraging this*, MJ imagined him thinking. *Alby's visits must be encouraging MJ to think she can insult me like this.* She was sure that Bernard considered this behavior to be unlike her. MJ could also tell that Bernard's increasing thoughts about

Alby fueled his intensified rage, and thoughts of forbidding Alby to visit again clearly must have tantalized him.

"Darling," Bernard said, as calmly as possible—and it was beyond problematic for him at this moment, "Catherine is dead. It has taken me a long time to come to terms with that truth. She is not here. She is not visiting you. She is not coming back. Not ever again. Trust me. I had a difficult time accepting this."

MJ couldn't help but feel a bit betrayed. As she lay there, literally dying a bit more each day, she believed that Bernard had just depicted an enduring love for his first wife. Originally, while falling in love with Bernard, she would state *I don't ever want you to forget about Catherine. I would never want to be with someone who swept away one of his loves just because he found another. There is room enough for both of us in your heart.* Somehow now, these thoughts escaped her, and they no longer described how she felt.

MJ hoped that Bernard continued to focus on her weeping. She believed him to be naïve to the reasons for her behavior. She imagined him feeling as if he was being punished for something of which he was yet unaware? And, just as she expected, Bernard's tone eventually presented itself as a bit more irritated than usual.

"After all I have done for you, *for us*," Bernard exclaimed as carefully as possible. "Your insinuations are like daggers to me. I just don't understand what you are trying to suggest here!"

"I am being haunted by her. It is the only possible explanation," MJ asserted, unwavering in her resolve. The more she pushed, the more she could see Bernard's confusion and distaste for the assertion boil to an untouchable limit.

"She's dead! Dead!" Bernard charged quite loudly. That was a first for him. As a matter of fact, MJ never remembered hearing Bernard's voice raised in the slightest, not even during the evening he drank more than he could handle. But for a reason she could not explain, MJ enjoyed the fact that he was stung by this conversation. As he paced back and forth, it seemed to MJ that Bernard was either deeply concerned about her emotional and psychological welfare, furious that she questioned the assemblage of photos dedicated to his former, dead wife, or exceedingly befuddled with no ability to comprehend the situation.

"I think it is time I begin working from home," Bernard, with unquestionable assurance stated, now more calmly than his voice was just moments ago. His attempts to calm the situation were noticeable.

"I couldn't agree with you more, Bernard!" MJ retorted. "I want you here! I don't want to be left alone any more. Things are happening beyond what I think I can bear. I'm afraid she is going to do something terrible to me."

"Stop it, MJ!" Bernard implored, somewhat dramatically. "Catherine is not back from the grave to haunt you. Really, this is getting me quite frustrated. I don't know what has gotten hold of you. I am very disturbed by this!"

"How dare you, Bernard," MJ cried. "I desperately tried to explain this to you in a completely rational way. But no matter how much I search for an explanation, and no matter how much Alby coaches me to consider rational ideas, the only thing that comes to my mind is this terrible instinct that she is trying to reach me, to harm me, to harm us!"

"Alby," Bernard huffed. "This is his doing, isn't it?"

"Bernard," MJ snapped back. "It is Alby that encouraged me to tell you about this, not to keep it hidden."

"That doesn't shock me in the least! I cannot hear this any longer," he said, furiously. "I love you, but I will not have you go stark raving mad on me. Yes . . . yes . . ." Bernard immediately continued. "I'm working from home from this point forward. My colleagues will understand. And if they don't, too bad, I'll take a leave of absence."

Bernard stormed into the hallway. This time he did not stop, not even for a brief second glance at the hidden pictures. MJ thought that it must be so wonderful for Bernard to walk away from the conversation either because of his lack compassion or his deficiency in understanding her situation; all the while the reality of her circumstances was quite simple. She was stuck in bed and could do nothing to escape it. For the first time, she felt as if a storm of fog was coming—felt as if she was one of those lush, overgrown Pacifica plants stuck in place, trying everything possible to reach toward the sun, unable to move, only to find itself soon enveloped by a sudden, rolling vapor. And while she was always one to appreciate its beauty before, this was also the first time she hated the fog.

MJ sat in her bed quietly, absorbing the tête-à-tête she just suffered. She was shocked and frankly dejected that Bernard did not come back to check on her.

However, just when despair was at its height of downward fall, moments later Bernard returned. MJ found herself struggling to look at him. She felt just like his colleague, Marcus, whom Bernard often described as wimpy beyond belief. In one respect, she sympathized with Bernard and appreciated the reasons for his prior outburst. When she pieced the story together, it was purely nonsensical. The facts were ridiculously obvious that she was:

A. Speaking ill of Catherine, who for all intents and purposes was likely a lovely woman and a wonderful companion,
B. Foolishly presenting herself as one of those detached people from one of those biography haunting shows—the kind of person that obviously needs attention, and
C. Finally, she was acting like an utter bitch.

Yet when she thought about it further, though she often questioned her sanity in the past few days, she *was indeed* confident in justifying the experiences surrounding this haunting as well. She knew what she saw and she knew what she heard. More important to her at the moment, she knew what she felt, and she knew the feeling wasn't normal or happy.

Bernard waved at her to grab her attention, yet she did not respond. He then positioned himself on the bed, sitting close to her face. When the time finally came for MJ's eyes to turn toward him, he peered into them, transfixing upon her saddened gaze. As he focused into her stare deeply, MJ just then realized Bernard finally saw her fear—a fear he had not seen from her since a year ago. She found herself suggesting to herself, *he almost forgot about how fearful I was when I was becoming ill*. The longer Bernard fixated his gaze on her, MJ knew the more he realized that she certainly must have seen something. Just what that *something* was, he could not begin to imagine at this point.

"MJ, I apologize for being irrational moments ago," he began softly.

MJ, in a state of guilt, addressed his apology head-on.

"Oh no, Bernard. I'm the one that is acting irrational," she cried. "I know that I am not imagining this, but I also jumped to conclusions."

"I believe you," he said, to MJ's surprise. "I can see you are doing what you can to hold it together. Let's just please try to discuss the alternatives to ghost stories first."

MJ was reluctant, but she agreed this plan would be best for now.

"Something makes me quite nervous, actually categorically nervous," Bernard continued. "You said you saw 'her' at the window."

"That's right," MJ replied, beginning to become noticeably distraught.

"Just calm down, darling, and help me understand."

MJ took a moment to collect her thoughts and still her nerves. She once again thought back to her time at the Churchill Theater, back to when she was a ballerina and, before every one her performances, without any alteration from her methods, she would take a 20-second pause, force herself into a tranquil state, and immediately unwind. She was proud of the fact that she could still place her mind into a state of ease, and for now, it seemed to be working well.

"Let's play devil's advocate for a moment," Bernard said. "Omitting the prospect that Catherine is haunting you, can you be sure that what you saw was a *woman*?"

"Yes. At first, I wasn't sure. The more I saw her, I knew it was a woman."

"And," Bernard, unsure as to why he entertained the notion, asked, "What made you determine it was Catherine?"

MJ hadn't considered the need to defend her theory. The truth was that she didn't know why she accused Catherine of this. But, while she couldn't champion this dissertation of sorts, she accepted this as reality. It instinctually appeared as the only possibility, though she was careful not to express this to Bernard. The last thing she aimed to do was to get him furious again. She did not like the furious Bernard.

"Bernard, who else would continuously come to me, angry, making me innately feel threatened, other than someone who was unfortunately robbed of her life with you?"

"But Catherine was not that type of person," he retorted.

Without any hesitation, MJ relayed, "I'm sure she wasn't, Bernard. But I guess death can piss you off."

For a moment, they both paused, and finally they briefly laughed.

"I'm sorry, Bernard," MJ said with a slight smile. "I didn't mean to offend you or Catherine."

"Don't apologize, darling," Bernard responded finally and fully back to his normal tone. "It is a relief to see you still have your humorous spunk."

MJ considered that the probability of what she claimed was very low, nearly mutually exclusive from reality. But she stopped herself short of brushing the accusation off. She knew something was happening to her, and as much as she loved Bernard, as much as she enjoyed Alby, she would not let their realism discourage her from believing what she saw, felt, and heard. MJ once again thought of her mother. A bottomless extent of melancholy hit her heart.

"I think I need my mother to be with me."

Bernard, though he was usually too often diplomatic about the Wendy situation, this time held nothing back.

"We've been over this issue several times, MJ. As unfortunate as it is, your mother has made no attempt to keep you in her life. Your failure to marry Jonathan, and your fall from grace in marrying me instead—both have convinced her to choose a different path then the one that led her to staying as an active participant in your life."

"Yes, but maybe if I called her . . ." MJ interrupted.

"I will not allow you to do this to yourself, darling. Why put yourself through this pain, leaving both of us to pick up the pieces into which you will shatter after experiencing her refusals once again?"

MJ knew this to be true. She was still not quite sure why her mother was acting this way, but she made herself incredibly stressed and actually sad thinking about it. It felt like it was time to take a 20-second break again, and so she did.

"I want to get back to this appearance at the window, MJ," Bernard continued, changing the Wendy subject quite successfully. "First though, I am going to ask you something, and I hope that you will not fly off the handle."

"Please, Bernard. No bull shit."

"No," he chuckled. "Nothing like that. I just want you to contemplate the possibility that . . . maybe you believe you are seeing Catherine as a way to punish me for keeping her photographs around."

"Bernard, I do think the photographs have something to do with it," MJ responded. "However, maybe you have not allowed Catherine to be free? Maybe you're holding on to everything that belonged to Catherine is allowing—no—forcing her to hold onto this life."

"Those things, those photographs," Bernard replied, "are the only happy memories I have left of her, before, before she was gone. They ground me in reality."

"Bernard, why are you with me?" MJ asked.

"Oh don't be ridiculous, MJ."

"Please answer me."

"Because I love you and you also ground me in reality," he answered.

"Maybe then," MJ said slowly, "maybe it is time to let Catherine go."

Bernard took a moment, and at that point MJ knew he was caught red-handed staring toward the hallway, and then stopped himself from doing so.

It took some time for MJ's message to absorb. Bernard paced the room. After a minute or two, he turned toward the window, then turned toward MJ, then toward the hallway, and again faced the window, staring into space. Watching him was making MJ quite nauseous.

"Maybe you are right," he responded to her surprise.

This immediately relieved MJ. She thought that perhaps this would change things, and more importantly, she believed that Bernard could tell that his willingness to take this action was comforting her. He quickly walked away from her toward the largest hanging portrait. Placing his hands on it, hidden by its musty sheet, he tugged it three times to be exact, popped it from its comfortable groove on the wall, and carried it toward the bedroom closet storing them deep inside one of the corners. Not once did the sheet fall, and not once did MJ want it to move, not even slightly shift. As far as she was concerned—and she certainly did not want to anger Catherine—but the less she saw Catherine's mug, the better.

Bernard walked back toward the bed and once again sat by MJ's side.

"Voila," he said.

"Thank you, Bernard," MJ sniffled appreciatively. "It's a first step."

"Now," he continued, "let's deal with the possibility that someone other than Catherine is doing this to you."

MJ truly felt that Bernard supposed this was all in her creative mind, not maliciously, but psychologically as a response to cabin fever. But he did not want to take any chances. If someone was truly scouting the house, and MJ in the process, he wanted the issue resolved to its fullest punishing potential.

"You took a first step," MJ responded. "I can meet you halfway and do the same."

"That's my girl," Bernard calmly stated.

"Who would do this to me? And why?"

"Surely I don't know, darling. Possibly some teenage punk?"

MJ laughed a bit. "You sound almost exactly like Alby," she said.

"Well we'll deal with the fact that you trusted to tell this to him first, before you told me," he retorted.

"Yes, I'm sorry about that, Bernard."

Bernard stayed silent. MJ knew he likely didn't think it necessary to respond to that apology, but instead moved onto his next thought.

"I believe the first thing I will do is start monitoring things myself. Maybe I'll place some security cameras around the house."

"Why not call the police if you think someone may be doing something creepy here?" MJ asked.

"No police, at least, not yet," he answered.

MJ thought this was a rational plan, so long as Bernard was confident in it. Bernard was typically right, of course. She wasn't eager for all of Pacifica to believe she was a loon, especially if she and Bernard weren't able to catch anyone in the act. Still though, she was pleased that Bernard, himself, was beginning to look more and more concerned about the situation.

"MJ, dear, it is starting to get late. I'm assuming you are tired."

"I am desperate for sleep," she responded. "I believe I haven't had a good night's sleep in so long—between dreams and boogey women. But . . . wait, you are not leaving me in here alone tonight, are you?"

Bernard shook his head considerably. "Like I said," he reassured, "it's time for me to start sleeping in here full time."

MJ was immediately overcome by comfort. After the silly little things Bernard would do to ready for bed, the two would lay with one another once again.

MJ, after minutes it seemed, drifted into a haze, much like a dying beach bonfire. And all felt good.

Though some unexpectedly relaxing time had passed, it felt like just a moment later when Bernard violently shook her. MJ was able to see the clock to the right of her bed. Exactly three hours had passed since MJ first closed her eyes.

"What did you say?" Bernard asked her, with a shaking that slightly subsided in the process.

"What?"

"I heard something. Was it you? No it couldn't have been," Bernard asked and then confirmed to himself. He glared around the room, and then quickly looked toward the window. MJ heard Bernard asking himself if it was all actually possible, if he too was now going crazy?

"Bernard, what's wrong?" MJ asked.

"I heard someone speaking. At first I thought it might be you, but the voice came from, I think, the other side of me."

The fog outside was as dense as dry ice. The weather that evening, to MJ's surprise—being that the report had anticipated a relatively warm, sunny day tomorrow—had actually caused biting frigidity in the room. And, as a result, she had realized that Bernard was clutching onto her for warmth. In reality, Bernard, her regular West Coast town's man seized hold of MJ—his weak, indefensible wife—out of pure fear.

"What did you hear, Bernard?" MJ asked. "Tell me."

MJ saw Bernard thinking frantically for a moment, grabbing his ears, yanking them a bit—just as one does to clear clogged water after an aggressive swim.

"No, this is just not possible!" He forced from his lips.

"Bernard, damn it!" MJ screamed. "Tell me! What happened? You are scaring me!"

"I am going outside to go check the grounds."

"Like hell you are!" MJ stated heatedly. "Don't even think about leaving me here alone. What the hell happened?"

"Tomorrow," he responded, "I am going into the city and getting a security system. I'm taking care of this once and for all."

MJ fumed. Better for her to douse this growing flame without delay, she thought, before she boiled in her own rage.

"Answer me right now, Bernard."

Bernard examined her lying there, looked back out the window, and then scrutinized the room with alertness.

"I heard someone say," he choked in disbelief, "I'm coming soon, and I am going to get you."

CHAPTER SEVEN

It was no surprise to her that she did not sleep for the remainder of that night, not even in the slightest sense. MJ couldn't tell, however, if it was due to her terrified state or her exceptionally felt reassurance. She was now quite positive that she had not experienced delusions of grandeur and in fact was undergoing something all too existent and tangible.

"Clearly someone is doing everything possible to startle you, MJ," Alby said, helping her to take a sip of water. "Bernard mentioned that he was going to get security cameras installed."

"He left earlier this morning to purchase them," MJ responded. "I begged him not to leave, but he insisted it needed to be done immediately."

MJ hadn't considered, until just at that moment, that Bernard was now terrified as well. The idea of MJ being stalked infuriated him, and as usual, she was grateful for his support.

"Bernard disclosed that he only heard someone speaking, not that he saw anyone. Is that correct?"

"As far as I know, Alby," MJ confirmed. "But he seemed so troubled by the entire situation, that when I asked him to stay, he told me that you would be here to keep me company very soon."

"And here I am," Alby also confirmed.

The weather report yesterday was correct after all. MJ's bed was propped into a practically seated position. She could see surfers in the water, just beyond Mori Point, enjoying the warm rays of the sun. There was not a hint a fog in the distance—no mist creeping over the hills, no precipitation silently lingering, waiting for an attack. The day was simply beautiful, and due to the severity of the state of affairs the prior night, MJ was almost tempted to have Alby carry her outside for some fresh air.

Noticing MJ's longing expression, unfortunate sorrow under the guise of restraint, he proceeded towards the window.

"How about some fresh air," he said, as he began to make a motion to open it.

"Touch that window and you're dead," MJ answered. "I'm not going to risk loosening it and then having it opened for the ghost to fly in while I'm alone."

"Ok, ok . . . no fresh air."

"Look," MJ continued. "I'm willing to accept that I was a bit delirious the other day. I guess anything is possible. I learned this when my life quickly began to sink down the toilet. But the possibility that I am being haunted is not very probable."

"Good, MJ. Good," Alby responded cheerfully. MJ knew this made him feel very comfortable.

"This, however, leaves me in quite a predicament," MJ claimed. "It means that someone out there is stalking our house, and has now threatened us. To be honest, I think I'd rather deal with the ghost of a jealous dead wife."

"I'm in total agreement," Alby said without hesitation.

CHAPTER EIGHT

Bernard arrived home approximately an hour after Alby left to go work on a wetlands project, which Alby of course described in nauseating detail to an impatient MJ during their earlier visit. For once, MJ thought Alby's departure couldn't come soon enough. To her, hearing about the project's description was like being forced to watch golf. She not only was prepared to face a ghost, but on top of that, she'd rather face a lingering intruder at her window instead of hearing one more issue related to the protected Pacifica frog and garden snake. As always though, she thanked Alby for his visit; and she truly looked forward to her time with him tomorrow. She only hoped that, although Bernard intended to spend more quality time at home due to the series of unfolding situations, Alby would still continue to visit her.

There was some relief with the turn of events that evening. The warm day, mixed with the typical cooling evening, did in fact create a less dense but equally as noticeable wall of fog. This was moving rapidly toward the shoreline. Following it was an unusual thunderstorm, equipped with passionate lightning. *Just perfect*, MJ thought. *Could this not be more like a television movie?* MJ was only comforted when, after having installed the security system, Bernard assured her that he was quite positive the 'weirdo' would stay directly indoors due to the storm. MJ wasn't sure if Bernard was trying to convince her or himself, but the reassurance calmed MJ's nerves, so much so that when Bernard mentioned he needed to leave for an hour, she wasn't as concerned as she thought she'd be.

"I just need to collect some files from work so that I can continue some of the research here at home," Bernard told her.

"I understand, Bernard."

"Now, you know what to do, correct?" Bernard asked her, his tone not in the least condescending, but more cautious than anything.

"If I see or hear anything strange, I am to shout the name of our town into the air," MJ responded.

"Pacifica," Bernard added. "I programmed that word to make it easy for you to remember."

"Yes, of course," MJ responded. "A simple 'HELP' would not have sufficed?"

Bernard laughed, and MJ could see that he admired the installation that took him most of the afternoon. In all reality, MJ respected his work as well. It included not just the highest quality security cameras on each side of the house, but motion sensors, and a voice-controlled alarm notification coded with the word 'Pacifica'—perfect for an immobile person who was unable to dial 9-1-1.

MJ couldn't explain her sudden strength. She believed that having Bernard's corroboration and validation made a world of difference. Yes, she was still quite disturbed by the things she had witnessed recently, but her sentiments began to progress from fear toward anger. Thoughts of ghosts were no longer weighing on her. Instead, it was becoming more evident to her that she and her husband were victims of discrimination at the hands of an imbalanced person. This was absolutely unacceptable to her.

It was apparent to MJ that Bernard searched for the appropriate time to kiss her on the top of her head. This often made MJ feel like an adolescent, but a show of affection was obviously the last thing to get her annoyed this evening. Her mechanical bed was still in the uprooted, seated position, as she had requested it be. While she agreed with Bernard that only the simplest idiot would go running around on a tempestuous rainy evening such as this one, she wanted to keep her body in a firm place in order to reconnoiter her surroundings if necessary.

"Again, I'll be back in about an hour," he told her.

"Please be careful," she responded. "I get very nervous when you drive late on Sharp Park Road. It is sometimes difficult to see what's around the next winding corner."

"Do you think," Bernard began, "I can't believe I am going to say this aloud, but do you think you need to . . . call Alby to keep you company?"

"Well, to be honest, I did think about it. But no I don't think it is necessary. I have a feeling he is out on a date this evening. God let's hope he's on a date and not saving more frogs and their surrounding plant life. I will be ok."

Bernard looked at MJ with pure amazement. To MJ, Bernard must have thought that this was the woman with whom he originally fell in love. MJ's spunk was finally returning, and her determination was committed. Illness or not, her mind was more focused. In some ways, this intruder, invader, or as MJ originally called her—this specter, was helping her to fight. More than this, she was conversing with Bernard more freely, including him in her daily thoughts, and he likely couldn't be more pleased.

"One hour," he called to her as he began to exit the house.

"One hour," she responded.

Door locked.

Silence.

"Well, this is a bit unnerving," MJ said aloud.

Silence.

"Maybe I should have called on Alby," she said aloud again.

More silence.

For a moment, MJ wondered what would happen if she shouted 'Pacifica'! Bernard would be furious. He'd actually be worried, and she did not want to put him through that. But the joke continued to enter her mind.

"Well," she said into the open air, "it's just you and me, classical music." Thank goodness Bernard had powered the stereo before exiting.

MJ scrutinized the room, "nothing there," she said. "And nothing there in that corner. Clock, you're still there ticking. Good clock. Window, stay shut."

As she continued to bolster herself of her absolute safety and normalcy, she walked the room with her eyes and thought *this way that I am acting—this is ridiculous*. Slowly but surely, she discovered some force of curious gravity once again drew her attention toward the hallway. She thought to herself, *those frigging pictures! I forgot all about them.* She didn't truly mind, but she did believe that, in a few days, the opportunity for Bernard to clear them out would become a reality. And she validated, in her thoughts, that this would behoove them both.

The classical music was, as it always seemed to be, soothing and hypnotic. Companioned by the atypical rain, especially at this time of year, and the natural strobe lights flashing through the sky, lethargy reared its presence within her once again. MJ could feel herself drifting into a sleepy state. At this point, she was shocked that her lack of rest didn't cause her to be instantaneously comatose. And for once, she was comfortable closing her eyes while alone.

"I'm making progress," she yawned. "Yes, I am making progress. Next week, I'll be dancing again and visiting my friends at the Churchill," she laughed. The thought comforted her. Further beliefs that she could possibly reunite with her mother—make her proud once more—also comforted her. Ironically to add, though she detested being in water in general, the sounds of the rain comforted her.

"Maybe," she said aloud, "I'll conquer that dream too! And this time, I won't drown." What a pleasant thought. MJ then closed her eyes. Thoughts of the Gull children from the *Happy House of Saddened Gulls*, drifting on the open water without their parents came to her mind. She again sympathized with them. As she knew that Alby often told her stories to pass the time, provide her with some solace, and present to her a world that she could only imagine in her current state, she could not help but continue to feel empty about the Gull children's experiences. The story, in some fantastical way, was so realistic to her. And the sensations she underwent as Alby told it remained within her.

Just as the Gulls lost their parents and entered an unknown and terrifying world, thoughts of her own mother's desertion of sorts burned in MJ's brain. Loss of her sense of pride as a result scorched her heart. She found herself not only wondering if the Gull children felt helpless with the realities of their story, but she also considered the possibility that she, herself, experienced a sense of vulnerability even before the tragedy of her paralysis. This was, in all respects, at last a bewildering recognition.

If the thunder hadn't crashed so sinfully loud, MJ knew for sure that she wouldn't have woken from her profound and almost subterranean sleep. The room was now bitterly cold and penetratingly dark—intense. She lied quietly, squinted as much as humanly possible in order to focus on the time displayed by the battery-operated wall clock. From what MJ could tell, it seemed as if only thirty-five or forty minutes had passed, and thus, Bernard still wouldn't be home for another twenty at least. MJ began to wish that he'd walk in at any moment. The power was now out, expired, and the darkness was suffocating her. She now not only hoped he'd walk in any moment, but that Bernard would indeed rush home, as unsafe as it was.

"Just grab your work and leave, damn it!" She said aloud. The dead silence within the house now forced her voice to echo from room to room. With this, her heart began to beat like a drum, and she so wished she could run from the bitterness she felt. The dark was breaking her, and she believed something was terribly wrong.

Sparks of light outside were becoming more frequent after each clash of thunder, and so too were MJ's anxieties. For an instant, the sound of the front door creaking ajar was as beautiful as a symphony waltz. Finally, Bernard was home. Steps toward the bedroom confirmed her safety.

"Bernard?" She called out. "Bernard, thank goodness. The power is out."

Footsteps. Then silence.

"Bernard?"

Slowly, footsteps again.

"What are you doing, Bernard?" She questioned impatiently. "Please come to the bedroom right away. I'm freezing and my head is beginning to throb! I'm getting myself nervous for no reason other than silly thoughts."

The sound of footsteps once again stopped.

"Can you check the generator, Bernard? I can't see a thing."

At once, the sound of footsteps could be heard again, this time at a quicker pace. They sounded lighter than a man's footsteps, causing MJ's emotions to stir quite suddenly. Things did not seem right. And with this, MJ felt nauseous.

"Bernard, I am going to be sick! Bernard, please answer me!"

The footsteps quickened further, and the closer they came to her room, the louder they became.

"Oh God, please help me!" MJ screamed, wanting to die on the spot.

"Please, God! Please let me die. I can't live like this any further!" MJ again screamed. She was, at this moment, unsure as to whether or not what she was hearing was imagined or as true as the rain outside. With each footstep, her heart pounded. She had only hoped, if the sounds were authentic, that the physical pain she felt would soon be over, and if it were to be something terrible, that mercy would come upon her. Outside, each time lightning struck, she could see her surroundings for several seconds at a time. She prayed for lightning to collide with something close by, just to be able to get a true perception of the things around her. But it was merely spurts of light that did little to make things clear. Furthermore, dead silence occupied the room again. To MJ, it was the worst part. She felt as if she was being watched by something invisible to her. She wanted to scream, *show yourself,* but she was too petrified—physically and mentally—to do so.

And then it came, what she had hoped would happen—a flash of light so rapid, so deep-seated, it was the antidote that allowed the walls to absorb any existing light left by the lightning's remnants. Regrettably her instant reaction rendered her terrified, helpless, and craving sudden death. She almost fainted at the sight of what she saw—a water-doused, drooling female face within inches from hers. She could feel water dripping on her neck, and the stranger's breath was foul and hot, trouncing MJ's intently shocked, icy skin. And then the room darkened, black again, as if the lightning never existed. MJ did more than scream. She wailed so loudly, her throat almost burst.

"HELP ME! OH GOD! BERNARD! HELP ME!"

She could do nothing to shield herself. If she hadn't truly been paralyzed, surely the fear would have immobilized her. The worst part was that she lost all serenity and instinct. The shock of the situation was enough to make her forget that simply ridiculous password to alert the voice-controlled security. She continued to lay completely still and scream until she began to choke. She could feel tears streaming down her face, and once again, she believed she was drowning. She could not help but think that possibly her dreams were prophetic? Maybe she symbolically foresaw her demise. Only then did the sound of a horrific, whispery, and unsteady voice break her sobs.

"I told you," the stranger said, now completely concealed by the obscurity of the room's powerful blackness. "I told you I would come get you."

"Who are you?" MJ screamed. "Oh God, shit! Oh God, help me!"

MJ felt a forceful jerk on the bed, and a yank on her duvet. It seemed like minutes had passed by, and with each heaving influence against her, her body substantially ached in a way that she had not felt before. Suddenly, she was completely uncovered—sheets and the comfort of her heavy blanket were now on the floor beside the bed. As she lay there, devoid of any barrier between her body and the night air, the room's draftiness pierced her at such incredible intensity. Then came several flashes of storm-fueled light. Though, she did not see the stranger anywhere close by—and she knew she was indeed close—she was grotesquely mystified by something that did catch her vision.

If she hadn't seen it with her own eyes, she wouldn't have believed that her body was bound. She was completely and physically strapped into the bed. Across her body in several different places, she could see shackles and choking chains. Looped around each wrist and ankle were small belts, wound to their tightest limits. Crosswise her breasts, her abdomen, and her legs were ropes digging into her skin. The sight of it made her body burn. She could see deep grooves within her flesh, and before the room went dark, she thought she could also see blood at an almost concentrated purple, surely as a result of the binding all around her.

"What did you do to me?" She screamed. "BERNARD! Oh God, Bernard! Help me! She did something to me while I was sleeping!"

Though she was horrified, and knew there was likely no hope for her, she had an abrupt and disturbing thought. *I am going to be killed!* And further, she considered the horrible reality that Bernard would once again find the most important person in his life dead, just as he found Catherine before. He would never recover from this, not a second time. She wept. She screamed. And then suddenly the word came to her. She was so foolish!

"Pacifica!" She shouted. "PACIFICA!"

At once, a siren—the superlative sound of it—rang throughout the room. Red lights flashed every other second, and she knew they came from the system Bernard installed above her bed just that afternoon.

"Pacifica! Pacifica! Pacifica!" She continued to scream. Surely this would scare the intruder away. But through the tearstains, dramatically blurring her vision, she could see the woman, soaked all over, at MJ's feet continuing to claw at the straps.

"Get away!" MJ cried. "Leave me the fuck alone!"

And then again that awful specter voice, "Move. Move now!"

MJ continued to cry. She could not imagine why this was happening to her.

"Move!" The voice screamed, appalling and vicious. "Move or you're dead! You will be dead!"

Precipitously, MJ found herself on the ground. She was in pain, and the weight of the overturned bed on top of her legs was numbing to the core, yet it seemed to be screening her, protecting her from this monster. Through the flashes of red, she could see the horrid scene of what looked very much like a half-dead, rancorous woman pulling the bed—surely to attack MJ.

And suddenly, MJ was free. The tumble to the ground and the force of the bed's collapse was enough to break the chains and ropes and free her from the horrid binds.

I will not let Bernard find me dead, she continued to think to herself. *I must move now!* Methodically to her shock, MJ willed herself to move.

She began to crawl across the floor, dragging her seemingly dead legs behind her, scratching against the grain in the wood beneath her. As she did this, she realized she lost a fingernail in the process. The blood oozed from the gaping wound just inflicted upon her, and her body throbbed with pain. *Keep moving,* she urged herself. *Don't stop!* She could hear footsteps coming slowly behind her, the monstrous invader's wheezing breath, and MJ knew if she didn't move faster, she'd be dead.

MJ reached the bedroom closet. Indisputably, if she could trap herself inside (she knew it locked from the inside) this would give Bernard enough time to get home and save her. With all of the might she had inside her, she scuttled up the door, lunging her body in the direction of its knob. It was painful to do so, but she turned it and pulled it open, feeling the heavy weight of the solid egress that was much too heavy for her weak physique. It may have been a miracle, or possibly the power of adrenalin, but her mind forced her legs to move, and without hesitation, MJ stumbled into the closet, just as the intruder reached her.

The pounding and screaming on the other side of her protective surroundings were deafening. *Please come home Bernard,* she yelled in her head. The closet was as dark as the room had been during the storm. Desperate to live, MJ felt around the walls, the floor, whatever grooves to which her fingers could introduce themselves. *A cable! A light switch cable,* she thought. Suddenly there was light. The power was back. She could once again hear the music that played before she slept.

Dead Can Dance: The Wind that Shakes the Barley. That song! MJ heard its echoes through the hallways, reverberating beyond the boundaries of walls between the rooms. Its ghostly sounds were evocative of a hypnotic and sad ballad, much like the sad tale that Bernard once told her was the source of the song. *It is based on an old Irish ballad,* Bernard said to her after having played the song several times in a row. *It was written from the perspective of a Wexford insurgent who loses everything, including his love, to fight in the Irish rebellion—resistance to British rule.* MJ remembered thinking about how sad it was that someone was so determined to march with resistance to something that he would sacrifice everything happy to him in order to do so. She then asked Bernard, *and why the barley?* Bernard simply responded, *the rebels carried it on them always, in their pockets, as a source of food and strength, but it only carried them so far until their ultimate demise—war—overtook them.*

Shaking her memories from her head, MJ had stared at the source of the closet's light fixture. The closet was now well lit, and MJ could see it packed to the brim. It consisted of old, musty clothes—some of them MJ's for sure, in better days now past, and other clothes had to be those belonging to Catherine.

The intruder continued to pound on the closet door from the other side. MJ tried safeguarding her ears from utter shrills coming from this beast. She again felt sick to her stomach.

"Leave me alone!" She screamed. "What do you want?"

"Come out here!" Screamed the woman. "COME OUT!"

The tears began to swell in MJ's eyes again. She was now curled on the floor, covering her face, laying in a fetal position, trying to grasp the reality of the situation. The sustained pounding was vibrating the closet floor. MJ would take short glances of her surroundings, just as quickly covering her face as much as possible. Through the corner of her eye, she saw Catherine's portrait vibrating as well.

"Oh God, why are you letting this happen to me?"

The tarp-like sheet that obscured the portrait then fell, like a graceful, slow-motioned ballerina in flight. The creases, piling upon one another onto the ground, flapped loudly to seize MJ's concentration. For the first time, MJ was face to face with the portrait. It glared at her unforgivingly. MJ slowly lowered her hand from her face, blinked three times to clear the tears, and slowly repositioned herself in the line of its sight. A traumatizing shockwave overcame her. She reached for her gaping mouth. Not one sound could be originated from her throat, though she tried. *It was impossible*, she thought. *How could this be?* A mix of emotions stirred inside her. She was stunned, terrified, suddenly paralyzed—again—with confusion and anxiety.

And then it came, finally, and had her senses not have kicked-in just at the appropriate time, MJ would not have appreciated that it was she in the closet, not the intruder outside, who made the horrible and amazing scream at the sight of the unbelievable scene she saw on the portrait.

PART TWO:

Bernard Matters

"A coward is incapable of exhibiting love; it is the prerogative of the brave."—Mahatma Gandhi

BERNARD'S ACCOUNT

Pacifica Police Station, Coastal Highway, Pacifica, CA

A pad of paper.
A dull pencil.
Stale coffee.
A lack of circulating air.
An offer of a cigarette. I refuse. Nasty habit. Maybe one?
What am I saying?

My left arm just above the elbow hurts like a bitch. It's oozing blood from a deep thrash, and it is throbbing where the medic provided the most ample service possible during this fucking incredible situation. It is bandaged tightly by gripping gauze, and six stitches are now underneath, carefully sewn through the torn skin. Several of the detectives have sporadically checked on me, asking if I needed anything further than the list I provided above (my pad of paper, a dull pencil, my stale coffee, no air, nasty habit, etcetera). They also have been checking my arm from time to time to see if I need further medical attention. Unfortunately, they couldn't offer anything more potent than acetaminophen to stultify the stinging throughout my body.

Just moments ago, I asked everyone in sight where she was.
MJ? They'd assume I meant.
Not MJ. I'd responded. *That thing! That awful thing!*

I knew MJ had already been taken to the university medical center, and it was good she was receiving attention. For now, I was stuck here reliving my account.

Again, I'd say, *where is she—that horrible thing?*

They would look at me with pity, utter repellant sympathy. They'd simply answer that it was all under *full control.*

Those interactions slowly ceased throughout the evening. And so, I have been deserted, left in this room to scribe my accounts. More like it, I have been left in this room to rot and sweat. Everyone, including me, has seen to MJ's security; and Detective Elphorantis has assured me of MJ's current care. Further, he has asked me to document everything I could remember about the situation. *Validation, references, certain versions of this jigsaw will need to be pieced together*, he claimed, and of course, the help I can provide will be of the *greatest importance.* He'd prefer to take my statement as written testimony rather than impressing upon me a moment of verbal pain.

I sat here for twenty-six minutes exactly before beginning to write this. I don't know what else I can provide beyond the interview I gave. Detective Elphorantis continued to insist this be done, and obviously it is my duty to provide every bit of detail possible. The truth of the matter—MJ was in danger. I articulated this in every way possible (morons), and they reassured me that they had no doubt in that fact. And now that MJ is in the University Medical Center, her care is being rendered, and the damage is being analyzed, yet I am stuck here helping them do their job. Fuck them.

What do I think? The injustice of this entire experience is unequivocally, unbelievably heartbreaking. After everything I built to put the ghosts of sorrow past me, adopt a new life, and live to my fullest potential, start my life over—happy, some bitch dives in and destroys it. Unacceptable. I'm tired. I'm frustrated. Are you reading this detective? I'm pissed.

How about this for starters? Detective Elphorantis asked me about my move to Pacifica—wanted to know when it took place, and whether or not I knew any of the town's people. Maybe signs of whacked neighborhood behavior would have been a clear prophecy to these events. I already told him that I did the best I could to avoid neighbors.

I moved from San Francisco's Hayes Valley to Pacifica after Catherine's death. We, Catherine and I that is, would formerly visit this town on warm days to escape life in the *City by the Bay*. Sunbathing here, where human surfers interact peacefully with marine life—the type of marine life disinterested in eating humans—was simply amazing to Catherine. Don't get me wrong, I could appreciate this town as well, but it wasn't until Catherine's death that I respected it for what it actually wound up being for me. It was pure protection from annoying disturbances. I could be left to myself with no one to annoy me, which is unless I wanted him or her to do so. Living here allowed me to be—me, without any apologies, left alone, and quite satisfied by it, mind you.

Like I already said, for Catherine, the beauty was much more about the town's interactions with her people. She absolutely loved to watch the surfers meet at Lindamar Beach, the crescent-shaped beach not too far from the Mori Point. To Catherine, and in fact to MJ as well, this town was a sheer reflection of beauty—Aphrodite's personal attempt to stare into a handheld mirror. Catherine would often say it was a place like no other—complete beauty captured in time. Catherine often believed this was where the most famous people in history escaped after they 'pretended' to die from society.

For MJ, she experienced peace here, especially on the foggy days. MJ often liked to discuss the fog as if it were a mystery of nature. She believed it was the environment's way of cleansing everything it encountered, removing the grit left by either natural or forced decay and harm. Things to MJ always looked much more clear after fog rolled in and then out of the scenario. In all honesty, I think MJ preferred the fog to warmth. Didn't matter to me. As long as I continued to be left alone by the surrounding people—fog, sun, didn't matter to me.

Me? I don't really care about the beauty, the wildlife, the surfers, or the weather. I came here to retreat and avoid others. And now it seems I'll need to do it all over again, damn it.

CHAPTER NINE

"Those disgusting scavengers," Bernard screamed aloud as he swerved in a treacherous manner to avoid hitting the gulls that landed in front of his driving path. Truth be told, his intention to avoid them had nothing to do with their safety, but everything to do with safeguarding his car. Bernard had no idea why MJ loved it when these damn birds landed on the sill outside of her room. She found them peaceful to look at. He found them to be noisy, harassing creatures with nothing to look forward to except the next live meal they were bound to rummage. If he could have moved past his ideas of the filth and disease that these nasty flying rats so surely carried, he would have had a profound respect for how as a colonized pack gulls were typically very bold in their hunt. He had once witnessed a rather large quantity of gulls attack a live whale as it surfaced for air, and he remembered admiring their tenacity. It was an example of persistence for him to follow. The problem, Bernard thought, they were too disgusting for his taste.

Bernard knew he should have driven along Sharp Park Road instead of exiting onto the freeway. MJ had warned him to drive cautiously on the winding trail, and upon thinking about it, he thought she was right. The weather was quite aggressive, and traveling on Sharp Park could indeed be treacherous, especially when his mind was rapidly wandering in so many directions. Among the obvious brusque turns and numerous blind spots, thoughts of MJ being terrified were ever present. And worse, someone was scouting the house. But now, having avoided Sharp Park's more direct route, he was behind schedule in getting back to his house quickly.

Fuck, he thought.

Bernard knew something like this was bound to happen. Life was sailing the treacherous waves too perfectly in the past year, and now the misfortunes of a happy man were quickly catching up with him. Of paramount importance at the current moment, he was quite sure that someone was attempting to scare him—them—him. He didn't know why, but regardless, Bernard was determined to protect them both. He entertained the thought of Catherine's haunting for one brief moment, and quickly brushed that to the side. *Even if something as ridiculous like that was true,* he silently supposed, *it would have surfaced some time ago.* Instead, he was sure someone was spying on them and trying to wreak havoc. Though he was frightened by the events, he couldn't bring himself to admit it. The possibility of this all swirled in his brain, and as a consequence, he pressed himself to feel outraged because of it.

Further still, he had an incredible amount of freeway traffic ahead of him. With the lingering work he was now forced to collect and bring home, he was bound to carelessly forget to pack something vital in order to rush back to MJ as quickly as possible. Before leaving the house, Bernard reassured her that this troublemaking spy could not possibly create any nuisance in such inclement weather this evening. In reality, his nerves were shot to their limits, and though he knew he comforted MJ, he simply wasn't sure whether his assurance was true or not.

Traffic was now at a standstill.

"This is just great," he sarcastically called out. "Perfect!"

He checked his cellular phone to make sure the signal was strong. At times, among the mountains on this peninsula, phone service was certainly less than satisfactory. He visualized the moment he decided to move to Pacifica, after Catherine's death. When making the transformation from city to town life, he could not have been happier. It was a wonderful retreat, perfectly far enough from everyone. Here isolation was not difficult to find. But if ever he needed to escape into a more frenetic civilization from time to time, for whatever necessitated him to do so, he needed only drive a minor distance in either direction. When making the transition to this town though, he knew if he wanted to enjoy it, it was essential to acclimate to the idiosyncrasies of the remote, mountains and ocean life—*like losing fucking cell service at the most freaking inappropriate moments,* he thought. It was imperative to be sure all cellular connection was clear enough to receive an alert from MJ—either by text or by the voice controlled alarm he installed. So far though, he had received no announcement whatsoever.

Eleven or twelve minutes had passed and the traffic reporter on the radio claimed there was an accident ahead. *Likely something small causing a lot of useless rubbernecking,* he quietly considered, more pessimistically than MJ knew him to be. In the meantime, Bernard made himself more anxious pondering the issues he would soon need to face, issues that were unmistakably ahead, and he considered everything—the police, the danger, the loss. It was almost unbearable for him. He was the one who now felt claustrophobic, like *he* was the one drowning, powerless with nowhere to go, much like MJ always claimed to feel after one of her nightmares.

The radio played loudly, cars trumpeted their horns like an orchestra's tuning itself before a show, and none of it seemed to register with Bernard. Too many thoughts caused him to drift through consciousness, back to several years ago when he lived in the Hayes Valley section of San Francisco. He remembered his time at his favorite watering hole, that very night of Catherine's demise as a matter of fact. And he zoned. His hands gripped the steering wheel so tightly that grooves appeared in the leather. Bernard continued to think about the avaricious nature of life, and he upset his calm. The moving headlights on the opposite side of the freeway approached his stillness in joust fashion, almost as if they had an unfair advantage against his inability to move. The lights were blinding, and their movement—while he was stuck in place on his side of the freeway—was irritating beyond explanation. Rather quickly, he thought about MJ's situation and understood how she must often feel.

That night was stormy too, Bernard thought. Thinking back, he forced himself to consider the details carefully. He remembered, interjected among her bouts of sobs, Catherine was incoherently screaming to him as he walked out the front door. He was so annoyed by their argument; he was lethargic and had no intention of exerting any further energy. He was interested in rolling down the sloped San Francisco street that embraced their old house instead of walking it, yet he knew the sight would embarrass him. All too often, his and Catherine's arguments were intensifying, and that evening's quarrel and the reactions that followed were yet another example of the weakening of their nuptials. Instead of sticking around for this nonsense, Bernard did what he did best. He escaped to his favorite place to drink beer, watch sports, view the occasional seedy scenes, and stare at the pretty girls.

Earlier that day, before the physical storm outside, and the mentally anguishing storm with Catherine inside, Bernard had a phone conversation with his brother, Alby. Bernard thought about it as he strolled slowly to the bar. He was becoming increasingly exasperated with

Alby's constant psychoanalyses of him. According to Bernard, Alby was treading into an area that didn't concern him; discussing personal issues regarding the declining relationship Bernard had with his wife was simply off limits. Still Bernard realized that Alby, for whatever reason, felt the need to pursue the issue, apparently out of concern for his dear brother and sister-in-law, Catherine. Sometimes he simply did not know when to stop.

"Bernard," Alby said over the phone, his voice at times seeming somewhat disconnected to the conversation. "In my opinion, I think you are trying to scrutinize my conversations with you a bit too much."

"I didn't seek your advice, Alby," Bernard retorted abruptly. "You are the one who called me. Things are just fine on my end."

As Bernard walked the dark street, determined to quickly introduce himself to a drink at the bar, he remembered his comment might have stung Alby a bit. Bernard felt a tad guilty for being so unpleasant. *At least,* Bernard thought during his reminiscing, *I apologized for it.*

"I don't want your apologies," Alby answered back quickly. "I am just tired of seeing you mope around like it is the end of the world. Man-up, Bernard!"

"That is so easy for you to say, brother."

"On the contrary, *brother,*" Alby mocked. "It is not in the least easy for me to say this to you. You are being a stubborn bastard. Your wife is, I am sure, still in love with you. It seems to me that you, *you,* are the one who is never around. Maybe *that* is the issue that has possessed Catherine all this time. Think about it."

Alby was correct. Bernard knew he hadn't been focusing on Catherine too much in the recent past. Could he be the problem causing their marriage to fall from grace? Possibly. Yet he was annoyed to admit it, and frankly pissed at Alby for addressing it.

"I appreciate the guidance, brother," Bernard coldly responded. "I think, for now, it is best for you to stay out of my business."

Click.

Silence.

Re-evaluating this memory caused Bernard pain. As he walked to the bar, his head intensely hurt because of the earlier argument he had with Alby, and the current argument he was having with Catherine. A drink could not come soon enough.

The bar was its usual opaqueness, with occasional flashes of neon. Its smell was a combination of beer, sometimes stale, and an aroma of a pungent bleach-product to cover the slightly noticeable smell of vomit from earlier in the day. He didn't fully know everyone in the bar, but Bernard recognized each of them as the typical customers, and they surely acknowledged him as a regular patron as well. In the corner, however, he did see two faces that he knew or at least recognized—a man's and a woman's—and he simply nodded politely at each of them before approaching the bar.

"What'll you have, mate?" the man behind it asked. Bernard believed his name was Kevin, though it certainly wasn't important.

"Whiskey, please. Straight up."

"Any particular . . ."

"It doesn't matter," Bernard interrupted.

Kevin turned, whistled toward the TV's announcement of the 49ers' touchdown, and then, before pouring Bernard's drink, briefly made a catcall toward the other TV's showing of jiggling boobs.

"Keep a tab going for you, mate?" Kevin assumed.

"Yes."

"How about those 49ers?"

"How about them?" Bernard asked with gloom, not in the least presenting the pretense of a question of any kind. "Frankly, my mind is elsewhere."

"A game like this?" Kevin announced in shock. "Dude, where are your priorities? It's the 49ers!"

"Just a lot on my mind."

"Oh man, I know that look," Kevin continued. "Problems of the female variety? Old woman's got you gripped by the balls is it?"

Bernard felt his mouth slightly turn upwards, even if not dramatically, and he bowed. "Something like that, I guess you could say."

"Well then," Kevin implored, "let me pour you another."

Bernard scanned the room. His mind was on Catherine, still furious from their recent argument, but still concerned for their marriage. He couldn't help, though, ogling the same TV-adorned jiggling boobs to which Kevin brought attention just minutes ago. Bernard could feel himself getting hard. The woman was rather trashy, but her body was fit and nicely endowed.

"You know, friend," Kevin motioned from behind the bar, "the real thing is coming out later. The pole is up, and the girls are performing tonight. Typical Sunday."

"No complaints here," Bernard responded, grasping his drink in tow, raising it a bit to toast the notion. Swigging the whiskey was likely not intelligent, but doing it made him feel strong and manly. As the whiskey burned slowly down his throat, his insides began to warm, and he knew the more he drank, the less serious the scene at home would eventually become. So he continued to order drink after drink, making small talk when he felt it necessary, and staying silent when it felt more appropriate. That said he was mostly silent throughout his time at the bar.

Bernard was not keen on touch, other than Catherine's over the course of the few years they had been together. It was therefore no surprise that the middle-aged woman's longer-than-comfortably-appropriate pat on his back caused him to jerk forward and then backward out of sheer unexpectedness.

"Well, if it isn't bright eyes," the woman said. Bernard could smell the cigarette stench reeking from the breath that hit his face after she spoke.

"How goes it, honey?" She asked

Bernard continued to stare at her face. The wrinkles around her eyes were as pronounced as the bad teeth that were visibly protruding out toward him like weeds needing a good pull. This was the woman to whom he nodded when entering the bar. He knew her, not by name, but by familiar face. This was his watering hole after all, and it seemed to be hers as well. And she obviously knew him enough to approach him. Maybe this withered woman could sense his anger and, in a Good Samaritan, slightly pushy way, decided to take it upon herself to offer some friendly assistance.

"Just enjoying a shot of what the doctor ordered," Bernard responded.

"I hear that, darling," she coughed. She helped herself to the empty bar stool that sat beside him. Bernard could see her sloth-like body clawing at the stool, grasping to get her ass situated on it. This was the last thing he needed—not just the sight of her middle-aged, flabby ass plopping beside him, but having her welcome a conversation that he clearly wasn't prepared to entertain. *Just leave me alone*, he thought. *Jesus, can't I just decompress tonight, have my drink, see some girls shaking their junk at me, and then head back to another unhappy evening with Catherine? Maybe things will be better when I get home. But I want to have a drink in peace!*

"Here to see some of our girls this evening?"

"Not particularly," Bernard answered. "Just out for a drink."

"You, looking for a good time, honey? Because my girls love to show a good time, for a good tip of course." She continued to cough, and for a brief moment, Bernard thought he was facing a literary character dying of Consumption. He had just about expected blood to spew from her lungs at any moment. The scenery was just too ripe for some type of bohemian story in the making.

"I'm a married man," Bernard insisted. There was, however, a twang of sarcasm in his voice, and the woman detected it.

"Guilty," she interjected.

"Guilty?" Bernard questioned. "I don't quite get what you are insinuating. I am guilty of what exactly?"

"Shit, honey," she laughed. "I meant same here, honey. Married. Married four times, actually. Think I finally found the one who gets me vibrating just right!"

And with this repulsive comment, she slapped Bernard's knee, laughed, and pounded a shot of liquor. The gesture, on top of her words, made his stomach turn. *Gross*, he thought.

"I'm sure he's quite a guy," Bernard responded.

"Got that right, honey."

She looked Bernard up and down. She had done it before during Bernard's previous visits to the bar. This time it was up close and personal.

"I'm sure you've got a sweet spot package yourself," she stated in a matter of fact fashion.

Bernard was not comfortable with this woman, and he wanted to drink even more now. He knew she was a harmless flirt, past her prime, begging for the attention she'd never get from him. She certainly seemed to be good at one thing though—bringing attention to the strippers she continued to pimp.

"You said your girls were coming out?" He asked, deflecting the focus from him to something else. He eyed the pole and the other surroundings carefully. The game was still the focus of half the room. Touchdowns, scores, commentators commentating, all in line with typical sporting theme one would expect. The others in the room looked like they were readying to touch themselves underneath their tables. Bernard questioned himself as to why he often went to that place, but the answer was quite simple. Again, things at home could be better, and he needed a pastime. To be fairly truthful, he didn't want to encounter what he thought he would obviously need to face at some point in the near future. Catherine was indisputably falling from grace—falling out of love with Bernard. He sensed it in the nucleus of his being, and it depressed him.

"Oh yes, every Sunday night," she answered. "I've seen you here before, eyeing up some of the lucky ladies. You're a bit more attractive," she continued, coughing every now and then, "a bit more than the typical guys who come in here."

"Well again, I'm married, and I'm just here to watch the game."

"Ha!" She exclaimed. "This ain't a David Lynch film, sweetie. We all got needs. Relax and enjoy yourself. Join me for a cigarette outside?"

"No thanks," Bernard responded. "I don't smoke. Never smoked."

"Oh honey. You feeling the need to confess or something?"

"Confess?" He asked.

"There is no need to defend yourself. *'I'm just here to drink',*" she said in a voice, mocking his own. "And *'I don't smoke, never did,'* and all that shit." She laughed a bit. "If you don't want a cigarette, no need to explain yourself. A 'no' will suffice."

"Point taken," Bernard responded.

"And you certainly don't need to feel guilty about staring at some of our girls here, married as you are or not."

"Understood," he replied. "I got it, Nazi. Thanks."

"Hmmm. I like a man who is a bullshit artist."

"Then," Bernard retorted, "You'll love me."

The woman leaned her loose hanging, wrinkly breasts over the top of the bar, shifted and lifted her weight somewhat over the counter, grabbed the bottle of whiskey and poured herself and Bernard another drink each.

"Hey Kevin," she called out loud. "Put this on my tab. Bright eyes is doing a shot with me, and I'm taking care of the service while you're back there playing with your thingy."

"Real class, you hag," echoed Kevin's voice from the bar office. "You never seem to surprise me, you bitch. Don't break the bottle again."

"I love my boys here . . . and my girls," she laughed. "Each one of them fuckers . . . I love 'em. Cheers, honey."

Bernard met her glass with a clink. The vibration rang a bit longer than he had anticipated, and to silence it, he took a quick swig of the burning whiskey. Again, it was great.

"Honey, if I may," the woman began before a momentary pause.

"I assume you will anyway," Bernard responded.

"Well done, honey. Well done," she continued. "Yes, I will. If I may, honey, you look like a man who is trying to grasp onto reality."

"Meaning?"

"Meaning you are suffering inside. Each of us progresses down the road of life, moving along like chess pieces on a board. We rarely think about the strategy ahead . . . simply move along the path that seems appropriate or planned for us, huh?"

"Where are you going with this?" Bernard asked without showing much appreciation for her philosophy.

"You seem to be holding it together . . . trying at least, honey . . . when inside you are crumbling to bust loose, let go, do something wild."

"Amazing," Bernard replied.

"What's that, honey?"

"I enter a bar, and a drink later, I'm speaking to Confucius." Bernard's sarcasm was thick like syrup, sticking to this woman's attempt at cheap conversation.

"Ok, ok, ok, honey," she responded. "Have it your way. But don't forget that each one of us, even those that try to take the straight and narrow, need to live once in a fucking while. Enjoy the show, honey. I'm going to smoke my stogie."

Bernard hadn't had much time to value his newfound freedom from the hag's nasty conversation before the music began. It was loud, porn-like, somewhat disturbing, and somewhat catchy. It shook the metal legs under each of the bar stools, including the one on which he sat. He could see a shadowy figure appear slowly behind the poll. Her face had not yet formed in his vision, yet her body seemed taut, ripe, and rhythmic. It was still dark inside the room, and he could not distinguish her features in detail, but the soft neon red light, pulsing to the music, illuminated her eyes. No face, but her eyes were clearly visible now. And they pierced the room. The music continued to beat, beat, beat, beat, and then . . . honk.

Honk?

Suddenly, Bernard was back in the reality of the present day. Traffic had begun to move, and Bernard could see the flares ahead. A police officer was cautiously directing traffic around an accident that was, to be quite honest, such a minor fender-bender that it didn't warrant the nuisance. Bernard knew his office was only just minutes away now that the flow of traffic seemed to be steady. He was eager to quickly move in and out of the office like MJ's fog, collecting what he needed to stay focused on his work while keeping watch over MJ and her well being.

Some minor time later, Bernard was still, in the parking lot of his glass-faced office building, brightly lit, looking similar to a modernized, highly technical fort. He sat in his car, thinking again back to Catherine's fateful evening, when he had just noticed that stripper's eyes peering at him.

Kevin was now speaking directly into a microphone that projected scratchy sounds over a hanging speaker. The whole contraption seemed to resemble cheap karaoke equipment rather than a club sound system. The music continued to play loudly, in between Kevin's words.

"Thanks for joining us again, gents, for another Sunday showing of our girls," Kevin shouted.

No one clapped. Guys just anxiously waited for movement on the pole. They too could see the shadowy figure behind it, and they were waiting for her to drop her panties; that was for sure.

"Starting the evening right," Kevin announced, "is our very own Miss Misty Moore! Give her a tip and she'll mist right in all the good spots!"

This is kind of disgusting, Bernard thought. Still, he was hard. He looked around at the other patrons, again recognizing them, seeing how desperate they were to get some excitement in their lives. Maybe that hag was right. Maybe these poor dopes were experiencing the type of agitation Bernard was trying to frantically avoid himself—a life of arguments, mistrust, and loveless future. He could no longer blame himself for wanting to now see those same panties drop to the stage.

"And Miss Misty Moore," Kevin continued, "that bad pussy cat . . . misty Misty, on behalf of the girls back there, would like to welcome you to another *Sunday Church Event* at—at the Churchill!"

CHAPTER TEN

Shoshanna grabbed her chest in shock. She hadn't expected to see Bernard standing at the entrance of her cubicle—the one that joined the wall to his.

"Good God, Bernard!" Shoshanna shouted. "Jesus! I didn't hear you enter."

Bernard stood silent, his eyes shifting to the ground at his feet, unable to move and feeling quite guilty for having startled her.

"What are you doing here at this time?" Shoshanna asked. "Isn't this when you reserve all of your time for home duties?"

"Yes, I—I came to get some work. Might take a few days as a *Work-from-Home* opportunity. I need to focus a bit more at home and care for things there." Bernard was careful not to elaborate on the details. He had no desire to share private information with others, but he certainly didn't expect anyone to understand the situation had he wanted to share it anyway. His thoughts immediately shifted to MJ, as he knew that protecting her delicate reputation was incredibly important to him and to her as a matter of fact.

Shoshanna seemed pleased at the suggestion. Eager not to show her satisfaction too hastily, she simply nodded and said, "I see. It's probably a very good idea to retreat home to focus on your project. It is very complex after all. You need some privacy."

Bernard was unable to see Shoshanna's reaction of relief as he moved to his side of the cubicle, slowly, then quickly sifting through manila folders, labels, and binders, spending approximately four seconds skimming the material on each page to decipher its importance, or lack thereof. Bernard knew that Shoshanna was still a bit uncomfortable around him. Ever since Catherine's death, things were no longer the same for him, and metaphorical loose boards now weakened the altar of respect where he believed his colleagues once placed him. He wasn't too comfortable around them either. *No love lost* as far as he was concerned.

"Shoshanna," Bernard called out. He obviously could not witness Shoshanna's eye roll.

"Um, yes," she responded with a forced diplomacy. "Do you need something, Bernard?"

"I'm looking for the project's pile of folders. I can't seem to remember where I placed them. Do you have any idea where they might be?"

"I'm sorry, Bernard," she answered. "I haven't the foggiest . . ."

Bernard's head popped up, now visible over the cubicle wall. Again, the sudden and unexpected sight startled Shoshanna.

"Jesus Christ!" She screamed. "Please stop doing that!"

"I'm sorry," Bernard responded. "Stop doing what?"

"You're creeping me out a bit, Bernard."

"I don't understand! What happened to the files?" Bernard questioned aloud. He didn't specifically mean for the question to be for Shoshanna, but any confirmation of the files' whereabouts would be prized.

"Bernard, I don't know what you did with your files," Shoshanna calmly stated. "Those are your responsibility, but I'm happy to call Marcus to have him come downstairs to search with you."

"No, no!" Bernard shouted. The sound caused Shoshanna to quickly rise from her swivel chair and stand, one hand clutching the other arm.

"Bernard, I think it's best that I call Marcus . . . just so he can help you look."

"So," Bernard insisted, "he can refuse to look me in the eyes—as usual?"

Shoshanna stood there, still holding onto her arm, somewhat resembling a child that was impatient to urinate.

"Just to help you, Bernard," she quietly repeated.

Bernard took a moment to gather his thoughts. He remembered MJ's trick of pausing, silently counting and calming the anxious situation in which she would sometimes find herself. He figured it would work for him as well, and so it did. He placed the files in his hands back onto the surface of the desk. Both hands, now firmly outstretched, gently swayed in plane-like motion as Bernard breathed in and out. He thought of MJ's Pacifica fog that rolled with such ease and grace, cleansing everything in sight; and as he considered this, he felt everything in him suddenly cool. For him, the state of affairs was once again tranquil.

For Shoshanna, Bernard was sure that serenity would be achieved once he left. He was correct. She wasn't comfortable around him. Since Catherine's sudden death, things changed in Bernard—his attitude, his concentration on work, his composure, and his increased reclusiveness. He knew that Shoshanna never considered him a friend, but before Catherine's freak accident, he was tolerable. Now, he simply frustrated her and he surely made her nervous. She wasn't the only one who felt this way either, he was sure.

"Fine," Bernard stated calmly. "Let's call Marcus. Maybe he can help me look for the files."

Shoshanna was once again relieved. She athletically jumped toward the phone, Olympic-style. Dialing it, she encouraged, "you'll see, Bernard. Marcus probably knows exactly where the files are."

"Yes, I'm sure you're right," he responded.

"Hello, Marcus?" Shoshanna said, directly into the receiver at her chin. "Yes, Marcus, could you come downstairs? Bernard needs your help looking for something."

Pause.

Continuation.

"Yes, that's right, Marcus," Shoshanna continued. "Bernard needs your help. Yes, he's right here, Marcus. Could you come downstairs to help him look please?"

Pause.

Continuation.

"Thanks, Marcus."

Shoshanna put the phone down on its receiver. She glanced up toward Bernard's side of the cubicle, and peered over the wall.

"That was Marcus," she said.

"Obviously," Bernard snorted.

"He'll be down momentarily. Could I get you some coffee?"

"No thank you," Bernard responded. "I'll be fine. I just want to collect my work and get home quickly. Things there are a bit challenging tonight, and I want to make sure everything is ok."

"Oh, yes, yes. Understood, Bernard," Shoshanna replied, seemingly anxious to get Bernard on the move.

Within moments, Marcus stood in front of the cubicle space. He glanced quickly toward Bernard's posture, and just as quickly his eyes shifted to a state of shame. As Bernard assumed, Marcus could still not look at him ever since Catherine's death. It was starting to annoy

Bernard. While it was true that Bernard did the best he could to avoid the population at large, he still did not appreciate being the subject of sympathy, especially any longer.

"Bernard!" Marcus said politely. "You're working late, aren't you?"

"Just looking for some files to bring back home. Do you have any idea where my project's pile is, Marcus?"

"I'm sure we can find it, pretty quickly," Marcus responded.

For a brief moment, Marcus looked at Shoshanna who clearly gestured a sign of appreciation for his presence. He continued to sift through piles of paper, helping Bernard search for the information he sought.

"Could it possibly be in the file room?" Marcus asked, continuously doing what he could to avoid eye contact with Bernard.

"No, I know that I left the information at my desk," Bernard responded.

As Bernard continued to search, his agitation began to surface, and the fever that boiled into frustration continued to seemingly disturb Marcus and Shoshanna. Bernard began crumpling papers, sliding them across his desk into the trash, flipping through files, letting them land harshly on the ground.

"Man, calm down," Marcus insisted. "It's not that big of a deal!"

"What?" Bernard questioned. "Not a fucking big deal? Thank you, Marcus. Thank you for your counsel." Bernard hadn't noticed that, as he was screaming, he was nudging, though not forcefully, Marcus's chest. Marcus still could not look directly at Bernard. Bernard was sure that Marcus recognized the pain he experienced. But in light of the current events, he also imagined that Marcus believed Bernard's unfortunate experiences of the past didn't excuse him from being an asshole.

"Bernard, I think you need to get your files and leave," Marcus implored.

"That's what I am trying to do, Marcus! Don't you think I want to do nothing more than find my work, bring it home, and spend time with my sick wife instead of being in the office every stinking day?"

"Bernard . . . Bernard . . ." Marcus attempted to console him, but couldn't bring himself to do it. "Bernard, listen to yourself . . ."

Bernard glared at Marcus. If looks could kill, Marcus would've been rotting in the ground. His gesture was so removed from anything gentlemanly, and Bernard realized he was letting stress get the best of him. This was not the Bernard that MJ knew. It was not the Bernard that he himself knew. He was becoming someone that was allowing others to trample on top of his weak emotions.

At the sight of what seemed to be steam rising from Bernard's head, Marcus's discomfort immediately intensified.

"You really need to leave," Marcus firmly stated.

Suddenly, this departure notice reminded Bernard of his time at the bar, the time when it was 'gently suggested' he vacate. His mind shifted his thoughts toward that scenario. As he began to dive back into the past, he noticed the files he sought were on the floor, in the back corner of the cubicle. He knew he hadn't placed them there, which would lead to conventional wisdom that someone else had, though Bernard didn't care. Without any further haste, he bent down, grabbed the files at once, tucked them under his coat to protect them from the pelt of rain outside, and exited quickly passing Shoshanna and Marcus without haste.

Rushing into his parked car, he threw the files onto the front seat beside his. He hastily tried to buckle himself into safety, too hastily as to catch his finger in the buckle. A surge of pain quickly sharpened his attention, and he cursed aloud. It caused him to suspend his current thoughts.

What the fuck is going on? Bernard thought. One moment, he was caring for MJ. The next moment, he was not caring, but protecting her from some psychotic town's woman who, according to MJ, is the ghost of his dead wife from the past. How'd it come to this? And on top of it, he was just rude to his coworkers in order to rush back to MJ's side.

He sat in a mess of rain-soaked leather, quietly, attempting to center his calm again. This time it wasn't working. His mind instead went back to the past.

* * *

"So you're name is Misty?" Bernard asked.

"That's right," she responded. "Misty Moore, as in more tips, more show. Do you catch my drift?"

Bernard searched his wallet. He couldn't believe he was about to squeeze a twenty-dollar bill between her strung bikini bottoms and her pink flesh, but it was the only cash he currently had in his possession. It especially seemed inappropriate as the normal Bernard would think it was too soon since Catherine's death some time ago. The last time he was in the bar, talking to the hag, drinking Kevin's whiskey, and staring at this strange girl's shadowy eyes—the only parts of her that were crystalized in his vision—he sat there, playing macho, enjoying himself while his wife suffered at home. He was usually overwrought with guilt these days. But something about Misty enticed him.

"Here's a twenty," Bernard replied.

"And here's a nipple," Misty said through her grinning teeth.

Bernard stared at her chest. Her nipples were the perfect size, round, firm, and amply placed on her beautiful, distended breasts.

"When do you get off?" He asked.

"Well, for another twenty, I just might do so right in front of you."

"That's not what I meant," Bernard responded.

Misty smiled and continued to shift back and forth to the music. She was quick to interject, quite proudly, "somehow, I knew that, stud."

"Well?" Bernard continued.

Misty stopped for a brief moment. "Look, bud," she said, "nice try and all, but that's not why I do this."

"I'm not meaning to suggest . . ."

"You know what," Misty interrupted, "it's really ok. It's just my time to go backstage. Have a good night, buddy."

Misty began to reach down to the dollar bills that blanketed the bar top by her feet. Bernard saw how athletic her legs presented themselves, and at that moment, he was finding himself attracted to her. She was not the type of girl that typically grabbed his interest. Maybe it was a mixture of emotions brewing inside him. It could have been the unanticipated conversation he had, months ago, with the bar hag who had urged him to not feel guilty living his life. Perhaps at that time he was no longer willing to accept that his former wife, God rest her soul, no longer wanted him in any way. Though this was the reality, he couldn't help but be depressed over her loss, and he hurt desperately for her loving attention that once shined through her very fingertips when they first met. Could he possibly be deflecting this toward Misty? He didn't care.

"You just deserve to be treated like a princess," Bernard responded quietly. Misty stopped walking, shook her head, and smiled. She knew she would regret going back to him, but after a momentary consideration, she did.

"Again, look . . ." she raised her hands, searching for a name.

"Bernard," he responded.

"Thank you. Look, Bernie," she continued.

"Bernard," he interrupted.

"Look, Bernard, I didn't mean to be rude. But I am sure you can assume the type of guy that may hit on a girl in this place. I appreciate you asking about my schedule, but it is just not a good idea."

"Coffee is always a good idea for a hard-working woman," Bernard retorted.

Misty smiled again. In the background, Kevin could be heard saying, "another Sunday Church event at the Churchill! Come enjoy our sinners dance around your face." Bernard thought this was utterly crude, but his focus remained on Misty.

"Bernard," Misty continued. "It is truly nice of you, but I don't think they'd allow it."

She jerked her head in a way that carefully motioned toward the hag in the corner. Next to the hag was a greasy looking Italian or Greek man, smacking gum through his teeth, and sensibly keeping his gape on Misty's whereabouts.

"You're not a hooker, are you?"

"Oh that's brilliant, Bernard," Misty responded. "Your chances just shot down real quickly."

"No, again," he said, "I didn't mean to insult you. I just don't understand the property thing you are projecting. If you're not a prostitute, why would they have an issue with you getting coffee with me? They're not your pimps, are they?"

"No, but they are my managers. They're all of our managers. And they don't take kindly to strange customers trying to get their way with us . . . messing up the merchandise, if you will."

"What if I promised to buy you a drink here?" He asked.

"I'm not allowed to drink at the bar."

Bernard shrugged. "You're not making this easy for me. Just once, I'd like something to fall into my lap."

"Now look, Bernard," Misty responded. "You're not going to feel sorry for yourself, are you?"

She padded his nose lightly. Though he hated anyone else's touch, other than Catherine's, Misty's felt natural, and he didn't intrinsically shift his body when experiencing it.

"It's been a few months since I have been able to come back here," Bernard continued. "It's actually been a while since I have been able to do much of anything. My wife recently died. We were often arguing about the stupidest things. But I know she no longer loved me. I did everything possible to get that spark lit again, but it became insurmountable each day. And suddenly, it was too late."

Misty stood amazed at what she was hearing. At first, she thought it was another desperate line from a guy seeking to get into her pants. The more she heard pour from Bernard's lips though, the stronger his posture and character seemed to become. She knew instantly that this story was true, and something clicked in her.

Bernard prolonged the story by concluding simply.

"When I found her dead, after her freak fall, there was no hope for her. There was no hope for us. I was depressed for months. I still miss her."

Misty actually believed a tear was forming in her eye.

"Bernard," she said, "I respect a man that refuses to forget the woman he loved. I admire your ability to be strong during your loss."

Bernard just looked at his empty glass of whiskey, wishing there was something filling it. At this point, any alcohol would have been just fine.

"You really don't know whether I am strong or not," he insisted. "At times, I feel the void is so large inside me, without filling it, there will be no hope for me to ever be strong again."

"Look, I can't promise anything," Misty continued, "but if you wait around a bit, maybe I can meet you out on the floor. If things work themselves out carefully, maybe we can go grab that coffee. There is a diner up the street . . . Fog City. Know it?"

"Yes," Bernard responded.

"Ok. Again, I'm not promising anything. But I'll come out on the floor in a few minutes or so."

"And I look forward to it, your majesty," Bernard joked.

Misty gathered her things in a manner that seemed more lady-like then when she was standing, legs apart, on the bar top. She winked at Bernard, and quickly mentioned, "don't be ashamed to go ahead and watch," as she slowly walked away from him, shaking her barely clothed hips.

Bernard could see that the hag in the corner did not seem very pleased. The man next to her, whose regular face was also familiar to Bernard, whispered something in her ear, and was certainly not hesitant to motion toward Bernard's direction. Bernard knew this meant that, momentarily, the hag and her lumpy ass would soon be sitting next to him, just like she had during the night of Catherine's death. And he was right—she waddled over rather quickly, with her gentleman Italian/Greek friend behind her.

"Well hello there, honey," she coughed. "Haven't seen you in some time, bright eyes."

Bernard nodded in obvious agreement.

"Yes," he responded, "it seems as if I can't keep away from you."

"That's funny, honey. You seem a bit more comfortable tonight."

"Do I?" Bernard asked. "I hadn't noticed the difference."

"Well I noticed that you were getting pretty cozy with Misty Moore," the man behind the hag called out. Italian. Bernard knew he had to be Italian.

"Now, now," the woman interjected. "Our customers are more than welcomed to talk with the girls."

The Italian simply stared at Bernard. It felt like daggers piercing him. Bernard wasn't sure if this was a *don't-mess-with-my-girl* warning, a show of power, or both.

"Do you monitor all of the girls this closely?" Bernard asked. "Seems to me as if she is here to do a job and then free to do what she wants after her shift is done."

"Honey, all of us are free. Free country. Excuse me," the hag said, sifting a handkerchief from between her breasts and coughing into it.

"Damn stogies. Gotta quit them soon."

"It'll kill you," Bernard responded.

"Let it try. Not much scares me off," she countered, laughing invincibly. She refolded the handkerchief, and this time placed it in her stretch-jeans pocket. For a moment, Bernard thought *are those truly jean-designed sweatpants she's wearing?*

"Like I said," the hag continued. "This is a free country. We just want to make sure nothing fishy is gonna happen here. I kinda feel like a protective momma over these girls."

"And I assume," Bernard said, focusing on the Italian, who despite the greasiness, was actually quite handsome, "that makes you the big brother?"

"Something like that," the Italian answered.

"Honey," the hag interrupted. "Lots of boys come in and out of here, looking for one thing. Don't blame them. I look for it too when I can. But I ain't running a brothel here, and I ain't into drugs. The girls here get offers all the time. Sex, line of cocaine, you name it."

"And I look like someone who is ready to cause problems like that?" Bernard questioned.

"You look like a man, honey—a man with a dick. That's all there needs to be. Trouble usually follows."

"And brother over there," pointing at the Italian, Bernard suggested, "his dick isn't a problem?"

This infuriated the Italian, who once again did not hesitate to show his authority over the situation.

"Yo, fucking asshole," he interjected. "I think it's time for you to leave, wise guy." The Italian moved in closely, as if to frame himself into a position to make Bernard defensive.

"Really, there is no need for this, tough guy" the hag continued to cough looking at the Italian. "Our friend here is just having a nice conversation with Misty. Besides, *bright eyes* here is married, right?"

"My wife died, the night I was here last," Bernard responded.

The hag glared at him, not knowing whether or not his response was a sick joke or a sarcastic attempt for Bernard to show his strength. Truth be told, she didn't care.

"Tough shit to handle, honey. My apologies. Come on," she pulled at the Italian's shirt. "Bright eyes won't be messing around where he knows he'll get caught."

The Italian continued to stare at Bernard, and before moving to follow the hag, stated very boldly, "I'll be seeing you around, wise guy."

Just about fifteen minutes later, Misty appeared from behind the bar. She was now wearing jeans, a scarf, and a light jacket—appropriate for the evening microclimate San Francisco weather change. She looked impressively gentle to Bernard, yet still rather sexy as if she were still standing in her stringed bikini.

"Seems like your friends over there don't like me very much," Bernard stated. Misty looked to the ground and shook her head.

"Yeah, this is a bit irritating. Sorry about that," she replied. "I'm suddenly feeling a bit more cheeky. How about that coffee?"

Bernard said nothing. He raised himself from the stool, stood firmly, and held his hand out to politely let Misty walk ahead of him.

"Just one thing more," Misty continued. "If we are going to get to know each other, feel free to call me by my non-stage name, the name friends called me as I was growing up. I'm MJ."

CHAPTER ELEVEN

"So after Catherine passed," MJ began to ask, stirring her coffee slowly but with purpose, "you immediately packed her things into storage and moved to Pacifica?"

Bernard nodded. While in recent weeks he was making peace with Catherine's loss, speaking about the reality of that evening was still somewhat uncomfortable. He knew, though, that he needed to make progress in that area, and he was therefore willing to continue the conversation. In the same respect, MJ, who really didn't understand why she asked this question, reached for a packet of sweetener, added it to her coffee, and continued to stir it.

"I really couldn't bring myself to enjoy being here any longer—in that house, in that neighborhood, in the city in general," Bernard responded. "Moreover, I really wanted to be alone. It bothered me to think about neighbors' pity or my own memories. Solitude was appearing to be the perfect solution to my situation."

MJ appreciated this completely. At times, she herself wished that she could leave the city. While it was home to her, and she truly was partial to it over anywhere else, she had sometimes wished she could go somewhere where no one knew her, a place she could vanish, and a place she could be at peace to start over. Further, if she was thinking this way, and had not even experienced a major event like the one that viciously intruded upon Bernard's life, she could only imagine the struggling memories and thoughts that led Bernard to move.

"Why Pacifica?" MJ asked. "It's beautiful out there, but I don't often go. It's actually really strange. It is so close, and yet I rarely ever go there."

"And you have just identified the reason!" Bernard said in a jovial manner. MJ didn't know Bernard, and really—who knew where this relationship would be going—but it was reassuring to see a smile finally break Bernard's bleak demeanor.

"Pacifica," he continued, "is so close and yet so far! Geographically, it is quite nearby, but appearance-wise it is very disconnected to the rest of the Bay Area. Once you cross the San Francisco threshold, and travel along 19th Avenue to California Route 1, you enter this magical land of privacy. True, it is splendid to the eyes. Driving into it, all one sees to the right of the freeway is miles and miles of ocean, houses on the beach, a pier where the town's people crowd every day, and the occasional mom-and-pop shops on the side of the road. To the left, the driver sees undulating hills, sometimes covered by fog, sometimes not. And it is then that he realizes he has found a gem—a beautifully landscaped town that rarely gets visited by the rest of the population. It's reputation of constant fog, which is a total lie by the way, and its lack of a town center is what I think keeps people away. For me, nothing could be more perfect. No, it's not the beauty per se, but the separation and peaceful seclusion one feels when living there."

MJ considered his words carefully. Bernard painted an enticing scenario in her mind. Yet, while she too would like to 'escape' from time to time, the thought of constant isolation seemed to be a bit disconcerting to her.

"What about the fog?" she asked.

"What about it?"

"On the days it rolls in, what's that like?"

Bernard could see MJ trying to picture it in her mind. For a brief moment, he looked over toward her just as she closed her eyes to imagine the scene. It was at this moment that he realized she was a city girl—probably always had been, probably also, as evident from her profession, she didn't get to experience the luxuries he had when he was younger—and the experience of nature and non-urban beauty was a novelty to her.

"Are you alright, MJ?" He asked.

"Oh yes, I certainly am, thank you," MJ responded. "I was taking a 'breather', just one of my moments."

"I'm sorry, am I disturbing you? Do you need a break?"

"Nothing like that," MJ said beaming. She opened her eyes. "It's a trick I learned at the bars. When I really don't want to face the crowd—usually out of disgust, to be honest—I take a 'breather'. I count to ten or twenty, center myself; I think of nature, and it usually helps me put everything into perspective.

"Since I have learned how to master this Jedi-trick," she laughed, "it has always been a good tool for me to use when picturing any scene being described to me."

"Well then," Bernard stated, obviously impressed by her explanation, "I'll continue with the description."

"Ok," still smiling, MJ replied. She then closed her eyes. Briefly opened one, fixed it upon Bernard and laughed. She then closed it like the other.

"When the fog rolls into town, appearing out of nowhere—from above the ocean—it crystalizes one's vision," Bernard described. "Things become clearer. It is also another way to remain hidden."

Bernard could see that this characterization suddenly took MJ by surprise. Her actions dictated that she didn't comprehend why she felt the way she did, but this beautiful vision he portrayed just moments ago didn't bond well with the word 'hidden'. She seemed to understand his desires to not be pestered by annoying neighbors and memories that solicited depression, but 'hidden' just seemed to continue to trouble her.

"Do you have any family?" MJ asked, changing the topic to avoid the discomfort she abruptly and unexpectedly sensed.

"No. My parents are gone. No family," he answered. "Well, not really. Alby, but he's really not part of the picture anymore."

"Who's Alby?"

"My younger brother," Bernard answered. "But we've had constant disagreements over the past several years. I don't trust him much any more, and he disappoints me frequently."

"That is never good," MJ responded. "Family members should always be connected. I wish I had a family. I would never stop working at keeping us close if I did."

"My brother and I simply don't see eye-to-eye on life's most important lessons," Bernard continued.

"And those lessons are?" asked MJ. "I am intrigued to know your views."

"I certainly have them," Bernard immediately followed. "And I have never insinuated, not for once, that my life is any better than Alby's, Catherine's, or anyone else's for that matter. It is simply that . . . well, well for example . . ."

"Yes?" she inquired patiently.

"So Alby is . . . gay, and . . ."

"Wait," MJ interrupted. "You are not suggesting his lifestyle has something to do with your disagreements about his life choices, are you?"

"Not in the least!"

"Well, I certainly should hope not," MJ responded, indicating a joking disposition. Yet, the reality of the situation seemed to be that MJ was unable to understand why anyone would have anything negative to say about anyone's lifestyle orientation. Bernard recognized that it was simply not in her nature to mind anyone else's personal business. He was sure she would have been utterly disappointed to discover that his disputes with his brother were a result of political and social discords. This would have immediately changed her opinion about Bernard's tender and gentlemanly progressive nature. Therefore, he knew it would be a relief for her to hear him declare this, and she was willing to take him on his word that his brother's homosexuality had nothing to do with their previous tribulations. She was enjoying his company too much to think anything differently.

"I believe I interrupted you," she stated firmly. "For that I apologize. I just wanted to make sure I wasn't having coffee with someone who was living back in the social stone ages."

"You needn't apologize," Bernard responded. "I am happy to hear that you are quite progressive in these matters."

"Oh please," MJ laughed. "I am certainly not enlightened, if that is what you mean. I find there to be nothing liberal-minded about this issue. It is just something, in my opinion, that should not even be a conversational topic. People are who they are, and it is no one else's business to dictate who people love."

"I agree," Bernard assured. "I meant to bring this to the surface in order to illustrate an example about his approach versus mine. Man, with advocacy like that, I'm sure Alby would enjoy your company tremendously."

"Yes," she sarcastically agreed. "I am sure he would."

"Well, again," Bernard, slightly stuttering, suggested, "I meant to only mention this as a point. Often, Alby feels the need to illustrate what is important to women. He will, on numerous occasions, describe to me in detail, the things I am doing wrong in my relationships with women. In my opinion, I have been doing just fine. I find it interesting that someone who isn't capable of having a sexual relationship with a woman finds it necessary to instruct me on my relationship with them."

MJ considered this. She seemed to not want to appear as openly disagreeing with a man who recently lost his wife to a tragic accident, but to some degree, Bernard believed she understood his point. He could tell that she didn't believe he was angry at his brother's choices, more frustrated with his brother's self-implied expertise.

"I understand, Bernard," she stated, "but I have faith that you two will patch things up eventually."

"I'm not too sure about that . . ." Bernard hinted.

"No, Bernard, you must remain positive!"

"Yes, you are correct. Being positive is always best."

"And," she continued, "Maybe someday you could introduce me to Alby? I'm sure we'd get along swimmingly. Remember, I am an advocate for him already!"

Bernard said nothing, but looked at MJ's coffee and smiled. He thought *this girl is very sweet.*

It seemed as if Bernard and MJ spoke for at least two additional hours. No topic appeared to be inappropriate for discussion—money, life in the city versus life on the coast, movies, books (when either of them had a moment to read), relationships past and present, family or the lack thereof.

"I take it you don't have a family then?" Bernard asked, somewhat intrigued. Could it be that he possibly found someone who was, like him, relatively alone in the world? Maybe Misty—MJ—whoever—would understand him more preciously than he had anticipated. Could she be the bridge over this chasm in his life?

"I do not," she responded quite emphatically. "I have not seen my mother since I was sixteen. That is over ten years ago. I never had a father, and no siblings either. I grew up in the slums of the city, which thankfully as I understand are not as slummy as other slums in other cities," she laughed.

"I believe that is likely true," Bernard smiled. "But I am sorry nonetheless."

"You seem like a gentleman, Bernard."

"I'm not special. I'm normal," he responded.

"Well, I don't normally feel comfortable talking about my past with anyone."

"I'll then take that," Bernard continued, "as a compliment."

MJ caught the attention of the waitress, asked her for more coffee, and then smiled at Bernard.

"You'd think," she implied, "that she would have noticed my cup was empty for a few minutes now!"

"MJ, you were insinuating life was not the easiest while you were growing up?" Bernard asked.

"Trust me," she retorted, "I was fine and could certainly care for myself. But I didn't really have any type of parental guidance. My mom was always cracked out on one drug, or another, or a combination cocktail of some sort. I don't even know where she is anymore. For all I know, she could be dead."

"That's a morbid thought," Bernard responded.

"Yes, I know it is. And what I hate about it—though probably true—is that I feel no remorse about it. I don't have any relationship with her, I have no siblings, I have hardly any friends, and therefore I have no connections. I wish I did, which of course makes me sad that you and your brother don't have any connections, but sadly I have nothing except for work and the people at the bar."

Bernard measured the possible reactions in his head before asking his next question. He surely didn't want to pry or offend her in any way, especially now that he realized finding someone like MJ was similar to discovering a pot of gold at the end of the spectrum. MJ was the type of person for whom he had been seeking, and kismet was naturally materializing.

"May I ask you something?" He began.

"Well, you just did," she amusingly responded.

"Very wise, MJ."

"Wisdom is my best quality," she laughed. He did too.

"I simply wanted to ask you how you got involved in dancing at that bar," Bernard continued. There was a noticeable pause after he made his statement, and he suddenly believed he delivered a blow to fate. He obviously insulted her.

"I'm sorry," he stated. "I didn't mean to meddle. That is one of the things I never liked about my brother, Alby. He meddles in everything."

"No, no, no," MJ insisted. "You aren't insulting me. It just took me a moment to piece it all together. It has been so long."

"I'd be really interested in hearing about it," Bernard reassured her.

"In addition to leaving my mother's house, I'd also been stripping for almost ten years as well. I haven't always been 'performing', if you will, at the Churchill. Jonny saw me doing my last gig at another bar and suggested I just absolutely needed to be part of his show at the Churchill."

"But what made you get into stripping?" Bernard asked. "Did you enjoy it? Was it a way to make easy money?"

"I guess a bit of both," she replied. "I mean, the money is great, right?"

"I would assume," Bernard responded.

"Well, it doesn't hurt. And to be honest . . ."

MJ stopped.

"To be honest?" Bernard, enticing her to continue, interjected.

"I'm concerned you'll laugh," MJ bashfully mentioned. "Why I am concerned, I don't know. I mean I hardly know you."

"Exactly," Bernard interrupted. "Go on and tell me, please . . . tell me?"

"As a little girl, I had dreams," MJ continued, "of being a professional dancer—in the ballet. I wanted to do it so badly, but I knew I didn't have the money, the connections, or the family support to help me progress to the necessary levels to get hold of that dream in the first place. I was a stupid girl. I thought that a stripping job like this would help keep me fit, help me raise some dough, and then finally I would put myself through ballet school. Ten years later, I'm still shaking my goods at the Churchill."

Bernard was really enjoying this. He felt like he was making a deep-seated connection with her. She was so similar to him in so many ways, yet also fresh and invigorating. A sensation inside him suddenly resurrected—an emotion he had not experienced since sometime before Catherine's death.

"Sometimes life takes turns we just don't expect, doesn't it."

"Ain't that the truth?" MJ responded.

MJ looked at her cellular phone. It had been a long time since she wore a working watch, and she often relied on her phone to keep her on schedule. The time was much later than she had thought it to be. Catching her by surprise, she motioned to the waitress once more and suggested the check was needed.

"What are you doing?" Bernard asked.

"I've really enjoyed our time," she said. "It was such a nice departure from being cooped up in the bar all evening—like I am most weekends. But it is late. I'm going to need to do some laundry tonight at the 24-hour Laundromat, and I want to make sure I get some sleep before going to the gym at some point tomorrow."

"Do you really need to go? Can't you do your laundry tomorrow morning?" Bernard implored.

"No, I'm sorry, Bernard. I really can't."

"Well," he replied, "you are certainly not paying for this coffee. That is on me."

"I won't argue with chivalry," she responded. "Please, be my guest."

Bernard stopped the waitress from delivering the check to MJ, and gently took it instead.

"Now there's a sweet man, deary," the waitress insisted to MJ. "You hold on to him tight."

MJ simply smiled, and quickly glanced out the window. She noticed the fog rolling into the city and imagined that it must mean that Pacifica was fully covered in it by now. She was comforted by the thought, not because of Bernard's description that fog hides things, but because the fog itself seemed alive and so peaceful. It also appeared to be safeguarding the areas it covered.

"Maybe," MJ stated, smiling the entire time, "if you are nice to me, Bernard—maybe you can take me to see Pacifica sometime soon."

Bernard smiled as he dished money from his wallet.

"I would be honored to," he replied. "When?"

MJ laughed out loud. "I don't know . . ." she responded confusingly. "It was a matter of suggestion. I wasn't aware we were going to plan for it this evening!"

"Why not? How about next weekend? It will give me time to clean my bachelor pad, food shop, and cook us dinner. My place? Next weekend?"

He knew that MJ hadn't expected to be put on the spot. Her confirmation that she would meet him for dinner must have seemed to be a bit rushed, but somewhat exciting as well. Bernard however knew that she agreed because of his persistence in gathering an answer from her immediately.

"Well," she continued, "I don't have a car, so I'll need to take the bus."

"Nonsense!" Bernard laughed. "You'll be doing no such thing! I will gladly pick you up."

"You mean, like a date? Like an old-fashioned date?" MJ playfully asked, but mocking the type of damsel that cannot wait to be in distress. She could see, however, that either the mention of 'date' or her joking nature had staggered Bernard's excitement. Thus, her demeanor became a bit more focused.

"Yes, Bernard. You are welcomed to come get me at my apartment in the city. We'll then drive over to Pacifica, and I will see the beauty you described earlier this evening," she said seriously.

"I look forward to it."

Bernard, happy to hear her interest peek, unexpectedly thought of the hag and the Italian. While their *threats* didn't concern him, he thought about the impact they'd have on MJ—whether or not they'd try to persuade her not to join him next weekend. This worried him.

"Tweedle-dee and Tweedle-dum . . . those two at the bar," he said. "Are they going to cause you any problems?"

"Like I said," MJ responded. "I can care for myself. I wouldn't worry about those two. They act as if they are our pimps. And I'm a bit over it."

Bernard was relieved.

MJ laughed. "It's funny. One of the girls called them the Tweedles the other day. Other people call them Bitchface-1 and Bitchface-2. Others don't even acknowledge them except to suggest *the asses have arrived* as they enter the room. And have you seen the ass on her? Good lord!"

This made Bernard grin, especially after the strange altercation he experienced earlier that evening. Eager to hear her response, he asked, "and what, pray tell, do you call them?"

"Jonny—well, really he prefers his full name—Jonathan. And the woman is Wendy."

CHAPTER TWELVE

Bernard knew it was time for him to leave his office parking lot. The exchange between he and Shoshanna and Marcus seemed very strange. He already established in his mind that they'd been uncomfortable around him since Catherine's death, but their interactions with him this evening were downright discourteous, *and somewhat uncouth,* he thought. Regardless, it was necessary for him to get home as safely and as soon as possible. Though he knew MJ was likely in perfect condition, thoughts of someone breaking into the house and capturing her still raged in his brain. He knew he was making himself anxious over nothing real, yet his nerves began to get the best of him.

I believe I'll take Sharp Park Road this time, he quietly considered to himself. The thought of running into another idiot's accident was not appealing to him, especially not now. Memories from the past continued to surface as he drove the windy trail. He wanted to push the memories to the side and focus. He couldn't help but think about the intense argument he had with Alby, almost immediately after Catherine died. He had wished things could be different between them, but it just didn't seem to be a possibility. Not any longer, at least.

Bernard also thought more about MJ, about meeting her that evening, and about her first time over his house in Pacifica—the site of what would become *their* house in the near future. He remembered she seemed nervous when he parked his car in front of her rather shabby apartment building, in proximity to Haight Street, aptly known as *the Haight* in San Francisco. She was outside, waiting for his arrival, wearing a sundress that presented her in a way that was much more innocent than the stripper girl he met the other night—the one who, to be quite honest, he had been observing every Sunday for months. As he held the car door for her, one hand holding hers as she lowered herself into the front cushion, he remembered feeling pleased with himself. As a matter of fact, he remembered having said to himself, *God, I'm a stud.*

The moment he led her into the house, things worked like clockwork.

Wine. Check. Classical music. Check. Food, slightly but not too burnt. Check. More wine. Check.

MJ seemed to be enjoying herself, though being in a foreign environment was surely unnerving, and he knew that she knew she was wearing it on her sleeve. MJ continued to drink the wine that Bernard had poured them both. He remembered MJ telling him that she wasn't a wine-drinker. Something about it always made her feel languid. However, Bernard was sure that MJ realized that he had gone through such trouble, just to have an audience with her; the least she could do was enjoy the evening to its fullest possibilities and live the adventure she had been dreaming to live for quite some time now. Everything she experienced thus far—including Bernard's house—was surprisingly not rustic as she had probably assumed it might be, but completely modern, impressive, and peaceful. Lastly, Bernard was confident that she loved his choice in music that evening as well, though it was likely adding to her wine exhaustion.

In the corner, by the contemporary gas-powered fireplace—made from oddly lit and strangely colored glass and stone, was the one rustic piece of furniture she discovered—a chest, hip-high. It was a firm piece of equipment—rugged and dense, incredible craftsmanship adorned the carvings alongside it. The top of the chest was polished brightly, and it hosted at least fifteen modern squares of chrome-plated picture frames. A few of the pictures inside those frames were Pacifica sceneries. One was a shot of the Golden Gate Bridge covered in fog—San Francisco, and the inner East Bay in the distance. Other pictures were of Catherine, or so MJ assumed. Bernard could see her pondering over the pictures and imagined that she thought it was inappropriate to ask about Catherine at this point. Behind the front row of pictures was another row that included a black-and-white, older image of a couple wearing older-styled clothing. It looked as if they were surrounded by cornstalks, and their faces were so solemn that for some reason it sent chills up her spine.

"My parents," Bernard interrupted, noticing her stares toward that specific frame. He rather enjoyed the fact that MJ was interested in his display.

"I figured as much," she replied. "They look, happy?"

"Is that a question?" laughed Bernard.

"I'm sorry," MJ responded laughing as well. "They just look very serious."

Bernard agreed with her assessment. "Yes. Farming was a serious business. My parents were from the Amish country, in Pennsylvania."

"Your family is Amish?"

"Oh no," Bernard answered. "Well, I think not. My ancestors, when coming here from Europe generations ago, mostly settled in the Northeast section of this country, like Pennsylvania, New Jersey, New York. My parents went to Lancaster County, Pennsylvania. They continued to farm out there."

"Did they ever live in California?"

"No, my father died while I was a young age," Bernard replied. "Alby was not even a year old. I was almost ten. After that, my mother was especially more unpleasant than she typically had been while I was growing up." Bernard paused.

After some time of reflection, Bernard continued.

"That was wrong of me," he said. "My parents were suitable parents, and they were never cruel to us. They were just serious and not very affectionate."

MJ gestured herself toward the couch as if to ask permission to sit. Without halting conversation, Bernard gesticulated the obvious. He knew it probably felt good for her to sit. MJ was still buzzing from the wine, and she still had yet to show that she was fully at ease.

"When my mother died, I had already entered college. By then, I had been more of a parent to Alby then my own mother was to both of us."

MJ continued to look deep into Bernard's eyes, and he back into hers. She seemed to fully comprehend this suggestion, and yet she also seemed to understand that, despite the lack of parental warmth, Bernard nevertheless seemed to profusely respect his parents, notwithstanding his desire for them to have been less serious all the time. Bernard gathered that this was not something she felt about her own mother, though she likely wished she had.

"I soon transferred to Stanford University," Bernard continued. "It was where I was going to be able to complete my graduate research studies. I determined this to be the case, and I made it happen. And because of this, it was only appropriate that Alby relocate with me, or so I thought. So he did, entering high school close to Palo Alto."

During the conversation, one picture caught her eye—a striking, chisel-faced, model-like young man. Bernard noticed her glancing at the picture, several times in fact. Yet, unlike his affirmation regarding the picture of his parents, he waited for her to ask about it.

"Is that Alby?" She asked finally.

Bernard remained silent, but nodded in confirmation.

"He is beautiful," she responded. To Bernard, she strangely looked a bit like a moth drawn to a flame. Alby's stare was gently piercing her. It looked to him as if, as she had stated at the diner a few evenings beforehand, she wanted to meet him. Bernard didn't understand his slight jealousy. He believed she positively was not sexually attracted to him, but she seemed to identify herself with his face. For MJ, Alby seemed to be someone whom she'd be able to trust and with whom she could build a friendship. This, of course, was unexplainable, and she was certain it was because of his good looks.

"Well he is certainly the ladies-man in the family," Bernard snorted. "Always has been, always will be apparently." He smiled.

"My, my, my, Bernard. I think you are jealous!" MJ joked.

"Oh, what's abnormal about minor sibling jealousy?" Bernard asked.

"Nothing at all," MJ immediately interpolated. She raised her glass of wine as if to toast the exclamation, and noticed it was empty.

"Oops," she laughed.

"I'll go get some more," Bernard assured her. He swiftly moved into the kitchen, clanked a few bottles, and reappeared without leaving her alone too long.

Bernard imagined her thinking that he was *such a gentleman.* As he continued to ponder about the wonderful thoughts crossing her mind, Bernard poured wine, almost to the brim of MJ's glass.

"Ease down, cowboy!" She snickered.

"Sorry!" Bernard laughed.

"And so am I, Bernard," MJ responded. "I was playing with you a bit. Your brother is handsome . . ."

"You know," he interrupted, "he is gay, 100 percent gay."

"Yes," she replied also laughing. "We established that before. Or I should say you offered that information to me the other night, several times."

"I just wanted to make sure you knew the ladies-man was off-limits, to the ladies at least."

"Bernard," MJ countered, "I was going to apologize for teasing you. I was about to say that, yes, your brother is rather handsome, but he is not my type."

Rather than making eye contact with him, Bernard saw her gaze toward the massive floor-to-ceiling wall of windows that exposed themselves in front of them both. He knew the view was captivating and hypnotic. And as she stared, MJ smiled at both the panorama and the implication she just made.

Beautiful, thought Bernard. He smiled as well.

"I must apologize, Bernard," she said. "Some of this wine is going straight to my head. I'm afraid I'm embarrassing myself."

"Not in the least!" He replied. "We can take a break from the wine if you'd like. Do you need any more food? I have several things left over from our meal."

MJ wobbled her head in what he deciphered as a 'no'. With that, MJ lifted her hand to her brow, and realized she was sweating a bit. It was true that she seemed nervous, partially from the excitement of being with this slightly older, really handsome gentleman—at least in Bernard's mind she was thinking this—but also slightly because she hadn't been feeling her physical best that evening.

"I think I may need to lie down for just a moment," she said. "I can't believe I said this! I can't believe I just invited myself to lie down in your house . . . and I hardly know you!"

She laughed. And Bernard's imagination further explored the countless possibilities. He envisaged MJ thinking *I can't believe that I am telling him what I am thinking about myself! I am not some flimsy, weak schoolgirl in distress. Maybe I caught the love bug? Wouldn't that be a twist?*

"My dear, MJ, there is no need to be embarrassed. If you need to lie down, please, lie down! I can grab a quilt or throw-cover to help keep you snug. Would you like some aspirin, or maybe club soda to settle your head and stomach?"

"No, thank you, Bernard. I'll be fine. I just think I have seen a bit too much excitement in the past week since having met you than I have had in quite a while."

Bernard was delighted to hear this. Of course he hoped she would not be ill around him, but the fact that she had expressed this much interest in their time together—and so quickly—was pleasing to him. Things seemed to be working out just fine.

"Bernard," she said, fairly feebly, "I know we discussed walking down by Mori Point, but I am just so weak right now."

"I understand completely," he responded.

He believed at that moment that MJ was thinking *this guy is really quite a catch. The waitress the other night was correct! What a gentleman.*

"I feel awful that you planned this stroll, even prepared me to bring a jacket because of the beach fog. You wanted me to see the Pacifica beauty you described the other night, even through the night's darkness. I remember you suggested it was even more graceful when the sun was down. And here I am . . . acting like a drunk from a few glasses of wine. I ruined your plans."

"Not at all," Bernard reassured. "No, not at all."

"I should have warned you," MJ continued, "that wine and I do not agree with one another. I always have quite a reaction to it. It typically makes me feel very drained and incredibly drowsy. I should have warned you."

"But my dear," Bernard said, stroking her hair as she outstretched her legs across the couch. "As a matter of fact, the other night you did warn me."

From that moment, the mood immediately changed.

CHAPTER THIRTHEEN

Through the walls, Bernard could hear MJ waking. He instantaneously evoked a scenario in his head, visualizing her thoughts in very detailed fashion. As she began to wake, he imagined MJ was shocked to hear heavy breathing. After some deciphering, she'd realize it was hers. This made Bernard laugh a little. In addition to this, her heart was likely rapidly beating. No, it was actually pulsating in her chest. She was incredibly confused. The pressure in her head was paralyzing. The unadulterated stinging in her temples, behind her eyes, and in the back of her skull was so intense; and with that, she surely could tell that she must have wept while she slept. She was parched, her mouth was dry and her throat must have felt scaly.

Then he could hear her having a conversation with herself.

Am I having a migraine? I can't even see clearly.
Oh my God, I am so tired, I can't even move.
Wait.
What the . . . ?
Wait!
Where the hell am I? Where the hell am I?
It's dark. It's cold. I can't . . .
Oh my God, I can't move. I CAN'T MOVE!

Bernard thought that MJ encouraged herself to attempt to fill the silence that was surrounding her. She was likely still feeling worn, and she was, only at this very minute, truly grasping the fact that she was terribly numb all over her body. This whole situation must not be making sense to her, and he imagined that she was growing increasingly frustrated. Again, he laughed, this time a bit more sinisterly than he had before.

"Move," Bernard heard MJ say aloud to herself. "Get up!"

Inspiring herself to exert enough force to lift her head from the pillow beneath it, she surely did, deploying her attention toward every detail that surrounded her. Now Bernard could tell that she moved her focus toward her body. And after she prospectively blinked several times in order to moisten the dryness that caused weak vision with the goal of manifesting the images in her line of vision, Bernard knew that she was sure to notice what he had done.

"DEAR GOD!" She screamed. The sound of her voice reverberated across the walls of the room where she laid. "Are those . . . straps? Am I strapped into this bed? Are those ropes? Help!"

There was nothing but silence. No sound inside the house. No sound outside on the land. The stillness was a complete contradiction to the sounds of the city that surrounded her each previous day. The novelty and her ignorance to the situation likely terrified her. Bernard held a hand to his mouth to try his best not to release the sound of amusement. He pictured her asking herself, *what the hell happened? Did Bernard do this?* Or then thinking, *did something happen to Bernard as well? What if he is in the room next door, in the same condition as I am? Maybe I should scream.*

And like clockwork according to Bernard's assumptions, she did just that. MJ screamed loudly. Demanding help, calling out Bernard's name, even screaming to Wendy and Jonathan, as if they were close enough to hear. The poor girl must have known they weren't anywhere close by, but she was surely desperate for someone to find her. Sudden images artistically floated into his meditations. Maybe she started to think she was dead, rotting in place in this bed, having been found years later by people saying 'if only someone knew she was there'.

She wailed.

"Where are you?" MJ screamed. "What are you doing? Please, let me go!"

Bernard could hear MJ struggling to get free from the ropes and leather belts that tunneled into her skin. Burns, bruises, and blood adorned her wrists, ankles, and abdomen—all places where the straps tightly bound her to the bed.

"You nutcase! What are you doing to me?"

Stillness. Dead silence.

Through a peephole he created in the wall, Bernard finally brought himself to survey the situation. MJ peered around the room encasing her. Light from the window reached her face; battering her in a way that felt like an assault. It seemed that MJ's body continued to attempt to recover from an excruciating headache, and the light's angle was almost unbearable. But, she looked as if she was somewhat drawn to the light, as if she knew that light from the outside was indication that she slept through the entire night.

MJ mustn't be aware of the time, Bernard assured himself, but based on the view from the window, fog was slithering around the topmost hills of Mori Point. This was surely a means to inform her that it was probably morning, before the fog dissipated, or rolled out to linger over the ocean leaving the land bare. He then saw that she recognized the Mori Point view, probably from her memory of seeing it last night from Bernard's parlor window.

Bernard laughed again, like a giddy schoolboy readying for a prank, and imagined her thinking, *I'm still at Bernard's. Where is he? Did he do this? Or is he hurt? Did someone else do this to us?*

Unlike the comfortable house that hosted her last evening, this place must have now felt taciturn to her, unyielding and rigid, a once hospitable alcove suddenly transformed into a squalid penitentiary. The light was different, the shadows were different, and obviously the mood was different as well. Whereas last night she was smiling and enjoying her conversation, viewing beautifully framed pictures so artistically preserved, Bernard was confident that she now saw something completely different.

He saw her attention focused toward the hallway, beyond the doorway to the room in which she was imprisoned—dusty and decrepit. On the wall of that corridor were pictures draped with cloths, some of them turned with their front-sides facing the wall on which they hung. For a brief moment, he continued to envision her thoughts, as in, *am I insane? Have I been committed to an institution?* While he bet she hoped it was possible, since the thought was better than the reality of being held captive, she probably knew this wasn't likely. The revelation must have caused her severe and immediate terror.

"Answer me!" MJ screamed. "Where are you? Oh God! What are you doing to me? I don't understand," she cried.

She continued to struggle, aiming to get loose from the torturous grip upon her, but as was expected she was unsuccessful. Each time she moved, the straps and ropes burrowed into her gashes even further. Bernard could see that her body reacted violently to the constantly changing sensations—burning one moment, completely numb-to-the-touch the next.

Again, Bernard considered the horror that was likely before her. He imagined her thinking, *not one person knows I am here! How will anyone be able to save me? There is no one. No one!* Tears swelled in her eyes, and lumps formed in her throat. From a sudden burst of energy, and due to MJ granting herself permission for self-pitying, MJ howled in ghastly sorrow. She beseeched God, promising to go to church every Sunday—real church, not the Churchill—if He intervened to allow for a miraculous saving on her behalf. Bernard was amazed at watching this. And when she instinctually surely believed that her response was unanswered, she made deals with the devil, promising her soul to him if he would loosen the bonds that instant. Nothing. There was no hope, and MJ must have known it. The weeping continued, even more dramatically than before. As expected, a combination of her bewilderment and her frenzied sorrow created a natural anesthetic within her; and it smote her into deep sleep.

CHAPTER FOURTEEN

It was later that day, or so MJ must have thought. Bernard knew that she rightfully had no concept of time, but the light that once shined through the windows, pressing on her weary eyes, was no longer visible. The day was on its way to becoming night, and the air outside seemed misty and dark. Interestingly, the pain that scorched throughout her body earlier that day seemed now to be controlled, localized in minor sections—her wrists, her arm, and both ankles. While still physically restrained, she could shift a bit more at ease since the straps were not causing the intensified burning they had before. Surveying the room around her once again, she was able to see the only items that looked familiar to her from earlier in the day—the pictures from the hallway that were covered by dusty cloths, a door that she assumed was an entrance to a bedroom closet, and the window that now accommodated condensation from the evening fog.

To the right side of the bed she saw something new. Transfixed upon a makeshift silver pole was a liquid-filled plastic bag and drip, hooked to a tube connected into her arm, which was of course still chained to the bed. This seemed to cause her tremendous angst, but after her initial reaction to it, it looked to Bernard as if she lacked the normal vigor to care about something like that any further at least. She seemed to be fading into the distance once again. And as she slowly began to close her eyes, Bernard could see that she saw his likely blurry figure standing in the doorway entrance to the room. She wanted to scream from the surprise, but she couldn't. She was utterly lifeless. Her eyes opened and closed, opened and closed. The lids were so heavy; Bernard knew that she couldn't control the desire to sleep. Yet, Bernard also realized that she also couldn't stop herself from feeling incredibly anxious as he moved one step closer from the entrance into the room. She looked as if she wanted to yell at his figure, but instead appeared to form the screams in her head: *what are you doing? Help me! Please let me go!* Not one sound came from her lips.

Her body began to convulse likely from dehydration and pain, but unquestionably from unadulterated fear of the moment. Bernard appreciated his figure appeared as if ready to ambush her, like an animal scouting its prey. He understood that he glared at her, and he could see that she was glaring right back—mutually from trepidation. Bernard laughed as he conceived her true horror and sudden unanticipated expectation as he moved heavily and quickly toward her, covering her face and vision all in one swoop.

CHAPTER FIFTEEN

MJ woke again, still obviously confused, still obviously in pain, but surely, according to Bernard's perceptions, feeling a bit more rested than before. Immediately focusing on her newly familiar surroundings, she once again began to beg God to either save her or kill her. Whimpers crept from her mouth, giving Bernard the impression that she had not just cried, but sobbed while she slept.

It was at this very moment that he realized that the sound of his sullen, hoarse breath, almost directly behind her headboard, shocked and chilled her. The room was still as dark as before, but *surely MJ knew she wasn't alone*, he thought. The air was dense and there was a fixed presence surrounding her. Although numb, there were definite shudders that seemed to stiffen her muscles and cause her to panic quite dramatically.

"Who's there?" MJ asked. "What are you doing to me?"

He did not dare to answer her questions, but Bernard continued to breathe heavily. One effort he made was to deeply exhale, and as a result of this action, Bernard knew MJ could sense movement toward her face.

"Oh my God, don't touch me! KEEP AWAY! KEEP AWAY! God, help me!"

Bernard placed his icy cold fingers on her forehead and slid them toward her hairline. Like a claw, each curled around a section of MJ's hair, separating it into pieces and combing through the tangles that formed over the past forty-eight hours.

"Silence," Bernard insisted as amazingly gentle as possible. "You must relax."

"Don't touch me!"

"Relax, MJ," he responded.

"Why are you doing this to me?" MJ screamed, her throat once again beginning to swell, begging to burst into a sorrowful whine.

"You must calm down."

"Who are you?" MJ asked. "What have you done with me? What have you done with Bernard?"

A gentle laugh, which started as a whisper, swiftly cultivated into a brooding roar much like wizardry madness.

"My dear," the madman responded, "I *am* Bernard, love. I'm here to protect you, my dear. I believe it is time to be treated like the woman you deserve to be."

And with these words, Bernard lifted the light switch by his arm, clearly allowing his face to materialize for MJ to examine. He bent over top of her, staring directly into her eyes, laughing sinisterly. Momentarily, Bernard could clearly see that MJ was moving toward a hyperventilating state. These are the kinds of scenes that happened in the movies he'd seen in the past. Pressure seemed to fill MJ's chest, and as she made the loudest, most blood-curling commotion she'd ever produced, Bernard saw MJ struggling as she felt the straps tightening around her. Obviously, her body once again was suffering from convulsions, and the pain indubitably stung as insufferable. Bernard did what he could to appease her.

"The more you move, my dear, the more you will suffer," Bernard averred. "Why do you want to continue to make yourself suffer? I am here now to take care of you."

"Holy God," she cried, over and over to the point of hysteria. "Help me! Please SOMEONE HELP ME!"

"Dear, I *am* helping you," retorted Bernard. "Please calm down. The fever has almost broken at this point. I've injected you with intravenous antibiotics. You need more rest."

"No please! I need to get out of bed! Please help me!"

"No, no, no!" Bernard said firmly. "You will soon appreciate my assistance!"

MJ continued to scream.

"Time to rest!" Bernard yelled with a decreased amount of patience that once controlled his gentlemanly emotions, shutting the light as quickly as he finished his statement, quite theatrically in fact. The harshness of his voice, and the reverberation throughout the room evidently shook MJ into disbelief. She simply scared herself silent. Bernard slowly walked away from the bed, and he knew MJ could hear him doing so. His steps were purposeful, and with each move he made, Bernard forced a statement of authority in both posture and gesture. He then knew what was necessary. As he exited the room, he once again tried what he could not to laugh aloud. He imagined the following:

MJ, just moments ago, surely heard his profound strides surrounding her. Suddenly, she would have heard nothing. She would then wait, and straining to hear, would continue to feel an emptiness and uncertainty that would cause her additional anxiety. It would only be when she heard distinct rattling by the entrance to the room, that Bernard was sure that she would begin to experience a sort of trauma that, sadistically, was causing him to enjoy the moment more than he had expected. Here, more rattling, then pausing, then more rattling again, further pausing, and finally he did what he had waited to do. Bernard's sharp jerk of the manacle in his hand created a monstrous roar of the chainsaw he tightly held. As he stood there, now unashamed to laugh aloud, Bernard further imagined MJ trying to assure herself that the sound was in her imagination. Only when the noise was too close to allow her to continue to fool herself, MJ would suddenly realize she needed to obey him.

As MJ burst into tears, screaming loudly, surrounded completely by darkness, she heard Bernard laughing as he calmed the machine in his hands. Now it only purred before coming to a full stop.

"Just a bit of humor, my dear," he said.

Suddenly, the door slammed, and MJ surely could hear his footsteps on the opposite side, echoing down the hallway. He believed MJ would be able to hear his childlike, mischievous laugh finally dim, and then at that moment she must have known she was alone.

"FUCK!" She screamed. She cried for what seemed like hours. In reality, by the time she had wept herself unconscious, it had been just about fifteen torturous minutes.

CHAPTER SIXTEEN

Bernard remembered it well, like it was yesterday.

For three or four weeks (possibly five) during that time—a time Bernard lovingly refers to as their *honeymoon period*, each day was the same. It consisted of MJ's consuming cries, deep screams, irrepressible panic, uncontainable vomit, chaotic excretion, more vomit, and despairing prayers. That was the period of time when the rapes began as well, typically once per night. At first, MJ would thrash about, fighting back with verbal appeals; statements that she surely hoped would bring Bernard back to his senses. He was a bit too refined for such feeble attempts, and as such, her efforts would fail miserably.

Bernard would return from work each evening to change her intravenous bag, checking on MJ first before doing anything else, including removing his jacket and shoes. He could see that MJ labored to understand why it was the case, and she surely wasn't pleased by the lack of comprehending it, but somehow he believed she seemed to think this was an appropriately loving gesture in a strange way. The intravenous served as both her meal ticket and her way to remain hydrated. In addition to this medical bag, newly added within the past few days was a catheter tube that he connected into her vagina. Easily the mess that MJ continued to make from her body's natural urination process was beginning to annoy Bernard. While he was sure he loved her—and that meant caring for her in every possible way—having to clean her every, single, fucking evening was something he was beginning to begrudge. It was true that the constant insertion, removal, and reinsertion of the catheter caused her increased risk for further infection. However, to Bernard it was necessary. He could no longer start his evenings with MJ by cleaning her urine filth. And the need to keep her catheter lubricated during this process aided in his ability to have sex with her whenever he wanted.

A fifth week passed, and then a sixth week. Soon two months had gone by, and during that time, Bernard explained only a few things to her, reinforced over and over to drive the point:

1) MJ was, at first, sick with fever and dehydration. This required attention, and like any loving caregiver he connected the intravenous medication during the first few weeks immediately aiding her back to health.

2) MJ was now no longer in need of the intravenous continued care. She was now sipping water on her own through a bendy straw that hung toward her face, begging to be used. This came from a glass of water on the tray table that hovered over her bed. Additionally, she was now eating the food he fork-fed and spoon-fed her. For his troubles in the matter, he believed he had demonstrated his love for her and expected MJ to return the signs of affection that he clearly assumed she had noticed.

Bernard tried not to think about it, but at times, the consideration materialized in ways that he could not control. He visualized MJ feeling like a hamster drinking from a water bottle attached to a cage. Additionally, he expected that she only prayed that God would have mercy on her soul and let her die before he experimented on her. These thoughts, which he was certain were crossing her mind, angered him.

She hardly spoke, but when she did, MJ would ask simple questions.

"Are you going to chainsaw me into pieces?"

"Don't be ridiculous, darling. I love you," Bernard would respond. "Sometimes I like to play a joke or two, just to get a reaction."

"Why can't I move?"

"Actually," he'd answer, "you can. It is the straps keeping you in the bed."

"Why have you strapped me in?" MJ would cry, pleading for an answer.

Bernard thought it was important not to upset her delicate situation. He'd try to explain it in a way that he believed was most appropriate.

"Dear," he'd start, "you are entering a new exciting phase in your life. Now that I have found you, I am not going to let anything happen to you. I am going to protect you from all those wolves of men out there who want to do nothing except salivate over your body while you dance for them. I am going to protect you from Wendy and Jonathan who don't care for you like I do. I am saving you from stripping. One day, you are going to dance ballet for me! But this change requires adjustment, just as a caterpillar requires seclusion in a cocoon. And until you have adapted to it, it is much safer, in your condition, to remain secured."

MJ continued to cry. It was evident to Bernard that she could simply not believe this was happening to her. He was sure she was wondering why he simply wouldn't kill her. She must have thought, *I don't even care what you do to my body after I am gone. Stuff it for all I care. I just want to be put out of this misery. I am never going to be saved.*

"And," Bernard continued, "every now and then, you need to be reminded about how close to death you have come—maybe not physically, but developmentally. This is why I try to remind you with quick bouts of fear *i.e. the chainsaw thing*."

MJ looked petrified; not just from fear but also amazement, *probably from the bullshit she continued to hear spewing from my sick mouth*, he gleefully thought to himself.

"Bernard, please?" MJ begged. "Please, I think you may need help. I think your wife's death caused you to go over the edge. You need some help. You need to talk to someone. *I* can be that *someone*. I will talk to you. Maybe together we can talk to someone about all of the pain we have both experienced—the pain of—losing your wife. Just let me go so I can start to help you."

For a brief moment, Bernard played along allowing MJ to believe her petitions resonated within him. The rigidity of his new face had slowly eased, and he presented himself as the serene person whom she'd met some months ago—the average, gentlemanly guy who was her answer to chivalry's endangerment. On the contrary, he redeployed his equanimity and began to laugh again, in a sound that was even shriller than what she had obviously noticed before.

"My dear, *you* are my wife. And you will be safely in my presence for the rest of your natural life," he responded. "Now relax for me, please. I need to remove your bedpan and reinsert the catheter."

Absolute despair seemed to envelope her. MJ's fear was unquestionably noticeable now, and Bernard could tell that she was quickly considering asking him to kill her.

"Please, Bernard!" She instead interjected. "Please, I am raw down there. It is so painful."

"Well dear, I cannot continue to clean you up each night," he retorted. "Since we plan to make love this evening, how about if I use a special numbing lubricant?"

"Bernard," MJ responded gently, likely hoping to gain some composure in the situation. "If you want me to appreciate our love and our . . . marriage . . ." she gulped, "I cannot be treated like an animal."

Bernard thought this was clever, but weak at the same time.

"I resent that my dear." Bernard's reaction was distant and cold. It caused her to pause, surely with great concern. Bernard assumed that MJ was beginning to recognize that she needed to carefully deliberate over her words before expressing them.

"Bernard, I didn't mean animal," she assuredly stated though nervous with each word she spoke. "I meant . . . patient . . . medical patient. It is difficult for me to be like this, cared for by you," she cleverly insisted, "it's demeaning."

"But," Bernard argued, "it is my pleasure to care for the woman I love. No, I will not have you say such nonsense any further."

* * *

The truth:

The astonishment of the situation continued to burst through MJ's thoughts. This man was clinically insane. *How*, she thought to herself, *could I not have noticed this?* Bernard was speaking about love for a stranger, and within the same breath discussing the necessities of keeping her restrained and afraid—as a reminder of her suffering before he 'saved' her.

* * *

"Please, Bernard, please don't put that tube back inside me. I can use the bedpan to pee as well," MJ emphatically implored.

"No, too messy."

"Really, Bernard. I am a woman," she said, again cleverly in a playful manner. "We women are very resourceful."

"I'm not sure about this . . ."

"Bernard!" MJ's voice was now the firmest it had been in almost two months. Even amongst the torture, the constant rapes, and Bernard's unpredictable behaviors, her resolve was never as persuasive as the way she'd just demonstrated. He was appreciating her efforts and starting to believe that she was adapting the way he had hoped she would.

"Bernard," she continued. "Think about this. Your wife, your love, has just asked for your permission to let her be the woman she wants to be . . . so she is not embarrassed in front of you any more."

Bernard stopped in his tracks, tilted his head toward her, and gaped at her body. Judging by her look, he was sure she was waiting on baited breath to see how he would react to her recommendation, frightened but interested. He knew she must be entranced. He insisted that she'd be. Bernard was sure that to some extent she had wished he'd react violently and finally end her misery. But he did the unbelievable. He did the opposite. Dropping the catheter tube to the ground, he began to tear into a blubbering mess.

"My dear," he said, wiping his eyes in a way he thought may have reminded her of a politician's fake reaction to the funeral event of a cabinet member or the head of some foreign state. "I am so proud of you. You are getting stronger each day."

"I think so too, Bernard," MJ responded. "As a matter of fact, I am starving tonight. Is it possible to start making dinner a bit earlier than usual?"

Finally, he thought. *We're making progress!*

"I am preparing duck for you, darling," Bernard gleefully stated. "I always found it to be a bit greasy, but it is high in protein, and definitely savory."

"Thank you, Bernard," MJ said through her imitation smile. "I believe I can get some rest before dinner now."

Bernard bent down, kissing MJ directly in the center of her forehead—right at the point where she was clearly feeling pressure from a sinus issue. Just a month ago, Bernard knew this action would have made her want to vomit all the more. Back then, he pictured her thinking, *so long as he doesn't kiss me on the lips, I can handle this a little bit more.* He now believed the situation was quite different, possibly not fully corrected, but unquestionably on its way to being the life he had hoped to build for the two of them.

Bernard exited quietly. He knew MJ could see him stop in front of the dusty cloth-draped pictures hanging in the hallway. His back was facing her body, as he stood there, trancelike, staring at these pictures.

* * *

The truth:

In reality, MJ wished she was loose and holding something heavy with which to hit him over the head while he was distracted in front of this strange shrine of spookiness. When he finally moved in the direction of the kitchen, MJ surveyed the room, just as she had done over the course of her imprisonment trying desperately to construct a marvelous plan of escape. Her straps were still quite tight. She looked toward the entrance of the room. Obviously the bed was not thin enough to make it through the doorway. *Maybe instead,* she thought, *if I shake sadistically while he is at work during the day, it will cause the bed to break and I'll be able to loosen these bonds?* She eyed the window to see if she'd be able to shake the bed enough to have it crash through it. She was more than willing to take her chances with a fall, broken glass, broken bones, or even some body parts severing at this point. She'd be out of the house at least, and certainly the commotion would help alert an audience from someone else in the town.

MJ looked toward the new digital clock—the one Bernard installed after hearing her numerous questions about the time. In just about fifteen hours he'd be leaving for work. She was eager to begin working on her escape. Though her mood had improved slightly from the thought, she was quickly dismayed after slightly turning her head to find Bernard above her.

"Jesus!" She shouted. "Bernard, you startled me. You came in so quietly."

Bernard said nothing, but placed his hand on her face. The chloroform was awful. It burned as she breathed it in, and panic once again began to take form inside her.

"Rest, my dear. You need rest," he said. "You will not get well without sleep. Just a little help to give you a quick nap before dinner."

It seemed only momentarily that MJ wakened with a terrible pain behind her eyes. She had experienced this pain within the past few months, and she suddenly realized Bernard had used the chloroform on her before. She was alone and crying, and Bernard was once again watching, unbeknownst to her. He could tell that MJ must have thought that escape was the only option before she lost the will to live altogether. As he watched, he could smell the duck almost completely prepared for dining. It actually smelled rather good, and Bernard knew the same smell probably confused her into wanting to stay, comparable to a bribe of the sweetest sense. He saw MJ glance at her body, noticing the straps had not moved. Upon further inspection though, he could tell her sheets and clothes were soaked, red and yellow.

"Oh no!" Bernard heard her whispered to herself. "No, please, please, please."

He blinked a few times, hoping this mirage would soon fade; yet it became more and more clear that she had urinated all over herself.

"Oh good God, help me!" He again heard her say softly. "Bernard will be furious with me!"

Was it possible that with the renewal of hope in an escape MJ no longer desired to be killed? Bernard thought death would now be fruitless to her and it comforted him to believe she may actually be conditioning nicely away from depression and would soon accept him as her own. The more he thought though, the more he made himself fretful. Bernard began to truly believe, though as impossible as he knew it likely was, that escape could be MJ's destiny. He envisioned MJ praying for a miracle, and this likely scenario incensed him to his core. Rage suddenly overtook his emotions in a way in which a man like him should be ashamed. Instead of erupting into what surely would be seen as an unfortunate disaster, Bernard did his best to remain composed, for the moment.

When Bernard entered carrying the tray of carefully positioned food items, the aroma was beautiful and sweet. Bernard saw MJ close her eyes surely to imagine the taste. She must have been hoping that he wouldn't notice the stain. The thought was almost amusing to him. He considered her thoughts: *Maybe even,* she likely reflected, *he'll place the tray over top of me, square on the stain. I could then suggest it was the grease from the food.* Rage this time got the best of him, and as a result whatever thoughts she truly had were now interrupted by a vehement crash of plates and tin.

MJ opened her eyes and saw food scattered all over the floor and wall. The tray had dropped—or possibly had been thrown—and Bernard was nowhere to be found. Crying now, MJ undoubtedly realized she was in serious immediate danger.

I hope this is fast.

Bernard burst into the room with the old-fashioned, hotel-styled fire hose he kept in the glass container stationed on the wall of the corridor. It was unraveled, taking on a life of its own. It resembled a python that was ready to squeeze the breath from her and coax the very lasting life that remained inside. For a moment, likely out of shock, MJ laid there completely still.

"I knew this would happen to you!" Bernard screamed. "I knew if I would let you have your way, I'd be left to clean up your mess, Catherine!"

"Bernard," MJ interrupted, without much success. "Bernard, it's MJ. Not Catherine."

"Look at you!" He screamed. "Just look at the mess you've made. You are sick! Why'd I let you convince me otherwise?"

"Oh my God, Bernard! Please! STOP! PLEASE!"

Bernard twisted the hose and let loose an astounding fury of angry waves of moaning, stinging, and vicious pounds of water. MJ screamed, but Bernard refused to stop.

"I must get you clean," he said.

The scene was like Bernard's description of Pacifica the night MJ went to the diner with him. Bernard acted like the fog that cleans everything in its path. When the water was not filling her ears, nose, and throat, MJ would scream while simultaneously trying to catch her breath. The waterboarding was constant and painful. To Bernard, it looked as if she was drowning, and in her bound condition, there was nothing she could do to secure herself from the onslaught. MJ was bruised beyond expectations, and he wasn't quite convinced that she'd survive the water that must have been pooling in her lungs. Bernard suddenly stopped the ambush. The room was saturated like a sponge. MJ was in shock. Bernard was pleased. He quickly undressed and, in between the straps and bonds, laid himself across her and injected himself inside her. As he moaned in pleasure, MJ writhed in pain. Thus, slowly but surely, MJ fainted, or zoned. It didn't matter. Bernard knew at that moment that she had given up any hope, real or not, of escape.

The water torture continued for another long month with an occasional break in the routine when Bernard was exhausted from work. However, breaks from the procedural event were incredibly rare. Instead, MJ's typical night wouldn't be complete without Bernard using the python fire hose to cleanse her physically. In his very own sick way, what typically followed after 'the cleansing' was even worse. Almost each night, the sequence of events included MJ's painful and unspeakable saturation in more ways than one. Her body was ridden by contusions and blisters. There was even a possibility that the enormous surge of water that hit her face one night was the probable culprit responsible for her sorely dislocated jaw.

After repeated torture in this regard, Bernard could see the sight and mere mention of water caused MJ unease. At times it physically made her sick to her stomach. For MJ, Bernard was pleased to know that each night was like a recurring night terror from which she couldn't wake. Simply put, it made Bernard revel in glory that for MJ the thought of water terrified her for the rest of her life.

CHAPTER SEVENTEEN

Almost an entire season had passed, at least five months now—*and that,* Bernard thought, *was probably being generously conservative.* Gradually MJ lost herself in an abyss of her own personal identity. To Bernard's pleasure, she simply could no longer exercise any attempt to provide herself with a sense of safety, freedom, and the knowledge of the life that she once knew—the one just months before she must have thought was unfairly clutched from her. Bernard continued to think that the most incredibly insane part of all of this, as unfortunate but true as it was, could very well have been the result of MJ being gentle and responsive to the severely psychotic world he created. *Had she only met me before her spiral downward, dancing and likely pimping herself, we could have reduced the need for me to save her like this,* Bernard thought.

From Bernard's perspective though, there was no use crying over what could have been, or where the spilled milk might have dripped. This all couldn't have worked more perfectly. He was stimulated by his work, and found it fascinating that his resurfaced graduate studies as a psychiatric researcher, with a specialization in criminal behavior and mental conversion, were finding their way back to assisting him with his own personalized case study. MJ was the textbook example of the type of victim Bernard absorbed during his academic tenure. She had no family, no friends, and no major job where she'd be missed. She was strong enough to have personality, yet delicate enough to understand his pain. She was a faultless completion for the void he felt after Catherine's death, and soon he knew she would feel the same love he felt as well. With some major work on his end, she would be his new perfect wife, without any resistance. He wasn't sure if he would eventually tell others that he was living with a beautiful woman—both tangibly attractive, and intently good-natured. If he had decided to do so in the future, the isolation of

Pacifica would be his perfect safeguard. For now though, it was best for MJ to understand that she was an invalid, hoping for a cure.

"Let's try to remember, my dear," Bernard said. "There was an accident, and then a rare immunological infection set in, causing you to be nearly paralyzed. It's been about a year, and sometimes it affects your mental capacity and memory. Your beautiful brain sometimes can not hold all of the wonderful memories you have," he insisted. MJ was so lifeless, so lackluster that it was easy, Bernard thought, for her to confuse memories she had for new ones he made for her. The most difficult task he faced was having MJ believe she was paralyzed, not by the straps, ropes, and belts that bonded her to the bed

Bit by bit, Bernard could see MJ's memories slipping from her mental framework. She seemed to be forgetting her young life in the San Francisco slums, the place she cared for herself when separated from her crack-ridden mother, which created a path that led her into the arms of stripping. Bernard instead continuously reminded her how fortunate she was to have been raised in a beautiful painted-lady mansion in the Pacific Heights neighborhood of the city. He insisted that her mother, 'Wendy' was a doting parent who was, more often than not, intrusively involved in all of MJ's decisions, including making decisions regarding with whom she would and would not have relationships. This, as Bernard so often liked to remind MJ, would exceedingly frustrate her. It was this vexation that enabled MJ, according to Bernard, to strengthen her charisma, and it was one of the reasons why Bernard loved her so much. He would remind her that she made him the happiest man on earth when she chose him over 'that man Jonathan', despite her mother's protests. Again, he insisted she was his pride and joy.

"Never forget this," Bernard told MJ reassuringly.

And MJ, lying perfectly still in bed, would blink and close her eyes while counting to ten, seeming to desperately aim to remember these images from her past. He could see that she recognized the name Wendy—from where, she likely had no idea—but she seemed to concede the name as belonging to someone who *appeared* motherly. Bernard knew his explanations were starting to resonate and simmer.

There was no mention of Misty Moore or her stripping. This character simply did not exist. Instead, Bernard, in a psychological effort to make her new life a bit more realistic for her, played on MJ's familiar, delightful ambitions. MJ was now told that she was the ballerina she always wished to be, famous for performing center stage at a fancy place called the 'Churchill Theater.' Jonathan, her choreographer, was not only jealous of her incredible talent, but also covetous of the attention she often received. According to Bernard, Jonathan surely had remembered what it was like when he, himself, graced the stage with such presence. And, bothersome as it might have been for MJ to realize at the time, in order to gain the attention back, Jonathan was determined to marry her. This, Bernard reminded MJ again, was not something MJ easily accepted as true love and a good faith arrangement.

"You have always been too smart, my dear, to fall for something like Jonathan's ploys," Bernard pleasingly said.

"My wife," he continued. "She's too smart for anyone!"

And finally, playfully, Bernard included a statement that resembled something like, "You showed him! You showed Jonathan that he couldn't play with love."

MJ nodded in agreement and slightly smiled. When her movement didn't cause too much discomfort, her agreement emerged more regularly. It appeared to Bernard that she was conditioning adequately. Bernard was very roused by the efficacious results of his experimentation. Yet, he was slightly more animated due to the thoughts of having a new wife that wasn't going to leave, nor threaten to leave—in reality, couldn't leave. And whereas his last one didn't, this wife would love him, goddamn it. He was fully in control of her history and her future. Bernard would be sure that his new wife would never stop loving him. Therefore, he would be sure to never let a day go by without reminding MJ of their fortunes.

While there was so much fortune in her life though, Bernard felt it necessary to also remind MJ about the misfortunes she inopportunely endured as well. Perceptibly, the paralysis was one. Additionally, due to Wendy's utter disappointment in her choices, and the fact she couldn't face her ailing "child", very likely out of guilt, poor mother Wendy lost much of her maternal instinct and thought it best to avoid her daughter outright. Jonathan began to focus on his new ingénue and in due time, truly forced himself to forget about MJ. And then, combating with her misfortunes like they were his, he constantly reminded her about the death of his first wife. MJ was, as Bernard would consistently tell her, *so supportive* of him.

He spoke of his office colleagues, and how each of them admired him, yet he was too reserved and shy to desire it. For Bernard, it was unfortunate that Catherine's death brought more attention to him, as he proudly stated.

"From that moment forward," he explained to MJ, "my colleagues could simply not leave me alone, especially when their happiness for my finding you was suddenly shattered when they heard you had been stricken ill. Some of them, mostly Marcus, could no longer look me in the eyes out of pure sorrow for my continual losses. But I endure, reminding them calmly that all is going well."

There were two major lies with this particular scenario. First, Bernard never mentioned to anyone—colleague or not—that he was now living with a new woman. The few people who surrounded Bernard were not especially intimate with him and likely could care less if he had a new life partner or didn't. Second, Bernard's colleagues took notice of him, not for his professional and skillful abilities, but instead for his eccentricity. To them he was a peculiar and disturbing man whose social graces were not just absent, but virtually nonexistent as well. They were bitter from working closely with him, and Bernard knew that his colleague Shoshanna had—several times now—requested her cubicle be changed from its current position. *Fuck that bitch*, he thought. *I could get rid of her easily, in a moment's notice if necessary, if only she wasn't so damn smart.*

Two more months passed, and as Bernard expected, MJ was adapting well. By this point, MJ's body had acclimated to the straps, and he believed, as evidenced by the lack of flinching, she no longer felt pain. Bernard made it his routine to do the following eight steps:

1. Make MJ breakfast each morning, feed and bond with her, emotionally.
2. Play music through the house's sound system for MJ's comfort. The music he chose varied, but it typically was classical orchestrated sounds—sometimes-spooky material to the common man, though none of it was known by name to MJ. The sounds were from his favorite collection—Portishead, Billy Holiday's *Gloomy Sunday,* Tori Amos's *Spark,* or even Irish Ballads, such as *Dead Can Dance: The Wind that Shakes the Barley.*
3. Go to the office and try, as humanly possible as can be, deal with the outside world.
4. Come home, clean MJ's bedding, remove any excrement, sponge bathe her, and remind her how lucky he was to have her in his life.
5. Prepare MJ's dinner and feed her.
6. Make love to her.

7. Repeat love making if he believed it was necessary.
8. Go to sleep.

Over these recent months, Bernard was pleased that MJ became disheartened about her situation. His pleasure was that she was displeased about her sickness—her fake paralysis, if you will. Though she couldn't remember the details of it, Bernard knew she missed her ballet dancing and believed it was unfair to have been placed dead center in this bad streak of luck. She could not comprehend how someone as her—someone in her prime with such an artistic ability with such devoted fans—could become paralyzed as a result of a freak accident and infection. *Why,* she surely thought, *why do terrible things like this happen to such good people?* For his part, Bernard did his best to calm her. He'd explain how there are some things that we, as inferior human beings, could simply not explain.

"Sometimes," he'd respond to MJ's cries for explanation, "there are higher questions that we are not supposed to understand."

Any outsider observing such conversations between Bernard and MJ would surely become sick to his stomach.

Depending on the day, and also depending on his own mood, Bernard repeatedly embraced MJ in order to enliven her. He could feel that MJ understood that Bernard was showing his affection, but abstruse to anyone but her was the sentiment of anger because of it. Here he was, enfolding his body around hers, completely capable of moving. She instead was as still as a statue. It was likely depressing her. He knew that MJ was still a woman of few words at that time, though her speech and conversation had improved progressively. Bernard recognized that she was more willing to have conversations with him, even if she simply didn't remember the details of her past, factual or fictitious. He was as giddy as a boy with a newfound puppy. His plan was working.

During her bouts of melancholy, Bernard suggested sex. Realistically, he'd present it as "making love" since that is how he preferred to refer to it. He surmised that MJ thought she loved him—knew, at least, that she was supposed to love him—yet, enigmatic to her, it seemed that she still rarely (if ever) enjoyed sex with him. Bernard assumed this was due to her belief in the paralysis, and furthermore presumed it was her unhappy thoughts blocking her enjoyment. Bernard could see that MJ very much yearned to be happy once more, and thus as a result she would not decline Bernard's offer.

* * *

The truth:

However, sex with Bernard was often the only time she could black out, sometimes literally. Bernard never seemed to mind. Everything was extremely confusing. MJ believed she was fortunate to be loved so deeply, yet she could not understand the feeling of emptiness and isolation. And with this, she would sleep until sex was over.

* * *

One morning, some time after, during a weekend when he believed he needed a break from the office, Bernard brought the typically cooked breakfast to MJ's bed. She had been staring out toward Mori Point, considering the beauty of the day. It was sunny and the fog had already scattered. Remnants of it could be seen peaking around the point, but in an awkward way, those remnants seemed to be incredibly shy and unwilling to take the risk to jump from their hiding place and into sight. MJ told Bernard about the feelings she had. She told him how she thought the fog's cresting actions were synergistic to her true feelings. It was obvious that she slept a bit longer than normal since the fog was in this position.

He was sure that MJ would notice that he had a fanciful step that morning. He didn't walk, but he gracefully strolled across the floor. And indeed, Bernard knew she had taken observation of this because she continued to tell him so.

"You seem a bit different today," MJ said, quite lethargically, but as pleasant as she could be.

"Do I?" Bernard responded in amazement. "My you are sharp-eyed and vigilant, darling."

MJ was not unintelligent, but she certainly didn't have an archive of scholarly vocabulary, like the one that Bernard often used. Bernard knew that this sometimes maddened her, but the usage of his jargon also helped her to gain insight into the types of words she was now expected to use. The more he had intellectual conversations, sometimes quite studious in nature, the more she began to adopt his vocabulary as well.

"The most . . . interesting thing happened this morning," he continued. "Interestingly, I think it is the best thing for both of us."

MJ seemed to experience a brief moment of anticipation as a result of this. She continued to seem intrigued by Bernard's announcement, and it was true that something new was needed to heighten the mood recently.

"I spoke with Alby this morning," Bernard mentioned as he spooned oatmeal into MJ's willing mouth. "You remember me speaking of my brother, right?"

"Yes," MJ said, drooling some oatmeal from her lips.

Bernard placed the spoon back into the bowl, clutched the dishtowel that hung from his shoulder, and used it to gently wipe her mouth.

"Oh, dear," he said in a laughing tone. "Looks as if I didn't give you time to swallow your food before answering. Apologies, my dear."

"No, Bernard. I'm fine, and thank you," she responded with some bewilderment. "I just have heard you discuss your brother with so much disdain recently. You and he haven't spoken for some time. I don't quite understand why you are excited by this."

"Again," Bernard insisted, "the experience was rather interesting. I didn't expect for it to happen, but it did."

He began to feed her again after she showed it was an appropriate time for him to do so.

"That's just it," Bernard continued. "Alby mentioned to me that he has wanted to speak with me for some time now. At first, I thought it was a sick joke. But then, it became clear to me that it was a real conversation. He wants to make a regular appearance, as much as I am ok with it."

MJ, still showing confusion asked, "And you assumed this was the best thing for the both of us?"

Bernard didn't respond. He only watched her watching him and waiting for a response.

"It's been a while that anyone else knew that my life was changed for the better after meeting you," Bernard explained. "Everyone knows about Catherine's unfortunate events. No one close or related to me at least knows that since that time I met you and fell in love. It has been such a tumultuous time in my life, and with you getting ill, I couldn't bear to have anyone pity us."

"We have discussed this before," MJ responded.

"Well, this was all true until today," Bernard interjected proudly. "Alby now knows about you. And he would like to meet you."

MJ wasn't sure what she thought about this new revelation. She, according to Bernard, had always wanted to meet Alby and develop a relationship with him. The idea, though, of meeting some stranger in her condition was not comforting to her. If she were to agree to this arrangement, it would take some delicate convincing.

"I know you may have some reservations," Bernard suggested. "But I do think you are quite prepared for this."

Bernard spoke in an encouraging manner and smiled at her.

"I think it would be appropriate for you to begin building a relationship outside of our marriage. You need someone to help you feel confident in yourself, in us, and he would be great company for you while I am at work every day."

MJ agreed to consider it, and while she explained that she had concerns about her appearance, she also expressed that the temptation of experiencing a more flavorful day compared to spending it the way she had in the past half year. Bernard knew that she would eventually agree to this arrangement. Pragmatically speaking, MJ readied herself to agree to a meeting with Alby much sooner than Bernard anticipated. Unknown to him yet, MJ had already begun to experience some unexplainable, concerning, and at times some chilling events. As a result she preferred to have company with her during the day while Bernard was at work.

* * *

The truth:

While she hadn't yet seen anyone specifically, she was beginning to feel a presence surrounding her. It was an eerie feeling, one filled with the coldness of the very fog that approached her window each evening. She typically suffered through this sensation when she was alone, and it seemed to be getting stronger each day. It was a feeling that made her question whether or not her sanity was at risk from cabin fever. It was a feeling that, as much as she hadn't ever thought it to be possible, made her believe that she was possibly being haunted by some type of force that was determined to bring her harm, physically and spiritually. She could tell it was growing, intensifying, and was preparing to soon appear, likely before she was ready to confront it. Helplessness soon overwhelmed her; and there was nothing she could do about it.

CHAPTER EIGHTEEN

As the rain poured in front of his car, Bernard continued to reminisce about the world he had created for both he and MJ. The more he valued the memories that played in his head like a pleasurable recording, the more he became disturbed with MJ's recent and what seemed to be frequent disturbing twist of events. He was convinced, if not before, with absolute foregone conclusion that someone was aiming to steal MJ from his control. This person, either a do-gooder, or worse—someone who had been spying on the two of them—had no right to infringe on the happiness that took a grassroots campaign of events to settle into place the way it had over the past year.

Bernard could feel tears of sadness and frustration welling from his eyes. He was not the type of man that often let his emotions get the better of him. But he had been through enough already, and this rapidly declining situation would cause them such devastation. He needed to do something about it, and rather quickly. But determining exactly what to do, without any preconceived knowledge of just who this shit-head do-gooder was, or without having caught this ass hole in the act, was causing him the trepidation that MJ must have surely underwent when first being conditioned.

At times Bernard considered that possibly Wendy or Jonathan found them, determined to wreak havoc on the situation. Perhaps they were planning to capture MJ and force her back to her days as Misty Moore, and obviously watch Bernard suffer as a result. *It must be them,* Bernard thought to himself. *Who else would it be? There is no one around here that knows her or is willing to take a risk like this if they did.* The thought crossed his mind—like a derailing train that was precisely bound to collide with all of his plans—that he should pay a visit to the Churchill, that disgusting hole that enslaved MJ to dance for all of those pigs that maintained their erections while she was performing.

"Try to take me down!" He screamed. "Just try to take her from me, you freaks!"

Bernard didn't want to envisage the possibility, but he was willing to accept anything—other than the possibility that his dead wife was indeed the culprit.

Alby?

Could it be Alby who was behind this? Or more realistically, could it be that MJ had convinced Alby to be behind this?

Bernard, deviating through the implausible amount of traffic detained by the inclement weather, began to think about some of the tales MJ would recite back to him after he rejoined her in the bedroom each night. To be quite transparent, Bernard often would pretend to listen for MJ's benefit of course. He truly was very disinterested in these fairy tales. These stories, either Alby's or her creation, made absolutely no sense to him. At times he remembered thinking to himself, *damn it I kidnapped a talker.*

On that particular evening, the first time she said anything about the stories Alby told her, Bernard remembered his amusement and initial interest in her trying to summarize the plots.

"Wait," Bernard responded. "Repeat what you just said please."

"Alby told me this very interesting story," MJ replied. "And being that you are quite a learned man, I thought maybe you could help me make some sense of it."

Bernard stood there in bewilderment. *Stories,* he thought. *Is she really going to waste my time with stories?*

"Bernard," I know you just came home from a long day at work, but typically when Alby tells me these stories, I know that there must be a deeper meaning to them. He is telling me these tales for a reason, and I know I am supposed to somehow assess the reason. That brother of yours is very clever."

"Indeed," Bernard responded, rubbing his chin and shaking his head. "I'm confused, MJ. How is it that Alby is telling you stories?"

"What do you mean, Bernard?"

Bernard simply smiled, trying to hide his frustration that grew more intense by the minute. Calmly, he replied, "I simply mean, what story is Alby telling you?"

"Just an interesting fable called *Happy House of Saddened Gulls*—about this poor family of children that are forced by their parents to live on the sea, only to be abandoned by them—you see they, the parents, were killed in a storm. And this is what forces them to face survival by depending on one another. The problem is that they don't even like each other. Never did."

Bernard was careful not to display the intense amount of rage that filled his body at that moment. He imagined himself as one of those cartoon characters, upon escalating frustration, simmering to a stewing point so scorching in nature that an exploding head was all too expected as a result. It all made sense to him. *A story about children who were 'forced' to live somewhere where they didn't originally belong,* he thought. *A story where the children needed to learn to survive,* he continued to examine within his mind. *What are she and Alby cooking here? Is something coming back to her? Does Alby know about this? Is this Alby's doing?*

With as much patience as he could humanly maintain, Bernard slowly moved toward the window by MJ's bed. He could so easily turn and strike her out of pure frustration; yet doing so would be incomprehensible and perplexing to her. He knew she'd question the physical aggression This was the conditioned MJ, the one who believed her prince had been found in the man that stood before her, not the MJ that was the recipient of rape and torture.

"Dear," Bernard said calmly. "Tell me this story."

"Oh Bernard!" MJ exclaimed. "You mean it? You will help me decipher the meaning? Alby is so difficult to beat at these games."

"Where, by the way, is my dear brother," Bernard interrupted.

"He left a bit ago, way before you came home, but did spend some great time with me today."

"And why did he leave?" Bernard questioned. "Was he aware that I was on my way, or was he planning to do something?"

MJ laughed a bit.

"He wouldn't tell me, but I am assuming he had one of his dates tonight."

Bernard thought to himself, *Alby is a fucking freak.*

"I am so happy for him," MJ continued. "He spends such a considerable amount of time with me to help me get through my boredom and displeasure here while I am not with you. He does so in a way that takes him away from his own interests."

"He *was* interested in spending time with you, MJ," Bernard corrected. "We've been over this. He is not stopping himself from doing anything he wants to do."

"I know," MJ reassured herself. "He has said the same thing to me. I just continue to get concerned for him."

"Well don't. I'm actually more concerned about where he goes at night. It has been some time since we actually spoke last. Can you do me a favor, dear?"

"Of course," MJ replied sarcastically. "You know full well that you don't need to ask me to do you any favors."

Bernard leaned down and kissed her on her forehead. He thought back to the time when doing so would cause her to shutter, and he'd imagine her wanting to vomit as a result of his conditioning affection. *My,* he laughed to himself, *how things have changes in such an incredible way in a relatively short amount of time!*

"The next time you see him . . ."

"Tomorrow, likely," MJ interrupted.

"Ok, tomorrow, ask him to stick around, or possibly come by to see me the following morning. I'd like to have a conversation with him."

MJ's look was a puzzling one. Bernard realized that his almost condescending tone coupled with his special request must be confusing to MJ at best. In an attempt to dilute the mounting apprehension, Bernard smiled brightly. He could see his attempt worked, and MJ beamed as a result. To be honest, her cheerful disposition just then was relaxing to his current anxious state. At the same time, Bernard could not help but to think that Alby was planning something, and he knew that he must get ahead of it proactively. *What is with this story? What is he trying to do here? What is MJ herself trying to do?*

"I am just interested in making sure he is not filling your head with crazy, scary stories that are causing you to be nervous while you are alone," Bernard confirmed.

"Bernard," MJ said softly. "I truly do love you, and I love how you care about my welfare so much, but I can assure you that is not what Alby is doing. He is not scaring me on purpose."

"Well, he always was a troublemaker," Bernard retorted. "He was always playing some type of prank that made things hell for everyone around him, me included."

"Come on, Bernard!" MJ laughed. "He is telling me stories to keep me alive, keep me thinking, keep me guessing!"

"So, are you going to tell me about this story, or what?"

Again, MJ laughed. Bernard could see there was a newfound excitement within her. She acted like a detective trying to decode the case file that she recently received. Maybe he had nothing to worry about after all and was simply being overly sensitive. Maybe Alby was not intending any ill will against Bernard. Maybe, truly, this was a way to keep MJ engaged in an active and interesting life.

"The actual story starts with characters known as the Gull parents. The father is a fisherman, and the mother seems to be a homemaker. The family does not have much money, but they live in a village that depends on the father's seasonal catch."

"Sounds delightful," Bernard interposed.

MJ rolled her eyes and suggested that Bernard calm his sarcasm to listen to the rest of the tale. As such, Bernard put his hand to his mouth, covering it and implying that he would remain quiet.

"Well, the problem that the village encountered was some type of mystical occurrence that caused drought, famine, and livestock issues—something like that. The fish were not coming as close to shore as they once did. This forced the father to leave for the open sea for bouts of time that lengthened each time he left. As a result, eventually, he and his wife decided it was best for the family if they all moved on a boat amongst the open sea."

"I can only imagine the thought you had, MJ," Bernard said. "Thinking about living on the open sea must have made you tremor, you know—with your fear of water and all."

MJ burst into amazed mirth.

"Yes!" She exclaimed. "I said to Alby that the idea made me sick!"

"See, I assumed as much," Bernard retorted.

"Ok, no more interruptions," MJ responded. "At least no more interruptions until I ask your opinion about the story."

Again Bernard motioned his hand over his mouth to portray a committed silence moving forward.

"The Gull children," MJ continued. "Their children, Sylvester, Daphnis, Holly, and Piper, were apparently not happy with this arrangement. Begrudgingly though, they eventually succumbed to their parents' wishes. What is very interesting about the story is that each of the children, all but Piper eventually, are depicted in a way that illustrates the spitefulness and egocentricity of human nature."

Bernard took a moment to congratulate MJ on her bold word choices. Easily, his lessons in grammar seemed to be having an impact on her. And furthermore, MJ appeared to appreciate the recognition.

"What Alby failed to describe to me the first time he relayed the story was that each of the children, though nasty they were, had reasons for being that way. The eldest son, Sylvester, was never given the respect he had hoped his father would give him. He apparently wasn't considered manly enough to take over the fishing business, and their father—who at first seemed to be this peaceful and loving man—was actually quite cruel to him."

Again Bernard thought, *what is Alby up to?*

"The second son," MJ resumed.

"That would be Daphnis, correct?" Bernard asked.

"Very good," MJ laughed. "How non-*egocentric* of you to be listening to the story so closely."

It felt good for Bernard to hear himself chuckle a bit.

"So yes, Daphnis," MJ responded. "He was actually stronger in character than the first born. But, maybe as a result of seeing how Sylvester was treated, he wasted no time in suggesting he wasn't even interested in the family trade. He instead preferred to focus on matters that were more dear and beneficial to him. He wanted to simply be an explorer, to find some way to move beyond his family."

"Well then," Bernard interjected. "Wouldn't this move to the open sea help him fulfill this need?"

"I thought the same thing," MJ replied. "But Alby helped me to realize that by moving there, he'd be in confined quarters with the very family he was trying to escape. The thought was quite stifling."

"Oh yes, I can assume. Poor Daphnis."

"And that's not the worst of it! The first daughter—Holly, she was kind of a slut."

Bernard laughed. He continued, however, to feel aggravated in the sense that this story was taking shape to be very similar to MJ's experience. *A person who was trapped and forced to live in an environment that was unforgiving,* he thought. Again he thought, *is she remembering her conditioning? Is Alby somehow figuring things out and telling her this information to make her think of it? No, it can't be. He's not that smart. Neither is she.*

"But she, like her brothers, never seemed to get any attention from her parents. And in some respects she was aching to find love. She finally discovered a boy from the town—named Duke, I believe—who fell head-over-heels in love with her. The second time Alby told me this story, the way he explained the feelings Duke had when he first saw Holly were so magical, so loving, so prolific and abundant with rich material. The vision I had when hearing it was so realistic, much like the dream I have when sensing the outside again, walking barefoot on the sand and smelling the sweet ocean . . . that is, before I drown."

The statement caused MJ to take a pause, and suddenly both Bernard and she snorted a laugh that was reminiscent of what Bernard felt when he made the decision to bring MJ into his life.

"And what happened?" Bernard asked, showing some type of eager anticipation that he didn't expect to have.

"It is so sad," MJ responded solemnly. "When Alby expanded on the story the second or third time, he informed me that the father caught Holly and Duke in a compromising situation in the boathouse one day. The two teenagers were, shall we say, close to consummating their relationship. Apparently, the real story became quite graphic at that moment, but Alby spared me from the gory details. All I know is that Holly's father punished Duke for coming close to his child and threatened him in such a disgusting way that if he ever came close to Holly again, he would punish them both even further. This left Holly with no choice but to join her family on the open sea."

"And what was wrong with the second daughter—Piper? What was it about her that caused her parents to make her suffer?" Bernard questioned.

"Actually," MJ replied, "nothing."

"Nothing?"

"Correct, sir," she confirmed. "Piper seemed to be the apple of her parents' eyes. Alby led me to believe that she hadn't always been accepted by her father, but eventually she was seen as the only child who was suitable enough to receive her parents' devotion."

"What was so special about her?"

"Alby hasn't detailed this yet, but he promises to do so," MJ responded.

Bernard grunted and showed he was absolutely ready to expire.

"All I know at this point is that there was a storm," MJ continued. "Something caused the parents to go overboard, the children became lost at sea, and Piper eventually takes it upon herself to keep everyone in line, the way that the father had anticipated she would in the future anyway. But I think there is more to this story."

"Well, clearly," Bernard retorted.

"I first felt sorry for the parents and Piper," MJ said. "Then after hearing more about the story the second time around, I understood more about the ways the other Gull siblings suffered. I then felt badly for them, and I was very angry with their parents. I still felt sympathy for Piper Gull though. She couldn't help that she was favored—or could she? That is what is unclear to me. And Alby is not budging on providing me with any clues. He says that he'll tell me the remainder of the story in due time."

Bernard continued to openly stare at MJ, trying to decipher the meaning behind her interest in the tale—which, truth told, he found annoying.

"To me," MJ persisted, "It seems as if the story is ever changing, that it is alive. I believe maybe the point of the story is not to trust my instincts. Each time I hear it, I have a different perception of the characters. I suppose by the time it is finished, I will have understood why the parents treated the children the way they did. Maybe there is more to the story that makes me feel sorry for the parents again? Maybe there is just a whole lot more to the story that Alby will eventually unfold."

Bernard, fuming from irritating thoughts of his brother, serenely responded when he was ready to do so in a way that demonstrated no frustration.

"Clearly."

CHAPTER NINETEEN

Bernard was jolted back to reality when his phone suddenly twitched and sounded a distressing noise. It startled him, causing a stir of emotions inside him. *This could only mean one thing*, he thought. Bernard, not once taking his eyes from the sight of the road, reached for his phone on the other seat, feeling around for it with the palm of his hand, and finally discovering it when the point of frustration was about to set in. Glancing quickly down at the blue glowing screen, he saw the code 'Pacifica' flashing. The sight of it almost caused him to swerve off the road. He wondered if the phone's text alert was immediate or if it was one that was delayed as a result of previous poor signal service.

"Pacifica," he mouthed. "Pacifica! Damn it!"

Bernard sped through the winding trail, rushing toward the sight of Mori Point, terrified to find what he had expected he would. Thoughts raced through his mind, and he was convinced, now more than ever, that someone indeed discovered his dirty secret—MJ—and this obvious stalker finally made his or her move by removing MJ from Bernard's custody. *How dare they intrude! How dare they do this! Fuck them! FUCK THEM!* He continued to race down the street. His house was now in sight.

Flashing lights came from the bedroom window that faced Mori Point. This surely drew attention to the neighborhood surrounding his home. Immediately, Bernard got flustered. He was in no way interested in having anyone from the vicinity call the police. He was determined to find the intruder himself and invoke bodily harm on the person for having interfered with his and MJ's happy life. Jumping from the car, he ran across the lawn, barging into the house. Bernard wasn't concerned with creeping quietly. He expected to catch the intruder in the act, and he was prepared to provide the ultimate punishment for the disturbance.

Yet everything within the house seemed normal. Not one morsel was out of place, but the sudden movement from the direction of MJ's bedroom finally caught his attention. His heart, beating so rapidly, may have caused him an unexpected attack if he hadn't reached the corridor to the room in time.

"MJ," Bernard shouted. "MJ, where are you?"

No one was in sight.

"MJ?" Bernard repeated.

Nothing. The background music maintained its play, but not one human sound could be heard any further. Bernard continued to progress slowly through the corridor. He noticed all of the pictures that hung there were no longer covered. Those that were turned facing the wall were now fully in view. He winced at them, covered his face, almost ready to cry. The memories of his life before were almost too much to handle at the moment. He also recognized that some of the smaller pictures were missing—neither on the wall nor the surrounding floor area.

Bernard cautiously stepped toward MJ's bedroom. Lights from the Pacifica-coded alert system he installed earlier were still discoing around the bed, illuminating sections of the bedroom at given intervals. He could see that someone had been in the closet. Hoping it was MJ he hurried toward it. There was no one there, but the inside of the door was scratched and nearly broken over portions of it. He examined scratch marks on the floor, and observed the same large portrait that MJ had, apparently moments ago, uncovered and in plain sight.

Bernard screamed, "MJ! MJ! Where are you?"

Out of sheer frustration, he exited the closet, slammed the door behind him in such a catastrophic movement that it shook the walls of the room. Bernard nearly fell backward from the fright of seeing, through the mirror in front of him, a ghastly looking figure in the corner behind him.

"Shit!" He shouted aloud.

Turning around, prepared to fight, he saw nothing. There was no one around him, nor did he feel a presence, yet he was still compelled to face the mirror once more just to make sense of what he previously saw. As a result, he viewed nothing strange in the mirror after all. Maintaining his stare upon the reflection, he watched the circling lights shine into the corner where the grim figure previously stood. It was then that he noticed a coatrack standing in its place. Saying Bernard's fear was immediately allayed was an understatement.

Something else though, much more upsetting and frankly appalling then broke his concentration. He turned from the mirror slowly to face it. Tilting his head slightly, he tried to focus on the inscription written on the front side of the closet door. Bernard hadn't noticed it before when the door was swung open. Now that the door was slammed shut, the writing on it was visible; and as he approached it, the writing became distinct and unobstructed.

I'm back
I've been watching
I have her

The inscription was finger-painted onto the whitewashed wood of the door. It was red. Bernard reached for one of the letters. Tracing his pointer finger around it, the liquid writing began to smear onto his skin. Analyzing it in his typical methodical way, he began to tremble.

"Blood," he quietly mouthed. "It's blood!"

Noticing the opened window, Bernard now realized the sounds he heard were likely MJ, gagged and bound, being dragged out if it. Bernard ran to the kitchen, stumbling over broken pieces of glass, tumbled corridor pictures, and other bothersome intricacies that were unnoticed earlier in the day. He pulled open the kitchen drawer with such force that it unhinged and cutlery came crashing to the floor, clanging as each individual piece dropped. Grasping a butcher's knife, he moved toward the front door resolute in finding MJ and this captor, whoever this monster was. Before leaving, he noticed the phone, dangling from its receiver, was now sending out a tone that almost dictated a desire to be merged back with the table unit where it once sat. He went back into the kitchen, grabbed a flashlight, and once again headed toward the door.

"MJ! I'm coming!" Bernard shouted as he headed through the doorway into the front yard. The evening was crisp, and the rain continued its cascading gush around him. His objective was clear, and he thought nothing of the rain and wind that hit him. He examined the vicinity. Bernard wished he had indeed landscaped his yard to remove the grass and replace it with a sand—or beach-like system like he intended to do for so long now. That way, he would have been able to locate muddy footsteps to follow. Instead, Bernard relied on sheer instinct, up until he finally saw what he had hoped to see, as clear as day—footsteps on his driveway, directly after a spot on the lawn where mud formed from work the town did on his sewer lateral pipe replacement some months back. One set of moving footsteps, followed by what resembled something or someone being dragged, stretched down the path, and finally disappeared once reaching the wet street. Their direction faced Mori Point, and this is where Bernard headed.

"MJ! MJ?" He continued to call out. "I'm coming to save you. Scream out if you can. Scream out!"

Yielding his knife forward, he raced up Mori Point, instinctually tracking the trails in front of him, analyzing every step he took. Bernard didn't care about the stories of previous coyote and mountain lion sightings in this wildlife protected area. He pressed forward with purpose, forcing brush away from his face as he sprinted toward any possible sign of movement or life. The rain made it difficult, and the fog covered the moon's light, thus dependence on his flashlight became his only tool for success. Just when despair was about to set in, Bernard heard a whimper—not too far from where he stood.

"MJ?"

Only slight movement could be heard.

"MJ, it's Bernard," he whispered. "Are you there?"

Nothing.

"MJ?"

As he moved additional brush away from his line of vision, MJ, huddled into a fetus-like position, appeared before him completely head-to-toe soaked and muddy, her face covered by her hands. Bernard, caught by surprise, jolted backward at first. MJ said nothing, but Bernard wasn't yet aware if MJ had seen him or not.

"MJ! It's me. You didn't answer me. Are you ok?"

"Why didn't you believe me?" MJ inquired.

"MJ," Bernard responded. "What are you implying? Believe you about what?"

MJ continued to peek through her fingers in a direction behind Bernard. Shaking from cold and fright, she continued to say nothing.

"MJ," Bernard continued. "How did you get out here? How did you get out of bed? How are you moving about? You are sick and paralyzed. Did someone break into the house?"

"I'm not paralyzed," MJ retorted.

"I don't understand, dear. I am so confused! Did someone break into the house? Answer me, MJ! Did someone break into the house?"

MJ nodded her head to affirm.

"Who was it?" Bernard asked.

"I saw the picture, Bernard! I saw it!"

MJ continued to shake. Over and over, she told Bernard that he foolishly hadn't believe her, and she questioned why that was the case.

"Help me understand," Bernard implored. "What did you see and what did I not believe?"

Partly Bernard wasn't able to reconcile whether it was the intruder who was the cause of MJ's terrified behavior, or if she was furious with Bernard, angry with him for being her abductor. He could only think, *did she remember?*

And then, finally, MJ spoke.

"You didn't believe me that Catherine was haunting me!" MJ cried.

Bernard, unsure how to react, was somewhat relieved yet partially disturbed at the same time.

"MJ, darling," he said.

"Don't 'darling' me in a condescending manner!" MJ screamed.

"Ok, ok! My apologies," Bernard responded. "I just don't understand."

"She's here," MJ said. "She's here and she says she does not like what you have become. Neither do I!"

Bernard could suddenly hear shifting within the brush behind him. While he was unwilling to believe his former wife was back from the grave, he was certain someone was spying on them, and tormenting MJ into thinking they were being haunted. And he thought for a brief moment, *let's face it. In her conditioned state, she's liable to believe anything.* Knowing that someone liberated MJ, Bernard was all too certain that this someone was standing near him, hidden within the brush. He was now the one who was terrified.

"Come out here, you bastard!" Bernard screamed.

MJ began to laugh uncontrollably. "She's watching you, Bernard. She doesn't like what you have become. She doesn't like what you have been doing to me."

Bernard, astonished, mouth gaping, continued to stare ahead, screaming, preparing to slash at the first thing that plunged forward.

In spite of Bernard's attempt to threaten this presence by his screams and yielding knife, the brush nevertheless stood motionless without any response. Suddenly pain shot through Bernard with an intensity to force him to drop his knife. Bernard gripped his arm, now oozing blood from a wound inflicted upon him from behind. He screamed from the agony, dropped to the ground facedown. A mixture of mud, blood, sweat, and rain blurred his vision, and he feared the vulnerability of his position. Bernard could hear MJ's laughing behind him transition into soft cries, not from sadness but from worry. He could tell she was not alone and was trying desperately to keep stable. He felt someone was with her, and the mere presence of this 'someone' was causing MJ undue stress. It was at that moment that Bernard finally saw a figure, still very blurry to him, but certainly broad and commanding. Sound protruded from it, and as the tones became more prominent to him, Bernard realized that they were screeching and wretchedly horrid, and they were made precisely by a female voice.

"You made a terrible mistake," the female, blurry stranger implied. "You underestimated her. And you underestimated me."

The stranger's voice was whispery like the invisible wind, yet mighty like the solid fog as it rolled past and overcame him. Bernard's eyes were clouded with mud and rain. He could no longer see MJ.

"What did you do to her?" Bernard screamed, still clutching his arm tightly.

"She is free from you," the stranger responded. "And I see you are still consumed with your own sense of reality, your own sense of power. Well, sir, this is about to change."

"Fuck you," Bernard screamed. "MJ! Where are you? Answer me! I can hear you crying. I'm right here."

"Sir," she interjected, "Do you not recognize me? I have been resting far too long now, and it is time for me to return."

Bernard lay on the ground confused, rocking the pain back and forth. *This cannot be*, he thought to himself. *I refuse to believe it.*

"Now," she continued, "it is time for you to . . . rest."

With a forceful march, the figure approached him, hitting him over the head with a metal rod. Though it broke no skin, surprisingly, the blow was successful enough to wipe Bernard unconscious.

CHAPTER TWENTY

"Bernard," a distant voice called, slowly coming into focus with each passing second. "Bernard, can you hear me, sir?"

Bernard shot up, studying his surroundings. The feeling was akin to waking from a horrid nightmare. He was now dry, wearing no coat, but still in his jeans and his white tee shirt stained with blood. Attempting to reach toward his arm and chest to measure the damage that was done, he noticed he couldn't. He was lying in a gurney, handcuffed to it, and a somewhat decently dressed gentleman stood in front of him calling his name.

"Bernard? Are you able to focus on me?" the man asked.

Bernard plopped his head back down, exhausted and in pain, blinked his eyes a few times and adjusted them to the bright lights of the room. He licked his incredibly chapped lips trying frantically to moisten his mouth with his own saliva.

"Water," Bernard responded. "I need some water, please."

The man motioned toward a mirror as if he were drinking from an imaginary glass. Within a minute, a homely looking female entered the room with a half-filled plastic cup of water being held against Bernard's lips. Bernard choked as the water rushed down his throat, spilling partially from his mouth.

"You can remove those," the man said to the female motioning toward the cuffs.

"But sir," she said.

"Officer," he insisted. "Bernard needs to drink on his own. And in a minute or so, I'll be asking him to write an account for me."

The female officer nodded and did as she was instructed, releasing Bernard's cuffs from their bind. She then quietly exited the room as the man thanked her once again.

"Where am I?" Bernard asked, rubbing his wrists. He took a moment to survey his arm and noticed stitching through the wound that must have been sewn while he was unconscious.

"You are in the Pacifica Police Headquarters," the man responded. "I am Detective Elphorantis. I assume you understand why you are here."

Bernard gave no indication that he was aware of the multitude of crimes he had committed just by keeping MJ in captivity. Merely instead, he continued to rub his wrists showing dissatisfaction with the pain the cuffs left and the aforementioned treatment he endured.

"Where is MJ?" Bernard asked.

"She is safe. We found her, and she is receiving medical care at the university's medical center."

"I need to see her. She'll be terrified without me!" Bernard insisted.

"Sir, as I said, MJ is safe. You will not be going anywhere right now. We are attending to you as well, but we also have some questions for you," Elphorantis retorted.

"What's this about?" Bernard asked. "You had no right to keep me here, handcuffed while I slept. You have no right to keep me from her!"

"Actually sir, we do."

"Correction," Bernard immediately interrupted. "Actually you don't! You cannot arrest me without reading me my rights."

"Now, now, Bernard," the detective claimed. "Who said anything about an arrest? If I was going to arrest you, I'd read you your list of Miranda rights now."

Bernard began to laugh. "This is about MJ, isn't it?"

"Is it?" Elphorantis responded.

"You must be very careful," Bernard insisted. "She is very sick. She isn't fully aware of what she says. She's living in an alternate reality."

Elphorantis sat at the stool opposite of the gurney bed, placing his finger on the side of his brow.

"Funny," he said. "I agree. And this is why I need your statement—a written one. I need to analyze everything you say and get to the bottom of everything I am being told. I assume that you have no problem providing me a verbal and a written statement, especially because you want what is best for MJ?"

"Yes, of course," Bernard said stiffly.

"Very good," Elphorantis responded, motioning his finger once again toward the mirror that faced Bernard. Bernard knew someone was on the other side. And as proof would have it, within seconds the same female officer entered the room with a pad of paper and a dull pencil.

"I'll need to know everything about this evening," Elphorantis pleaded. "Additionally, I need to know about MJ's illness, how long she has been living with you, where her family might be, any type of arguments you might have had, whether or not you have any proof of strangers lurking about, that sort of thing."

"Easy," Bernard replied.

"Oh yeah," Elphorantis mentioned before leaving the room, "and one more thing. I'd like an explanation about the photographs we found in your house."

"Photographs?" Bernard questioned, rather anxiously.

"Yes, photographs. The ones that we found covered by sheets. Some strange shit, sir."

Bernard lowered his pencil and additionally, he lowered his face and closed his eyes. After a moment of pause, his eyelids lifted and the eyes inside rolled upward. He coldly stared at the detective, gazing at him, wishing the detective were vulnerable.

"I think," Bernard said slowly. "I think I'll be needing my lawyer before I answer anything further."

"Oh sure thing, Bernie," Elphorantis answered.

"It's Bernard."

"Oh, pardon me, Bernie, I mean Bernard. You're welcomed to contact your lawyer. Maybe while you're at it, you can contact your brother as well."

Bernard continued to scrutinize the detective's whereabouts. He greatly wished he could pounce on him and stab his pulsating jugular.

"And what," Bernard asked, "What does Alby have to do with this?"

"MJ informed us of her bond with Alby. He was a great source of comfort for her during this relationship of yours. A relationship we're trying badly to understand. Not too much of a champion for you, that brother of yours, at least according to MJ, he's not. We're simply trying to locate him at the moment so that we can ask him a few questions as well."

Bernard shook his head from disgust, and slowly but surely began to menacingly snigger.

"Something funny?" Elphorantis questioned. "I'd truly like to know. I'd like to get to the bottom of this and go home. I'm sure you would as well."

"Elephantitis is it?"

Elphorantis smirked cautiously, somewhat respectful of the sinister sense of humor, "Detective will do just fine if you have trouble with my name."

"Pardon me, detective," Bernard continued. "Old *BERNIE* has trouble with ethnic names at times."

"And," Elphorantis continued, "You were laughing because . . . ?"

"If it wasn't for my brother," Bernard began to snort. "Oh my goodness, pardon me! I can hardly contain myself!"

Bernard continued his hysterics, laughing and rubbing his chest.

"If it wasn't for your brother, then what?" Elephorantis asked again, patiently awaiting Bernard's continuation.

"If it wasn't for my brother, MJ would have never learned to trust me in the first place," Bernard, still guffawing, claimed.

"Are you suggesting," Elphorantis assumed, "Your brother is part of this—part of whatever it is that you need to acknowledge to me?"

Bernard, now wiping the tears that formed from his eyes, began to soothe his laughing state and gain composure. Still, with a chuckle now and then, hardly able to comfortably speak, Bernard responded, "Detective, I think you will need to question Alby. Ask him about his involvement."

PART THREE:

Alby Matters

"Freedom is fragile and must be protected. To sacrifice it, even as a temporary measure, is to betray it."—Germaine Greer

ALBY'S ACCOUNT

University of California-San Francisco Medical Center,

Interview with Attending Physician, Dr. Armstrong

Alby: Doctor, I was pleased that you contacted me. I am very concerned for MJ's welfare. Thank you for seeing me.

Dr. Armstrong: Actually, Alby, it is a pleasure to meet you. I know you also agreed to speak with the police, but I do appreciate the time you took to speak with me first. I too am very concerned for MJ. Can you help me understand the different things you witnessed when visiting her? Do you mind if I record this, for the simple purposes of helping with MJ's reconditioning?

Alby: Of course.

Dr. Armstrong: You should know that this recording could be requested as evidence for a future trial. With that being said, do you object to my recording our conversation?

Alby: No. I understand that this is what needs to be done.

Dr. Armstrong: You are very brave, Alby. Thank you.

Alby: You must understand, doctor, it is very difficult for me to do this.

Dr. Armstrong: Because you are speaking for and/or against your brother, I assume?

Alby: He and I have not had a close relationship for a good period of time now. There is no hiding that fact. I believed we were building something strong again when he met MJ—or as I thought, 'met' MJ. I guess in reality, he abducted her.

Dr. Armstrong: It would seem so.

Alby: Despite our differences, and our failing bond, he is still my brother and I feel a bit remorseful for speaking against his cause in this manner. I am sure he is going to need every bit of defense he can warrant in the next few months.

Dr. Armstrong: That too would seem to be so. One item of consideration though, Alby, is that it is very possible that Bernard, not just MJ, needs help. You can provide this in some way by helping the police and me. Alby, can you tell me your side of the story? MJ is in such a delicate situation after experiencing the abduction and conditioning. I fear that questioning her once again will bring her over the edge. She might not return, and in reality, were we ever to be able to provide her peace in the future, we'll likely need her to testify.

Alby: You mean testify against Bernard, my brother.

Dr. Armstrong: Yes, unfortunately, that is what I mean.

Alby: I'll do what I can. When Bernard first described his relationship with MJ to me, I found it curious. Don't get me wrong, I certainly was happy for him. He had just a year prior lost his first wife to a terrible accident. I thought he'd never recover. It hurt me to watch him go through that pain. For so much of my life, he was like a parent to me, and I didn't want to see him suffer. Yet, something about the sudden meeting . . . the sudden, shotgun marriage . . . the sudden illness . . . it just didn't sit right with me.

Dr. Armstrong: Please continue.

Alby: I had doubts that the story was completely accurate, but during my conversations with MJ, I had noticed that she seemed to be very fond of him. I now understand he conditioned her to be so.

Dr. Armstrong: Yes, that is likely correct.

Alby: Further, I didn't want to question it. I had not seen my brother for a year following Catherine's death. We lost all contact and our relationship was non-existent. I figured I was not around to witness the development of any new relationship between my brother and MJ so who was I to question it?

Dr. Armstrong: Thus, you accepted the relationship then.

Alby: I know, it was incredibly stupid of me to do so. I should have trusted my instincts.

Dr. Armstrong: There is no judgment here, Alby. I am recording every piece of information I can in order to help everyone in the situation. Please simply state what is on your mind. You are not on trial here. Your input is incredibly advantageous.

Alby: For such a long time, MJ was covered head to toe in blanket over blanket, each of them tightly tucked into her bed and underneath and within the crevices of her body. Bernard was very particular about MJ not being touched. He claimed her illness caused her immune system to be very weak. And he said MJ was often in in pain, so I was not to go near her, touch her, or move anything from its rightful place. The blankets hid the straps that kept her in bed. The poor girl! She had no idea she was being held prisoner. She thought she was paralyzed!

Dr. Armstrong: It is quite a sad situation. Believe it or not, I have seen worse situations, but this is something that is certainly very disturbing.

Alby: I accidentally noticed the straps one day. That is when it all began to go downhill.

Dr. Armstrong: I'm very interested in understanding your account of that situation as well. First, can you help me understand MJ's perception of something she continuously repeats, or I should say someone she continuously mentions?

Alby: I'll try my best.

Dr. Armstrong: Catherine. She claims that Catherine has haunted her for some time. She claims that Catherine saved her from the abduction. She further claims that Catherine did so out of sheer disappointment in the way that Bernard developed after her death.

Alby: Correct me if I am wrong, but you are aware of just who it is who saved her from this abduction, aren't you?

Dr. Armstrong: Am I? I'm not quite certain. I don't deal with the paranormal, Alby. I work in medicine. I therefore commit myself to science, and, of course I mean to apply no pressure on you, but anything you know about the Catherine situation would itself be useful to this conversation.

Alby: Yes, of course I understand. But you see Doctor; I too deal with the world of science.

Dr. Armstrong: Yes, MJ said you were a botanist, is that correct?

Alby: It is.

Dr. Armstrong: Well I can then certainly understand why we are both puzzled by this claim. Do you believe that Catherine's ghost gravitated back to earth and saved MJ from this calamity?

Alby: In reality, Doctor, with all due respect, if you believe you know what truly happened if it wasn't the Catherine's specter, what harm would it be to let MJ know what you believe to be the truth? Otherwise, perhaps MJ needs a bit of paranormal presence looking out for her just now. If that is what is enabling MJ to now survive, why not let her continue to think that?

Dr. Armstrong: Alby, I am not opposed to using whatever treatment is necessary to help MJ survive this ordeal. In order to do so, I need to know about the details of this nightmare as much as possible. Is there something related to the Catherine issue that you are able to share with me?

Alby: I'm feeling a bit uncomfortable again . . . a bit like I am selling my brother up the river.

Dr. Armstrong: Alby, we can take a break if you believe it is necessary. I just implore that you recognize the impact of you not sharing every detail with me will have on everyone involved—MJ, Bernard, and you as well.

Alby: [Deep breaths] I understand. I only meant that after I pieced together everything I needed to know, I went to get help.

Dr. Armstrong: Help? As in you went to—physically get help?

Alby: I sought help from anyone who would listen, and lucky for MJ and for me, forces in this town surrounding MJ, proved themselves to be her saving grace.

Dr. Armstrong: Just so I am clear, Alby, you are suggesting that you sought out Catherine?

Alby: [Laughter] Obviously no, Doctor. But beyond the help I enlisted from someone close in proximity to MJ, something else appeared. I mean possibly someone else.

Dr. Armstrong: [Long pause] I'm not quite sure I comprehend what you are suggesting, Alby.

Alby: When I figured out what Bernard was doing to her, I knew I couldn't deal with this horrid ordeal on my own; and I didn't want to face the reality that my sick brother abducted this poor girl. I know many people in this town, unlike my brother, and I decided to get someone involved. For MJ's sake, if she believes it to be Catherine, then that is probably what is best for her right now. To be quite honest, I was with MJ every day, and I still cannot explain all of it. I myself am starting to believe Catherine was somehow involved. Maybe you can also help me figure out just what the hell is happening.

CHAPTER TWENTY-ONE

Alby carefully considered MJ's claims. He could see how she struggled to make sense of what she told him she saw, and he knew there was a simple explanation beyond ghosts. The truth of the matter was Alby, unbeknownst to MJ, had started to untangle the weave of deception that he believed Bernard was creating. As a result, he made many efforts to protect her. He, however, wasn't yet ready to share with MJ the information about his plan. While he felt confident with his support for her, some of this ghost talk she described was concerning him. *Being tormented was not part of the plan*, he thought to himself.

"You say you saw her, first standing on Mori Point, up there, by the cliffs, those cliffs just beyond the break there—the ones that face your house?"

"Yes," MJ responded.

As Alby looked out toward the cliffs, he could see nature at its best. Clouds were forming, the ocean was calm but misting, and several seagulls were gathering to attack something that clearly had no chance in defending itself. Alby knew that gulls were not often viewed as specialized, yet their way of skilled hovering and sharp, focused landings was a respected attribute among nature lovers. Gulls also seemed to be heavy migrators, sometimes to distances that must seem so foreign to them. Though he knew that these types of birds typically learn to survive because of the trust they place within their community. They support one another, and though many people often believe them to be organisms of meaningless forage, they are actually quite complex and versatile in their ways of teaching one another to scope territory and prey.

"And then you saw her standing . . ." Alby paused. The thought was chilling and somewhat frustrating at the same time. ". . . She was standing by your window?"

He believed it was obvious why he sought clarification, and with this, he was finished with his line of questioning for the moment.

MJ simply stared up toward the ceiling. A single tear formed in the crevice by her eyes, slowly rolling down her bruised and shapely cheek. Alby could see that she was in pain, and he felt a desperate feeling of loss and a desire to support her further.

"Yes," she answered calmly, with intense sentiment—one that showed that she was not just concerned but confused as well.

She obviously, Alby thought, *is terribly disordered. This poor girl is scared out of her wits. What the hell is Bernard doing to her? What types of cruel acts did he perform to force her into this condition?*

Alby once again quivered at the thought of someone appearing at the window, causing MJ a near panic. Alby knew that MJ was unaware that he had recently partnered with a new acquaintance of his—someone who was willing to help him develop a plan to protect MJ. This acquaintance seemed to appear from nowhere, like a miracle waiting to happen, just when he needed her. Though he was pleased to work with this apparent neighbor, he feared his plans were now at risk—changing as a result of the eavesdropping for which his acquaintance must be carelessly and disappointingly responsible. With new information about a woman's appearance at MJ's window, Alby believed he was accountable for having possibly created a monster. When first calling for this woman's help, he assumed he had found the most reliable, most appropriate person to assist him in discovering MJ's real story. He dreaded at that moment that he possibly made the wrong choice.

Alby knew it was once again time to meet with this woman, as they agreed some time ago; and he dreaded the thought for one very simple reason. Each time he met with her, her image was becoming darker and more sinister. Frankly, the woman was starting to terrify him.

CHAPTER TWENTY-TWO

"Finally," Alby whispered to himself staring at MJ. "Christ, she takes forever to fall asleep!"

MJ seemed at peace for once.

Alby knew, according to MJ's own testament, that too many nightmares—likely the result of whatever suffering she had endured over the course of time—kept her from sound rest. He was pleased to know that his visitations were providing MJ with solace, enough so to ease the tension that currently was building insider her. Yet he knew that while she was in her latent state, he would need to make the visitation he dreaded. Though he was the one that asked for MJ to be guarded, he did not ask his helper to stalk her, and certainly not haunt her.

In order to safely have the conversation he needed to have, Alby allowed MJ to rest, and thus made his exit before Bernard returned. He soon found himself outside, in the spot he and this woman agreed as their general meeting point, waiting patiently for her arrival. Other than the street lamps at each corner of the neighborhood, the night was densely dark, wrapped in fog from sky to treetop. This is the type of weather MJ expressed as beautiful, embracing, comforting to say the least. It was the kind of weather that Alby hated. He felt forced to act in it, never able to grasp the harmony of the situation when choked by this mist.

Familiar noise slowly began to grow around him, echoing from one point to the other, providing clarity as it circled, yet also static as well. Bushes rustled, a few small raccoons ran from one end of the street to the next, and his situation within the cul-de-sac changed from a lonely, solitary sensation to one that was matched with an undeniable presence. Alby still did not quite understand the force that emanated from this strange woman, yet it made him uncomfortable. Still, he reminded himself that he was merely appreciative that she was willing to watch MJ while he wasn't around.

"Is that you?" Alby called out, a meager murmur is all he could bring himself to utter. He trusted that she would be able to hear him despite the soft tone he chose, but more importantly, he certainly had no interest in waking MJ. At that moment, a broad, unkempt figure slowly appeared from the brush that once hid her. She was elevated from his viewpoint, standing on the rising slant of ground in the short distance in front of him. The street lamps surrounding Alby blinded him as he looked upward. This made it difficult for him to identify the blur that stood in his presence.

The figure whispered back and Alby knew it was indeed she, his secretive helper—the one he met some time ago.

"Yes, I am here," she said.

Alby continued to squint, hoping to clarify her image, yet unsuccessful in each blinking attempt. Throughout his time in this world, Alby tried diligently not to bear any hatred toward anyone or anything. *Hate*—he viewed it as such a wasted, meaningless emotion to have. He truly believed the word was far too often used to describe the most nonsensical nuisance. And unfortunately, he believed too many people did not take its overexerted treatment into account. That being said, he absolutely abhorred the sound this woman made. Every time she spoke, something about her speech unnerved him. It was disconcertingly commanding and authoritative in a deviant way. On one level, finding this woman and making her acquaintance was an unexpected blessing. On another level, the more conversations he had with her, the more he began to regret the agreement they made.

She was scantily dressed, and as such, he considered the possibility that she might be cold in the evening fog. It seemed appropriate to ask about her welfare.

"Mister," she responded. "Are you more concerned about my comfort, or the safety of your friend in there?"

"My apologies," Alby remarked somewhat nervously, but sarcastically as well. "I simply felt cold myself. Stand there naked if it makes you comfortable."

"I assume you need me to continue to watch her tonight?" The figure asked.

Alby tried to shield the blinding rays of the lights. It was obvious to him that they were bouncing from different vantage points of the walls of fog that surrounded them.

"I will be leaving soon," Alby replied. "Your continued help in this matter is much appreciated, ma'am, especially tonight. I'm afraid there have been some further developments. I am seeing more marks on her body, and I believe she thinks herself physically sick when in reality, excluding her emotional state she's likely physically well.

There was silence. It was as if this acquaintance had no concern about MJ's welfare whatsoever. This angered Alby enough to build the courage to address his concerns about the possible panic-creating window appearances.

"However," Alby continued as diplomatically as possible, "before we discuss any of that, there is something that I want to bring to your attention."

"Mister, let me make this quite clear," the figure indicated, intruding upon Alby's statement. "I loathe poor little ladies who are addicted to pain. I am not interested in helping to rescue a damsel-in-distress. Nothing is worse that a woman who believes that the hand that beats her is the one that keeps her; and I certainly have my own problems to consider."

Alby thought to himself, *I chose the wrong person to help me with this. Damn it. I totally fucked this one up.*

"I don't understand," he replied firmly. "Why did you agree to help me then? If you are not concerned about the assumptions I explained to you some time ago, why involve yourself in this?"

"After listening to your pleas and suppositions I was intrigued to do what I could," she continued. "While I said I have no interest in assisting a weak woman who wants to be abused, I am also not interested in letting a bastard, regardless of whether or not he is related to you, exploit someone he has trapped in a terrible situation."

"You have my word, ma'am," Alby retorted. "Something in my gut tells me the whole relationship they apparently share is fixed. Something feels terribly wrong. I know she is in some type of trouble."

"Turn the bastard into the authorities then."

Alby struggled with the notion.

"The bastard is my brother. It is not as simple as you suggest," he said.

"Nothing is," she retorted with a harsh grunt. "I feel no remorse for you as you struggle with the guilt of confronting your bother. If he did something wrong, it needs to be addressed!"

"I do agree that something must be done," Alby responded. "Obviously, the woman lying in there needs our protection. But I also want my brother to get the help he needs. He'll never allow me to provide him with that help if he knows I am behind this, making my move while you watch over her in my absence."

"Yes, well," she sounded eerily through gritting teeth, "I am not interested in that either. A bastard is a bastard and no bastard deserves help."

Changing the subject rather quickly, she coldly made her statement.

"I'll watch her tonight, as agreed."

Her voice, similar to the wind that surrounded them, was cold yet resounding.

"Thank you," Alby thought appropriate to respond. "But, just backing up to one more thing—what I was going to say earlier. Do you think you could be slightly cautious not to get too close to the house? MJ has already seen you on Mori Point. That's not so much of a concern of mine. But she recently saw you scoping the house. It frightens me that you risk our plans—if you are not careful, we will be forced to stop watching over her."

The figure lifted her arm, and brushed her hair behind her ear. While Alby could still not clearly see her face, he could tell that she was quite angry.

"Scoping the house?" She asked resolutely.

"Yes."

"And by scoping," she continued, "I assume you mean from the cliffs on Mori Point or from other distances?"

Alby, determined more so than he expected, repeated his statement.

"She saw you recently staring at her through the bedroom window the other day," he said. "She and I just earlier had a conversation about it. It scared her and frankly me a bit as well."

"Sir," she said after a brief pause. "You asked me to observe the situation, and to report back to you if there was anything strange happening while you weren't present."

"Yes, I know," Alby responded. "You have been incredibly generous with your time and your help. I shouldn't be making those types of demands. I just think you need to be careful in case anyone, especially Bernard, finds you while you come comfortably too close to the house."

Rage filled the air almost immediately. It was as if the night's fog was sliced by a clever that swung forcefully at it.

"How dare you," the figure sternly retorted. Her intensity alarmed Alby to the bone. "I have done nothing of what you suggested, sir." Again, she hissed through her teeth as clearly as the gust surrounding them.

"I have been on Mori Point, monitoring the situation as closely as I could. If you think for one moment that it has been easy for me to watch this bitch, you are sorely mistaken."

Alby was confused. There was no clear reason why this woman was so harsh, no reason known to Alby at least why she was so intent to insult MJ. She made it very evident that she was not a fan of women who were vulnerable, but Alby also didn't believe MJ deserved this type of treatment.

"No, I am sure this has been difficult, and again I appreciate your assistance . . ." Alby insisted.

"But you are wrong, sir."

"Wrong?" Alby asked. The melody of her changing tone was again confusing to him.

"Yes, sir. You are wrong. I have not once approached this house. This is as far as I have come, up here in the brush—watching and waiting to find something to report back to you."

"Wait, wait, wait," Alby responded. "I, I don't understand."

"And you can trust in one thing, sir," she continued. "If I see something strange, of course I will report it back to you as I agreed to do. Yet, if I see something that presents immediate danger for her, I'll take matters into my own hands. I won't wait, despite what you expect me to do."

"But you say that you have not approached the house as of yet?"

"Am I not clear?" she asked harshly. "I have not come close to the house at any time. Nor have I seen anyone else come close to it. The only person who regularly circulates it from time to time is the owner, Bernard."

"My brother."

"As you say," she responded.

"But she told me that someone, some woman came to the window, glaring at her, threatening to come get her."

"Perhaps she imagined this," she abruptly interjected. "If you want me involved in this, I am willing to continue to watch because of the possible crime and strangeness you described. But I am sure as hell not going to be caught lurking about someone's house, looking through someone's window. I actually reject the insinuation!"

"Look," Alby responded. "I apologize, and again I thank you for your service. But now I am a bit concerned that someone else is prowling about, loitering to cause some kind of problem . . . maybe theft? Maybe worse?"

CHAPTER TWENTY-THREE

"MJ," Alby said as mildly as he believed was possible. "I think you need to start training yourself to make an attempt to move from your bed."

MJ's glare pierced Alby with painful surprise. It seemed as if MJ was deeply insulted by the suggestion, as if Alby believed the suffering she endured from her sickness could easily be forgotten or ignored.

"Sure, Alby, I'll work on that immediately," she responded sardonically. "Should I grab you any tea while I am up?"

Alby clearly saw that MJ was on the verge of tears.

"How can you say such a thing to me?" She asked.

The more insight regarding the entire situation that Alby was beginning to collect, the more he knew he needed to tread delicately with her. Progressively more so, he believed MJ would be traumatized once the shock of her reality was revealed to her. Alby thought it was obvious now that MJ was definitely being conditioned. Somewhere deep in his memory, Alby remembered hearing Bernard speak of his almost psychotic research work in psychiatry. It was becoming an obsession of his, and Alby knew that Bernard was just ill enough to experiment with his fixation on MJ. *No*, Alby thought, *MJ will need to face reality on her own, in her own due time. But to get her there, first she must try to move.*

"MJ," Alby continued, "Bernard will be home soon. And as it is, we don't have much time before I'll need to leave. Wouldn't you like to work with me on trying to get you well again? Wouldn't this be a wonderful surprise for Bernard?"

"Of course I want to be well, Alby!" MJ began to cry.

"Look, MJ," Alby responded quite harshly. "I'll have none of that victim's weeping now! You are a strong woman. You can do this. If you are as fond of Bernard as you say, I need you to focus with me and encourage yourself—no, force yourself to start to move."

"It is impossible!"

"MJ, there are two reasons why you need to build the mental and physical strength to begin moving again."

"Oh this is fantastic," MJ exclaimed in a mocking fashion. "I can't wait to hear this."

"It is not just the gift of a lifetime for your husband to see his wife moving again—a gift only you could give," he said. With this, Alby could see MJ contemplating about the suggestion. It was true that the thought of surprising Bernard must be appealing to MJ, and for a brief moment, Alby saw MJ's attitude change. It was as if she willed it, she could indeed walk again.

"But, if what you claim about this stalker is true, then there is a problem," Alby continued. "If this strange woman by your window did in fact say that she was coming for you, then it is also best that you are able to escape if she does indeed mean you harm."

"But how could I possibly do this?" MJ sought urgently. She surely understood the crucial need to improve her health in order to be protected from any impending harm, but it was likely that she simply could not envision herself walking again.

"It has been so long since . . ." she began, stopped briefly, and resumed her position. "It has been so long."

Alby shook his head. Looking down to the ground he thought about his brother's actions—whatever they were, they must be horrible, and he asked himself, *how could a human being do such a disgusting thing to another human being?* He knew it was his job to encourage her as much as possible, yet he also knew he wasn't solely able to protect her. This is exactly why, unbeknownst to MJ and Bernard, that Alby sought the help of this neighbor in the first place. It was now a few weeks ago when Alby began to develop the agreement with this woman. He continued to hope that together she and he would be able to move MJ to a safe place before she experienced any further harm from either Bernard or now, from some mischievous snooper.

"MJ, you have become so accustomed to living like an invalid, you think you are one. With some effort and positive reinforcement, you can improve. I know you can."

"What do I need to do? We're going to try to surprise Bernard, right?" MJ asked.

Alby nodded in agreement. While his efforts were certainly not for the purpose of pleasing his brother, he knew this was the best way to get

MJ focusing on improvements. It was good enough for him to play along at the current time.

"I think," he added, "I think that tomorrow we will start to work on searching through your mind a bit, trying to recount some of your history, even if it is out of my own interest."

MJ lounged completely confused.

"I'm not quite sure I understand what you mean, Alby."

"I want to encourage you to revisit and discuss the happy things you are able to remember, just to get your positive spirits moving again," Alby responded. "With a good attitude you will have won half the battle and you'll be walking again in no time."

MJ seemed to be pleased by this answer. For the first time in such a long period she was now acting as if she was aspiring to be well again, almost acting as if she had finally rediscovered her purpose. She insisted that she did not want to wait until the following day. Beginning immediately suited her just fine.

"No," Alby responded to this suggestion. "Bernard will be home, and remember, I'll need to leave soon. We want to be sure to surprise him. This will be such a wonderful gift for him, won't it?"

All the while, Alby truly understood the painstaking process that must have occurred for Bernard to have MJ trained or hardened in such a way to have her convinced of her state. He knew that this task was not simply about getting MJ to think positively, but to get her to remember her own truth. He was still unaware of the full and true reality of the situation, but he knew now more than ever that her past wasn't as she had described over the course of their meetings.

"Well," MJ interjected. "In the meantime, as we work toward getting me well again, what do I do if she comes back? What do I do if this woman comes to get me?"

"Let me see what I can do," Alby responded, once again thinking about intercepting the neighboring acquaintance. Alby still thought it possible that neighbor was indeed the culprit, and possibly was too surprised to admit she had been caught.

"Do about what?"

"MJ," he answered. "I am going to do what is necessary to make sure that you are not in danger. If I need to be with you every day while Bernard is at work, I will be."

Once again, MJ seemed pleased. This immediate comfort must have been overwhelming, and he knew that she believed she was fortunate to have Alby in her life. She told him that she must once more remind Bernard how happy she was to have both men surrounding her. She was equally happy that Bernard had his brother back in his life.

Alby momentarily measured the scenario encasing them. Amazingly, without any second guess, everything was beginning to crystalize and clarity was impressing upon his thoughts. It was almost too difficult to contain his reactions to the truth. He completed the puzzle, so suddenly, and he was amazed he hadn't considered it before. While astonished at what he began to realize, Alby knew once again that he must be cautious not to overwhelm MJ. Considering the best time to break the silence, Alby no longer thought it was randomly unfitting to change the mood. He looked at MJ, still basking in the mental image she made of Bernard, and he began to question her.

"MJ," he said. "Have you ever heard the story of *Happy House of Saddened Gulls?*"

"I can't say that I have," she responded in kind. "I assume this is a story you are about to tell me in nauseating detail I am sure?"

"I do find it interesting," Alby laughed. "And quite fitting for anyone willing to listen to it. It has been such a considerable amount of time since I last heard it told to me, and I figured you might be interested in hearing it as well."

MJ smiled, willingly nodded, and wet her lips as if waiting for a meal she savored. She always seemed to like Alby's tales. They helped provide her with temporary escape from her ill condition. Since Alby was quite a good listener, she believed he'd likely interpret the story in such an exciting way that the thought immediately made her anxious to hear it.

"What type of story is it?" MJ asked. "I am hoping it is not something that will worry me more than I already am. You know, the last thing I need is to hear a story that will cause me more anxiety."

"That's not my intention, no," Alby responded. "But it certainly is the type of story that provides a different message or moral for the various types of people who hear it."

CHAPTER TWENTY-FOUR

The Gulls were a family of four siblings. Their relationship with one another always seemed to be distant and unpleasant. To make matters worse, there was no way to avoid one another. The siblings didn't live in a house at all. Truth be told, they eventually lived on a moderately sized boat, deep in the middle of the ocean. The irony of it all, gulls—the species, not the family—are animals that prefer to remain coastal, or even inland, never wandering into the far outreaches of the sea. Yet, this is not how the story should begin.

Before the move, their father was a fisherman who often needed to leave his coastal home for an extended period of time. When the season was right, to fulfill his duties as the family provider, he would take to the sea, completely focused on his trade away from his family. This deeply troubled him. As such, in order to be a more effective and present benefactor, one day he told the Gull siblings to pack their bags with only the utmost essentials. Their former house, and the acres of land that accompanied it, would be sold to the highest bidder. They were about to experience the wonders of the sea—full time. As you can imagine, the reactions were varied.

Sylvester Gull was a sturdy soul. The oldest of the siblings, he found the arrangement to be quite proper indeed, but not necessarily for the reasons his parents considered proper. Sylvester rationalized his father's news as an example of his father's methodical work and determination, but not for his pointed concern for the family. "Where you go, father, I'll follow."

Daphnis Gull was not as understanding as brother Sylvester. He instead believed the move to be irrational. He had responsibilities in their current village. The plan was not one that could provide him with any benefit in the least. Daphnis hated fish, and each time his father came home from one of his trips, Daphnis was determined to suggest that he was on the verge of becoming vegetarian, just to cause his father frustration.

"The sea is not for people, father," Daphnis would insist. "It is not natural for us to live out there. You will see one day that this idea is quite possibly the stupidest one you have had yet."

Holly Gull, the eldest of the sisters but younger than Sylvester and Daphnis, was appalled at the suggestion. While like her brother Daphnis she viewed the plan as one that could not provide her with any benefit, the advantage she sought was not village responsibilities and earthy respect, but her reputation. For Holly, her popularity with the village boys was something that was very important to her. The village girls on the other hand likely did not have the nicest discussions about Holly when they were parted from her behind closed doors. Nonetheless, they admired her popularity, and when with her, they aimed to get her attention much like a disciple would. Holly's fortitude during her father's announcement was so delicate that she nearly fainted at the suggestion of it. Daphnis caught her while Sylvester fanned her, all the while rolling their eyes at her dramatics.

It was only Piper Gull, the youngest sister and Gull sibling, who acted naturally—a reaction that her father anticipated. The idea surprised Piper, then upset her (she too would miss her friends and duties), but then she appreciated the reasons for this decision. Piper was only a mere thirteen years of age, but she promised to remain helpful to her father and mother as best as she could.

"Father, I know this must have been difficult to tell us," Piper responded to her father's news. "We'll survive this, as a family."

Sylvester, Daphnis, and Holly despised Piper when she acted this way. Sylvester believed his role as eldest sibling meant he was the one to be considered the rational leader. Yet, no matter how he tried, Sylvester's attempted support and authority was never believable. His behavior was often contrived. In the same respect, Daphnis sometimes saw Piper as someone who was weak, agreeing to do anything she was told. Holly, on the other hand saw her sister as a nuisance—someone who consistently aimed to steal the spotlight. Holly considered herself to be the pretty one, and thus she believed she should be the one getting her father's attention, not Piper.

As he always had, father considered everything his children said. But most important to him was the counsel he received from their mother.

She was his partner in life, his best friend, and the one whom he was most excited to see at the end of every fishing trip. When he received her ultimate blessing, father was convinced that they were making the right choice.

The time came and went, and soon the family parted for the open sea. After the Gulls were all settled on the boat, amply named *The Sea Gulls*, their mother became a homemaker—quite a good one at that—and, beyond her daily duties, she would gleefully clean the catch that her husband brought to her at the end of each day. She knew rather well that her husband was doing the best he could to provide for his family. Observing the passion that energized him to excel in his trade made her love him more each day.

Things seemed to be going very well for the Gulls. It was true that Daphnis and Holly moped about, aiming to convince themselves (and anyone else who would listen) that the move was a ridiculous mistake. It was also true that Sylvester still maintained he was the main source of support for both his father and mother. Though other than repeatedly stating how much he was keeping everyone together, Sylvester truly did little to prove it. In the depths of the sea where they now found themselves, the fish were plentiful, and the work was good. Father knew that when the time came to dock, the abundance of fish he caught would provide his family with a sturdy payment to live for at least the next six months.

Piper observed her family. She was proud of her father's strength, touched by her mother's love for him, confused by her siblings' actions, but still happy to be part of the Gulls. Though, an uneasy sensation was recently jerking at her emotions. As the days wore on, increasing storms and various strange weather patterns were upsetting her, both physically and intrinsically. Father seemed to handle the storms with ease. Obviously, he had likely seen quite theatrical and spectacular forces of nature during his previous fishing trips before the family moved to sea. *For this reason*, Piper thought, *father is showing me there is no reason to be concerned.*

On one particular evening though, the waves were rather intense, rocking the boat back and forth like a feather caught in a swift breeze. Holly hung over the edge of the boat dramatically poised to vomit, like Rapunzel trapped, crying and demanding that her viciously cruel adopted mother be more sensitive to her needs. Daphnis shook his head, encouraging himself that he was right all along—this was proof that there was no sane reason for the family to be living on the open sea. Sylvester sat there, saying nothing, offering no counsel to his sick and dramatic sister, or calming his discouraged brother. He instead let the rain hit his face and thought, *yes—surely this will soon end. It must. We'll soon need to be sleeping. It is getting late and this storm is not appropriate.*

Father and mother rushed up from their cabin down below just as Piper noticed the storm worsening.

"We need you to move," mother screamed. "We need you to move down below, without hesitation! That is an order!"

"Obey your mother," father insisted. "This is no time for games. I need to pump the water from the deck while mother steers us on course. Please do not argue. Please move down below."

Father's voice, though it started as a stern and forceful juggernaut, became quite solemn at the end when pleading for his children's safety. Yet, if father hadn't had his back turned toward the direction where his children once were, he would have already noticed that most of his children, except for Piper, had already absconded to the shelter below. Piper stood there steadfast, anchoring her leg around the rope-attached sail that swung from above, hoping to gain composure during the stressful situation.

While she was a bit seasick, she also experienced tense emotions of fear for the safety of her parents, and disgust for the cowardice of her siblings. It was as she swayed to and fro, continuously trying to maintain her posture in the tumultuous situation, that father turned to check on his children. While Piper was preoccupied, concerned for her parents' safety as well as her own, she could not help but decipher the surprised look her father gave as he gazed at the sight of his daughter alone. He looked utterly saddened, immediately abandoned by his children. Despite his insistence that they take shelter, Piper was sure that her father had hoped that his children would have protested.

Saddened. It was an emotion that did not come easily to her father's generally positive attitude.

Saddened.

The emotion stirred sentiments of fear an unease in Piper's soul.

"Piper!" Father called to his only remaining steadfast child. "Daughter, my strong and reluctant daughter! You must go under and strap yourself safely to your bunk."

"I cannot leave you and mother," Piper cried over the sound of crashing waves and roaring thunder. "How can I help? Let me know what I can do to assist you!"

Father, face dripping from irritating crashing water, slightly and crookedly smiled out of appreciation, but lovingly and gently objected.

"My dear," he screamed over the continued sounds of the deafening water. "Mother and I cannot control the situation if you are up here taking our attention away from it. I need you to obey me."

At that moment, mother joined in the command.

"Piper, my love, listen to your father! Go down below!"

Piper, not sure it was the correct choice, but certainly sure of her continuous fear, nodded at her parents. Crying, she moved toward the ladder that brought her to the lower bunk; and she climbed down, reluctantly but with perfect pentameter.

Below, her brothers were huddled as if their curled bodies would protect them from nature's roar. Sylvester sat in the corner, fetal-like, head in hands, surely wondering when the moment would end. As always, Daphnis approached the matter slightly different. This brother who was so determined to find fault in anything that went against his benefit, cursed the storm, and furthermore cursed the sea for bringing him into such a susceptible circumstance. To Piper, the sight of Daphnis pumping his fists at the open air, screaming aloud and scourging Mother Nature herself was a shameful, distasteful way of dealing with the seriousness of the situation. Further, neither of them seemed to be concerned about their sister, Holly, who was nowhere to be found.

"Brothers," Piper shouted.

No response. No sign gave her any confidence that she was heard. The only thing Piper could hear was the wind, the crashing waves, and painful sounds of shifting noises above—noises that made her more fearful for her parents' welfare.

Nothing.

The lack of response was insulting.

"Brothers!" Piper screamed again.

And once again, nothing.

"Sylvester! Daphnis!" Piper called.

This time, whatever inflection Piper used at that moment seemed to finally grab the attention of her preoccupied and self-indulged brothers. Both raised their heads, and stared at their sister as a result.

"Holly," she mouthed. "Where is Holly?"

Piper might as well have spoken a language unfamiliar to them. Her brothers reacted in a way that showed disarray, puzzlement and confusion.

"Piper?" Sylvester questioned. "I feel sick. What is happening?"

"Sylvester," she responded. "We have no time for this. Where is our sister?"

At that moment, Daphnis was knocked to his feet by a swift and unexpected sharp rise and fall of the boat. Piper immediately thought of her parents above, and she silently prayed that all was fair and unscathed. Her attention then focused solely on her brother, and at that moment she approached closer to him in order to help him up.

"Daphnis," Piper shrieked. "Are you alright?"

"Quiet!" Daphnis responded harshly as he rose from the soaked floor.

Piper considered the fact that Daphnis was undoubtedly embarrassed from the fall, and somewhat ashamed at the blow to his manhood from defending himself against Mother Nature. Still Piper cared less about his discomfiture and, out of slight anger from his response, had to convince herself not to push him down again.

"Daphnis, Sylvester, whomever wishes to respond would be quite fine," Piper implored with a sense of determination that didn't always come naturally to her. "Where is Holly? Where is our sister? Is she safe?"

"Calm down," Daphnis retorted as the water rolled down his chiseled chin. "She is underneath her cot! She threw herself there as soon as she slid down below."

Piper jerked herself to the floor and crept her face toward the underside of the cot. It was dark and wet, and she was poised in a way that resembled how an explorer might look into a deep and unexplored cavern. With the constant sway from the storm, it was difficult for Piper to see her sister in full detail. When Holly finally came into focus, Piper saw that she had been crying. Her face was stained with tears, not just seawater, and her body was covered in vomit that smelled like the two-day-old fish, squid, and urchin caught by their father. It was actually quite disgusting to witness and experience.

"Holly," Piper called to her sister, doing her best to ignore the repulsive scent. "Come out here at once!"

Holly seemed to have no intention of moving from her safe spot. Piper was saddened by the image. It was at this moment that Piper took a brief pause from her actual and current fear as she focused solely on her unexpected sorrow. She was stricken by grief, actually, witnessing the destruction of her happy family—or what she thought was a happy family at least. The Gulls, in all of their failed attempts at striving toward perfection, were at least a family nonetheless. Now, they were tortured animals, unsure of what the future had in store for them. Piper was literally and figuratively seeing her family members sink into despair.

"Holly," Piper whimpered with actual tears flowing down her face. "Sister, please come out from under there."

Holly screamed, a sign that eased Piper slightly. At least her sister was not in shock and could express her distress through loud and shrill, but ever present shrieks.

"No!" Holly retorted. "No! I—can't—go—out—there!"

Piper insisted that her sister move, if not for Holly's own safety, but for Piper's comfort.

"I need my big sister, Holly," Piper beseeched. "I apparently can't rely on our brothers. That is something obvious."

At that moment, a shriek came from the corner of the room where Sylvester sat cradled.

"Wait a minute," he began. "What do you mean?"

Piper ignored her brother's question.

"Holly, please?" She implored. "Let's take care of one another. We need to give each other support right now."

Holly was obviously disoriented, saddened by the confusing events swirling about her, but further distracted by the unexpected feelings of fear and solitude. Yet, Piper was shocked that Holly finally submitted to her advice. Slowly, Holly reached toward Piper, sliding from underneath the cot and gliding toward the open floor where Daphnis recently laid. The struggle to slide to that section of the room was a difficult one. Yet, with Piper's help, the two girls stretched and clawed, scraped and scratched in order to position themselves into a place of safety. The scene was like the birth of some wild beast that was doing its best to explore the world away from its mother's womb.

"Thank you, thank you, thank you, thank you," Holly continued to say, out of sheer traumatization, clutching onto Piper. With each thanks, Holly heaved more deep, sorrowful breaths, hyperventilating the words as they barely escaped from her lips.

Sylvester, who observed the situation without offering any assistance, was confused by this image. All the while, as Holly's grasped tightened with each totter of their boat, Piper knew the longer her parents attempted to wait out the storm on deck, the more precarious a situation they created for themselves. Remaining as realistic with the situation as humanly possible, Piper had no idea what to expect other than more saddened thoughts to come for sure.

And so it was, as the storm subsided, that Piper and her siblings coerced themselves toward the upper quadrants of these wrecked quarters, afraid of what to find, but surprisingly not as shocked as what they expected when finding nothing. No parents. No fish caught in nets and stored in iced boxes. No loose trinkets. No parents. No parents. The thought was sad, and for the first time, the Gull siblings felt alone and forsaken. Sylvester experienced a vacant feeling, like a pit in his chest, aching inside him. Daphnis's thoughts meanwhile were overcome with moments of despair. While her brothers struggled with ways to deal with these unexpected emotions, Holly succumbed to dejected sentiments of dismissal. And Piper felt guilt.

After reminiscing, Piper was confused by the saddened sensations her father transmitted to her. Now she was dumfounded by the sense of responsibility she laid upon herself. Had she stayed on the bridge of the boat she may have been able to stop whatever came to destroy her parents. But now nothing was able to stop her from blaming herself for abandoning her parents in their time of need. She wailed. She wailed so loudly that the sounds frightened her brothers and her sister. It frightened them so intensely; they never spoke of the scene again.

CHAPTER TWENTY-FIVE

As time progressed, several months now since the storm that purloined their parents from them, roles and responsibilities within the Gull siblings changed quite dramatically. Their once happy house was now a floating shack imprisoning them to the unexpected tortures of the sea. Daphnis, who yielded to a now more aggressive Piper than he knew before, developed himself into a more naturally submissive being. He made the mistake of once attempting to make the best of the conditions, suggesting that the sea be viewed as an adventure from that point forward. This was obviously a remarkable departure from his previous criticisms about his family's move to the open water. Piper simply stared at his suggestion—which again he merely saw as an innocent attempt to lighten their despair. Daphnis knew her stare to be one that should not be challenged. And as such, he went about his standard duties of attempting to catch fish for his siblings, no longer suggesting such silly ideas.

With each fish that Daphnis caught, scarcely at best, Holly gutted and cleaned them. As she did, she wiped away blood and ooze, smearing her ratted clothing and her once soft skin, now sun torched, bruised, and scaled by harsh wind. Her historical beauty was austerely diminished; another major departure from the normalcy of the Gulls (or what Holly saw as normal), and thus this was seen as further punishment for their survival over their parents. Or so, Piper thought this to be the case.

Sylvester attempted to keep the standards with which he was raised. He was indeed the eldest Gull sibling, and as such, saw it as his duty to keep the family concentrated and orderly. That being said, he underestimated Piper's control over the unfortunate reality for which they were now forced to endure. At times, to Sylvester, Piper appeared hurt and desperate for justification for why her parents suffered such horrible demise. It was obvious to Sylvester that Piper sought forgiveness for abandoning their parents. More though, he knew that somewhere deep within the chasm that existed inside his sister, that Piper struggled to understand how it was conceivable that one minute her parents were here and ever present, and the next minute they were gone without any admonition. He was saddened by how Piper wrestled with this. Unfortunately though, Sylvester believed that Piper overcompensated for her writhing inner emotions by treating her siblings cruelly.

Brutality was a strong word to describe her behavior. Piper did not seek to be malicious or vindictive toward her siblings. Instead though, she seemed pitiless about their equally realistic situational agonies. Each time Sylvester made attempts to confront Piper with his growing concerns for each of them, she showed no emotion, but provided stale measures and flat interest in his disquiets. This saddened Sylvester even further. He asked himself, *what has happened to our family?* It was at this point when Sylvester finally confronted Piper and suggested that she lost pity for their siblings. Piper reacted unexpectedly in a pugnacious way.

"It is you, Sylvester," Piper responded boldly. "You and Daphnis and Holly—you are the spiteful ones. All of you, so consumed with your own interests and your inner selfish needs, you—each of you, you are the ones who never showed any concern for our parents. You never expressed any true support for father's desire to provide a better life for us. Instead, you each mocked him by criticizing his plans to take us to sea . . ."

"The very sea that killed them, you mean," Sylvester strongly interjected.

"You, Sylvester, you killed them, not the sea!" Piper responded. "You all killed them by never once showing them the affection they deserved. Each of you thought about how father and mother's decisions would benefit your own needs. I am disgusted when I think about the way each of you treated them. I'd rather face a stormy sea over ungrateful, disengaged, and self-absorbed children any day. I am quite sure our parents felt the same way."

Piper quickly rushed toward the side of the boat, overlooking the water, calm in its state except for the ripples created by her falling tears. Behind her, a shaken Sylvester made every attempt to maintain composure in an utterly disturbing situation. The realization of Piper's perception about the rest of them saddened him immensely. Slowly, Sylvester retreated to the lower deck, saying nothing further.

Maybe it was her way of correcting the mistake she believed she made the night her parents were lost at sea, maybe it was the shock she felt as she confronted her brother. Regardless, time passed rather quickly the rest of that day, and this time Piper kept her stance on the deck. As determined as she ever had been in her life, Piper did not shift one foot in either direction. She was alone. It was dark. It was cold. And still, Piper stayed in place, staring at her reflection in the water, begging to understand in some form or capacity, why it was that her parents were now suddenly gone. The thought tormented her profoundly, and coaxed her somehow gently into having a conversation with two careworn and influential voices within her.

The first, a more stable character, made every attempt to calm her ache. Piper could hear, as clearly as if someone was standing in front of her, a voice in her head begging her to jump overboard.

"Join your parents," the first voice said. "There is no reason to stay with your siblings. They are pathetic examples of what your parents were, and they will never live up to the potential your father had in mind for the Gulls."

A second voice, actually moderately intrepid in nature, but just as lucidly heard, engaged itself with the first voice, and suggested that Piper not cave to its inappropriateness.

"The events of your parents' demise is terrible indeed, my dear," the second voice said loudly. "This does not give you the right to bring demise to yourself, nor to your brothers and sister for that matter."

"This is foolish," the first voice interrupted. "Look at the water."

Piper continued to do so, quite longingly for that matter. The first voice continued its attempts to convince her further.

"It would be so easy to leap into the waves and let them carry you to your destiny. Your father loved the sea. Make him proud and end it now. Your siblings do not care for you. They are weak and undetermined. You recognized this yourself already, and suggested as much to your brother earlier today."

"Weakness is subjective," the second voice pleaded. "It would be feeble for you to stand strong and progress. Life is filled with complex arrangements that sometimes make it difficult to remain positive. You can overcome this."

"And what of want? What if I don't want to overcome this?" Piper asked the second voice. "Who said that I desired to remain strong anyway?"

"That's just it, my dear," the first voice interjected as Piper began to slowly shift her weight toward the railing that stood between her and the open sea. "You are choosing wisely."

The second voice made one last effort to challenge Piper to consider the obvious.

"Piper," it said serenely—in a way that was so tender, it reminder her of her precious father whom she missed terribly. "If you destroy yourself, you will destroy Sylvester, Daphnis, and Holly as well. They need you. Think, my love. Your parents knew this. They knew you were the one who would eventually be able to cradle them, care for them, and keep them in line. You know this. You truly know this."

Piper heard the first voice cry in disgust, and at that very moment knew that particular voice had just lost the battle. She had just heroically maneuvered a way to convince herself to calm her anxieties, woes, and guilt, and to focus on the realities that were ahead. Yes, it was true that life was no longer the normal 'happy' she once considered it to be, but it was her life indeed—her life to live, and neither she, nor her siblings, nor any thoughts that quarreled with one another in her head, had any rights to tell her to end it otherwise. If there was anything she could do to honor her parents, it was to carry on and live her own life. The realization of this importance was so relieving to her, she summoned the energy it took to go below, face her siblings, and deal with the realities that were clearly ahead of her.

Her steps were heavy but determined. Each move she made closer to the lower deck made her more aware and alert. Before descending, she stopped. The wind blew through her hair, and Piper shut her eyes to absorb the moment. A new precision had entered her thoughts, and she was reminded about how easily life can play tricks on people. Though the next thoughts frightened and further saddened her so, she knew what she needed to do next.

CHAPTER TWENTY-SIX

Alby monitored MJ's reactions with interest. MJ seemed to express curiosity in the story while suggesting the material put her into an immediate mood of melancholy. His intention was not to depress her further, but instead to help her understand the true mystical nature of the details—something for which he was sure that MJ would appreciate.

"I did not mean for you to become sad," he said to her.

"The story brings about memories for me," MJ replied.

With interest, Alby showed MJ that he waited for her to continue her thoughts about this.

"I know this is a fable, and I know you are likely to continue the story and eventually tell me the moral, but it struck a chord in me that I wasn't expecting."

"Was it a strength in a specific memory?" Alby asked.

"No," MJ responded. "I know what it feels like to be abandoned. Somehow, I am experiencing these thoughts of rejection or of careless neglect, yet I somehow can't put my finger on the details. I feel very sad."

"I am sorry, MJ," Alby responded. "I did not want you to feel that way. Instead, I was hoping you understood how powerful the Piper character becomes. She battles the demons in her life and moves forward to come to an even more powerful realization."

MJ laughed.

"I'm not depressed," she answered. "I simply feel this strange sense of emptiness."

"I see."

"Anyway," MJ continued, "I'm eager to hear the end of it."

"Some other time," Alby gently protested. "It is time for you to rest. As intrigued as you might be, the end of the story is not yet ready to be revealed."

Alby was able to recognize that MJ, in a mysterious way, understood what he meant by this.

CHAPTER TWENTY-SEVEN

"I must say that I am surprised to be speaking with you," Bernard exclaimed. "Not at all what I was expecting, but I am going to make myself very clear. If this is a game, I'm not interested and I will figure it out."

Alby remembered the start of his now months-old conversation with Bernard quite clearly. He remembered thinking that Bernard was partially delighted with his social call, yet apprehensive with incredible caution. At that time, Alby considered it only appropriate to approach this visitation with restraint but resilient effort to build their relationship back to what it may have once been. After taking a much needed break from the energy it took to positively reinforce MJ, Alby reminisced more about the moment when he reintroduced himself back into his brother's life.

To his recollection, it went as such:

"I must say that I am surprised to be speaking with you," Bernard exclaimed. "Not at all what I was expecting, but I am going to make myself very clear. If this is a game, I'm not interested and I will figure it out."

"Brother, I thought it best to put our differences aside. It has been so long, and I figured you could use a friend," Alby remembered responding.

"Is this some sort of joke?" Bernard asked. "What do you take me for?"

Alby ignored the question. He took some time to observe his surroundings and absorb the strangeness of again being in his brother's presence.

"My, you have done quite well for yourself, Bernard," Alby responded.

Bernard stared, bewildered, growing angry.

"Are you not interested in having a friend right now?" Alby asked.

"I have a friend, and I'd like to keep her just as she is, thank you," Bernard strongly emphasized.

"She?" Alby asked in astonishment. "Now I am the one caught surprised, brother."

"Stop saying that," Bernard said, remaining quite angry. "Stop calling me brother!"

"Look, Bernard," Alby continued. "I know things did not go well between us in the past. To be quite honest, it has been so long that I can't even remember everything that caused our rift. But I'd like to work on making things better between us. You have been through such a horrible ordeal. I know you miss Catherine and I want to support you. I want to be the brothers we once were."

Bernard looked amazed. To Alby, Bernard's steadfast glare was beginning to show that he was succumbing to his disbelief, all the while expressing a yearning to have a true friend back in his life.

"I'm still really confused by this," Bernard said. "I don't know whether to believe you. This is very strange, and I am not going to let you make a fool of me."

Alby remembered having the instinct that Bernard had noticed a dedicated inflection within Alby's voice, deep, and penetratingly different than how he remembered his younger brother's voice to be. But Alby could see that his persuasive and caring words began to resonate with Bernard. Alby knew that Bernard had not woken that morning anticipating a visitation. He had indeed been 'dead' to Bernard in recent times.

The more Alby held his conviction though, the more he knew that Bernard was becoming assured that nothing happens by chance. Alby imagined Bernard asking himself, *could it be? Could it really be that Alby has come to reconcile with me?* And then he felt something much worse; something that Alby knew only an incredibly selfish, disturbed person would ponder, turning a tender reunion into a negative scheme. Alby further imagined Bernard thinking, *I could really use your help with a scheme of mine.*

"Are you going to invite me in, Bernard?"

"You're already in the house," he answered.

"I meant to say," Alby continued, "I'd like you to invite me back into your life."

"I see," Bernard responded with a brief pause.

There was silence. Alby was utterly disturbed, and he regretted having come for the visit after all.

"You see what?" Alby asked.

"It is a matter of speaking, *brother*."

Alby sensed a mocking trepidation that Bernard attached to the use of that word. *Brother.* Alby realized that if he were ever to fortify this relationship again, he would need to be patient with Bernard's acceptance.

"Bernard, I'd like to be part of your life again, simply put."

"I see."

"There we go again," Alby laughed. "You are quite insightful. I'd like to know what it is exactly that you see."

"Let me ask you something," responded Bernard, collecting his thoughts in the process. "I'd guess that you know your visit is surprising to say the least. I'm not quite comfortable with you being here."

Alby waited. He knew that Bernard was intending to ask something, but nowhere did Alby locate a question in Bernard's most recent statement.

"You said you wanted to ask me something?" He responded after another awkward moment of silence.

"Why are you here?" Bernard interjected fairly quickly in reaction to the question. "Truly, why are you speaking to me like this? What purpose does this have?"

Alby actually saw the interrogation as a very fair inquiry. He wasn't expecting Bernard to welcome him with open arms, as if he himself was the prodigal brother returning to feast in the glories of the current day without taking any responsibility for his torrid past. The question was actually a good one, one that took some clever and truthful deliberation on his part. Alby took a few deep breaths, inhaling the fragrance of confusion, fear, and frustration that circled him like the fog that appeared outside. These breaths gave him new life, a rebirth, and with this notion, Alby found the courage to reply, though he knew his answer would bring further questions.

"I can't actually explain it, Bernard," he countered. "I know my response will likely bring more confusion and distrust, but I am hoping you'll be open-minded enough to listen to my explanation."

Alby looked toward Bernard for his visual confirmation. He thought to himself, *I want to see Bernard's eyes. I just need to make the connection with him again. Once he sees I am sincere, he'll be ok.*

It wasn't long after these thoughts that Alby received the validation he awaited, and the gleam of interest that peeked from Bernard's stare was an endorsement enough to continue his account.

"I've been awakened," Alby continued.

"I beg your pardon," Bernard retorted quickly. "And what the hell does that mean? If this is some religious rebirth explanation, I'm not interested."

"Please, Bernard. You promised to keep an opened mind about this."

Bernard laughed sinisterly.

"I promised nothing of the sort," he responded.

"I saw the promise in your eyes," Alby insisted. "You may not believe anything that comes from my mouth, but one thing is for sure. You are curious and anxious to hear my explanation. I know you well enough for proof of that."

With skeptical hesitation, Bernard finally told Alby to proceed.

"I haven't all day," he screamed. "You've awakened from what? You've awakened from a hibernation perhaps?"

"Obviously," Alby continued, "I am not suggesting I have been physically asleep. But I do not fully know what led me to you. Bit by bit, I have been getting the instinct, as much as I have fought it, to come speak with you. It's almost a guttural emotion that keeps pulling at me, as if you need my protection. Does this make sense to you?"

Bernard scowled with disdain. His dagger glare painfully pierced Alby causing him to actually grimace in place. Alby could see that Bernard's blood was coming to a boil, and he assumed the probability that his offer to shelter him from whatever needed safeguarding was a risk.

"You?" Bernard laughed. "Let me get this correct—*YOU* need to protect me?"

The air in the room was still and stale—the worst kind of air. It was completely contradictory to the scene outside—crisp, somewhere between cool and California-warm. The obtrusive silence caused Alby to sweat profusely, and he became nervous at that moment, not willing any longer to continue to provide Bernard any further elucidation.

"I think," Alby softly said, "I think I should just go."

"Oh, no, please!" Bernard contemptuously asserted. "Please, *brother!* You are the one who started this by coming to 'speak to me'. I'd like to know exactly how it is that you will be protecting me."

Alby thought, *and there it is again—his sarcastic use of the word brother. Coming to see him was a pure miscalculation on my part.*

"Well?" Bernard questioned, waiting for Alby's response. "I apparently need your protection. And from what, prey tell, is it that I need your protection? And how is it that YOU are the one to provide it?"

"Bernard," Alby responded. "I'm not trying to insult you. I am not suggesting that I am here to protect you with physique. Obviously, that would be a joke."

"You've got that right," Bernard interrupted.

"I've simply been having a nagging feeling, waking me, helping me to remember things—or at least see things more clearly. Part of this experience has led me to feel the need to be around you. I believe you might be in danger, or something, I don't know. I just think that you need to have someone watching out for you, watching out for your back."

Alby sighed loudly.

"I guess," Alby continued, "I guess this makes absolutely no sense at all. Just forget it, Bernard. I'm going to leave. It was really good to see you, though."

Alby saw Bernard considering the situation carefully. Something seemed to click in Bernard's mind, and Alby could not make heads or tails of it. He was instantly reminded about the thought he had moments ago—that Bernard may have silently considered, *I could really use your help with a scheme of mine.*

A scheme.

The word rang in Alby's head over and over again.

A scheme.

Bernard finally spoke.

"You've gone to such trouble," he said when ultimately breaking the stillness. "I am actually intrigued by this. Having someone to watch out for me is not necessarily a bad thing. The saints know I can't do this all on my own."

Alby's sensations were an anguished mixture of respite and bewilderment.

"I'm—I'm—I'm not sure what you mean," Alby said.

"You wanted to look out for me, correct?" Bernard asked somewhat ironically, in a clandestine way that Alby did not appreciate.

"That is what it feels like I am supposed to do, yes."

"Well, I could indeed use your help after all, as it seems," Bernard suggested.

"Does this have something to do with the 'she' you mentioned a bit earlier?" Alby asked hoping Bernard would not take the question rhetorically. Undeniably, Alby waited for a direct response to this question. "Have you met someone? Have you been spending time with someone, a Pacifica neighborhood friend perhaps?"

"Actually," Bernard responded. "I have."

"Is it someone you have known for a while?" Alby asked. "Someone who you just met? I guess moving here from the city was a good idea after all!"

"Brother," Bernard responded in a way that, from Alby's perception, seemed to still cause Bernard discomfort. "I have taken a wife."

Alby's reaction must have been inappropriate at best, at least suggesting shock. He saw that Bernard wasn't exactly pleased with the face he made, and for this reason, Alby tried as best as he could to further temper his response.

"I don't mean to question your choices, Bernard," Alby answered. "But with Catherine's sudden and violently tragic death—do you think it is wise to jump into a relationship like that?"

"Pardon me if I might," Bernard interposed. "Let's not begin to discuss what is and is not wise. You lecturing me on 'the right thing to do' is certainly not appreciated."

"I was merely suggesting that I was concerned you might be rushing—that you might not be ready for such a commitment. That is all I meant."

Again, Bernard scowled.

"I mean . . ." Alby continued.

"You mean what?" Bernard asked. "You are *meaning* to clarify everything you are saying lately, aren't you? What is it that you *mean*?"

"I just mean that you seem to still miss Catherine in a very sorrowful, desperate way."

Alby looked down toward the hallway of shrine-like pictures that hung fully draped and hidden from clear view.

"Aren't those pictures of Catherine?" Alby inquired. "You've made quite a statement by covering them up in such a methodical way, Bernard. It's ok that you have, but I think it proves my point."

Bernard's scowl became worse.

From Alby's vantage point, it looked as if Bernard grasped his own wrist to investigate a pulse, closed his eyes, probably counted imaginary numbers in his head in order to calm his nerves, and forced his body from convulsing into anger-wrought effect.

"If you know what is good for you," Bernard began serenely, "you will never refer to Catherine's pictures again. Never."

"I'm sorry, Bernard, I didn't . . ."

"I said never refer to them again," Bernard repeated. "That means immediately. Understood?"

At that point, Alby made the decision not to argue the matter further. He expressed his surprise, and for him, doing so was enough to make the declaration he thought was necessary.

"Well," Alby said. "When do I get to meet your bride?"

Bernard, still suffering a bit of an irritation from Alby's recent impulse reaction, breathed slowly yet heavily.

"My wife's name is Misty," he said, motioning toward a room at the end of the hallway.

Alby looked down the hallway, frantically aiming to avoid the pictures that hung between him and that room, paused, and then looked back at Bernard.

"Misty?"

"Misty."

"Sounds like a . . ."

"I know exactly what the name sounds like," Bernard interrupted. "Trust me. She is no whore. She goes by MJ."

"And," Alby continued, "MJ is in that room down there?"

"She is."

"Well, is she deaf? Is she asleep? Hasn't she heard us speaking quite loudly? Why hasn't she come out?"

"And that is what I want to speak with you about—you know, your offer to protect me," Bernard responded.

"What? Oh my God, please tell me that she's not dead and you are doing something disgusting with the body."

"It seems," Bernard interjected quite quickly, "that you have a sense of humor, brother. This is a side that I wasn't aware existed in you. Good for you. No, it is certainly nothing like that. But I do need to warn you about her."

"Warn me? What the hell does that mean?"

"Yes, maybe it is better to suggest that I need to make you aware of something," Bernard confirmed. "And I am hoping that you would be willing to come by, as often as possible, to keep her company when I am not around—while I am working and such."

"Now I am the one intrigued," Alby retorted.

"You think you are intrigued now? Just wait until you meet her," Bernard laughed. It was one of the jovial, belly-shaking chortles that made Bernard feel quite pleased with his response, but left Alby believing he was being kept from some type of sinister inside joke.

Bernard continued when he was finally able to regain composure.

"Intrigued?" Bernard questioned again. "I'll be the one who is intrigued to see how the two of you interact with one another. Oh what fun."

CHAPTER TWENTY-EIGHT

Back in the present day, Alby continued to think about the time that had elapsed. After giving thought to the past, certain images, situations, and realities began to mature progressively in Alby's mind. Alby remembered that it was then, during his past conversation with Bernard, when it became quite obvious that he was dealing with an incorrigible and illogical monster. To make matters worse, he knew this monster was a virtuoso of disgusting intelligence and an architect of sick games. MJ was dealing with the same monster. And Alby knew that the instinctual attempt he had to shelter her from an acute and genuine peril was indeed after all his responsibility as he had expected from before.

Alby remembered when he was first introduced to MJ. The time he spent with her progressed. One day turned into two, and then into four, and finally Alby was repetitively visiting her each time Bernard left the house for work. Alby had agreed, several months before, to do so as long as he would not spend too much time with Bernard either before Bernard left the house or after he returned. On one of those days, in the beginning stages of his relationship with MJ, Alby stared at her as she reclined sleepily in front of him. He was sure that MJ's exhaustion was from the horrors she tolerated during her conditioning. Without any forced determination at all, Alby now understood he was there to protect *her*, not to protect Bernard. That is why he found himself in her presence. He realized that his original visitation had absolutely nothing to do with Bernard. It had everything to do with MJ instead, and the fraternal relationship he thought he had desired to fix was now obviously not corporeality.

Alby continued to remember the past. As he was astutely realizing something was terribly wrong, he thought to himself, *I am weak. How will I be able to do this on my own?* With that, Alby scanned the room, glancing out the window, his vision focused toward the setting sun behind the mist that was forming quite solidly in the sky at that point of day. Alby remembered that Bernard would soon be home. Again he asked himself, *how could I protect her on my own? I need help. But whom can I trust? Is there anyone I can trust? Is there anyone who can help me through this horrible situation?*

And with a sudden, unexpected jerk that caught him by surprise, Alby finally saw everything unmistakably. *I can only protect MJ if I seek 'her' out—she has the type of strength I need, the strength I do not have inside me, the strength to help MJ.*

CHAPTER TWENTY-NINE

Increasingly beyond his prospects, Alby was becoming invigorated by MJ's courage to speak to Bernard about her concerns and fears. Alby's plan for helping her to build strength was proving itself successful; and he was confident that the subservient nature of the conditioned MJ was vanishing ever so slightly. Still unsure about the exact history that made MJ who she was—this girl, Misty, who he knew so little about—Alby was happy to know that MJ finally informed Bernard about the haunting she believed she was experiencing.

It was true that Alby provided MJ with very little information about Catherine. Most of their conversations centered on the obvious—how MJ was feeling, how Alby was feeling, MJ's insistent interest in Alby's love life, whether or not either of them had good rest the night before, and more recently, what type of hauntings MJ encountered. It was Bernard who filled MJ's head with information about Catherine, literally and figuratively. It was also Bernard who told MJ stories about Alby, thus forcing MJ to build her own perspectives of the types of people Catherine and Alby were. Somehow though, MJ continued to believe that Catherine was indeed haunting her.

"It's not that I cannot accept a *haunting*, as you put it," Alby responded—several times at that. "It is simply that Catherine was not the type of woman who would cause anyone harm. Bernard adored her."

"That's because Bernard is a wonderful man," MJ responded.

Alby said nothing.

"I'm afraid that maybe Catherine, in suffering such a terrible accident," MJ continued, "isn't ready to move forward and release Bernard."

"Trust me," Alby answered. "It isn't that difficult to release Bernard from your life."

MJ laughed.

"Sibling rivalry," she stated. "What you two shared as brothers is obviously going to be different than what he shares with his wives."

"I apologize, MJ."

MJ didn't respond, but Alby knew that he was forgiven. MJ instead continued to view the invigorating scenery outside her window, looking as if she was longing to be in the center of it. Bernard knew it was likely best to change the topic from Catherine's haunting to something else. *Small steps*, he continued to suggest to himself.

"Remember you told me about that dream of yours, the one when you were swimming in the ocean?"

"When I was drowning?" MJ countered.

"That's the one," Alby replied. "Were you an avid swimmer beforehand?"

"No."

The response was cold and decisive. It took Alby by surprise.

"Wow, I didn't mean to strike a nerve," he suggested.

"I hate the water."

"There's that word again," Alby interjected. "You have a distaste for the water you mean. You don't have a hatred toward something inanimate."

"I hate it," MJ reiterated. "Just thinking about it makes me cringe. It makes me feel helpless and trapped like an animal caught in a snare."

"Out of curiosity, why is that the case? Did you have some sort of experience as a child?"

"You know," MJ replied, "I have never quite known why that is the case. I don't think there was any dramatic event, or anything like that. Before, I would dream only of drowning. But now . . ."

Alby now saw some glimpse of uneasiness in MJ's eyes as she paused from completing her statement.

"Go on," Alby insisted. "Maybe this is something to uncover! Maybe this is something that can help you build your strength to get the hell out of this fucking bed once and for all."

"Oh I doubt it is anything like that," MJ responded.

"MJ!" Alby screamed causing her to break her trance-like focus. "Work with me here. You were about to continue your dream."

"I meant to say that I would dream only of drowning. But recently, I started to have strange dreams—visions—dreams, whatever the hell you call it."

"Well," Alby continued. "What are you seeing, asleep or otherwise?"

"I started dreaming about someone hosing me down."

Alby's confusion was quite noticeable. He wasn't particularly confident about what the interpretation of such a dream meant, but he believed it to be a clue for something that would be relevant.

"And," he said with a shy laughter, "When you are being hosed down, does it typically happen after you come back from a roll in the mud?"

"It is just such a strange feeling," MJ reacted to Alby's question. "It has only been a few times that I dreamt this, but when I do, I wake feeling incredibly alarmed. I actually believe, for a brief moment until I realize that I had been dreaming, that I am being tormented or punished for something terrible that I did."

"Are you sure?" Alby questioned.

"Sure about what? That I feel this way?"

"Not at all what I was suggesting," Alby replied. "I meant to ask if you were sure you were dreaming?"

"Sometimes you amaze me," MJ remarked. "I think you would agree that we have grown close, and yet sometimes you say things that are so contradictory to what I think. I almost think that sometimes you suggest something just to get me to debate you."

"Well, maybe I do."

"Well," MJ responded, "It is not very nice."

"Life ain't always nice, sweetie," Alby laughed.

The room grew silent for some time. MJ clearly felt some relief from it. To be quite honest, Alby was enjoying the reticence as well. It was like a welcomed momentary break from tension.

"Did you really mean what you said?" MJ finally asked, breaking the silence.

"Sorry, MJ," Alby replied. "I was enjoying a bit of a rest. You'll need to remind me of the nonsense I was saying."

Again, MJ laughed.

"You implied that maybe I wasn't dreaming. Is that what you meant?"

"Actually," Alby interrupted, "I did mean just that."

"Can you—and I warn you to please tread carefully—but can you explain what you mean by that statement?"

"I'm asking you if maybe you are remembering something from before, something that caused you this major distaste for water?"

"No," she replied.

The response was as equally as decisive as before.

"Got it. Understood," Alby confirmed. "I think you should be opened to exploring ways to regain your thoughts and strengths. This may have been a bad example, but take a look at other dreams that you can remember, and consider from where the source of them fueled."

"I'll try," MJ said to Alby's pleasing amazement.

What? He thought. *She's listening to my advice? Actually heeding some of my recommendations? Shocking!*

"Its just that . . ." MJ continued.

"Just?"

"Simply that the idea of rediscovering the pain I experienced, possibly the pain that brought me to this paralysis, is something that truly alarms me. I almost feel like Piper as she struggled with the two voices that tried to convince her which action was most appropriate to take. It seems that when things became evident for her, she was sad and alarmed. And that is where the story stopped."

"I get it, MJ," Alby comforted. "Truly, I do get it. I'm not expecting you to perform miracles here. Remember, the goal is to get you strong again, and to regain composure and a belief in yourself is all about taking the first step."

MJ, after a long hiatus, blinked in agreement.

"And speaking of alarm," Alby persisted. "That is some doozy hanging above your head."

"Oh that," MJ motioned with her eye roll. "It is Bernard's quite methodical and nearly perfect plan to protect me. The alarm system."

"For?" questioned Alby. "I am hoping it is for protecting you from a stranger lurking about?"

"Yes."

Alby was satisfied by this response. While he knew MJ needed protection against the very person who installed the system, he supposed that the arrangement could somehow be used to their advantage in the future.

"And forgive me for asking such a crude question," Alby started.

MJ began to giggle. It felt decent to smile so frequently again.

"No need to continue," she replied. "I need to call out a password if something dangerous happens. I'm not expected to physically key a code or pull a lever. Obviously that cannot happen in my current state."

With her eyes, MJ motioned to her bedridden condition.

"You've surely suggested to Bernard that you are being haunted," Alby stated. "You've already told me as much. But what finally caused the installation? I cannot fathom that he immediately believed you about this haunting."

"Let me get this straight," MJ retorted. "I'm not suggesting that you have me convinced—that there is no truth to the haunting. But the more and more I discuss the issue with Bernard, the more he is helping me to understand that someone is out there disturbing us purposely. He's become so protective over me now."

Alby found himself becoming increasingly silent in response to some of MJ's accolades for Bernard, purely out of respect for her feelings. He simply thought to himself, *I'm sure he is certainly becoming more protective over you—because I believe he sees you as his property.*

"I just think that the two situations are coincidentally connected," MJ completed.

"Remind me again?" Alby requested. "Two situations?"

"Either some creep is taunting us—situation 1, or some bitch is haunting us—situation 2," she replied.

"Oh yes, yes, of course. But again, what made Bernard seriously consider getting the alarm finally?"

"We were sleeping the other night. It was so wonderful to be lying with Bernard, hugging him, sleeping comfortably," MJ claimed.

Alby wanted to gag.

"And as I started to wake," MJ continued. "Bernard was a nervous wreck."

"In what way," Alby inquired. "What was he nervous about?"

MJ recounted the memory in her head. It was appearing quite clearly in her vision, just as if she was watching an episode on the television.

"He said, '*what did you say?*'" MJ replied. "I asked him what he meant by that and he responded that he had heard something."

"And what was it that he heard?" Alby questioned with anticipation. "Damn it, MJ! You should write stories. You never finish your statement and you always keep me hanging on every word that drips from your mouth. It's actually intriguing and annoying at the same time."

"Bernard kept asking whether or not the sound he heard came from me. But then he assured himself that these sounds could not have been me at all."

Alby took some time to absorb the scenario and glanced around the room. He almost believed that he was, at that moment, being watched. And he knew if someone were to burst into the room and disrupt the conversation, the action would cause him a certain panic. To suggest that Alby was tense at that moment would have been an understatement.

"It's funny," MJ insisted. "Bernard glared around the room, just as you are now, and then quickly he looked toward the window."

Alby was afraid to look. He thought to himself, *if I see someone standing there right now, I'm going to piss in my pants.*

"I continuously implored, over and over, that he tell me what was wrong with him," MJ articulated. "And finally, he suggested he had heard her."

"Heard who?" Alby asked, confused and nervous as ever.

"He said, '*I heard someone speaking. At first I thought it might be you, but the voice came from, I think, the other side of me.*'"

"What did he hear?" Alby asked.

"Exactly!"

"Exactly what?" Alby screamed. "Damn it, MJ!"

"No, I am not trying to annoy you, Alby," MJ insisted. "I asked that exact question as well, right at that moment."

"What was his answer?"

"Before suggesting it was impossible, and then further suggesting he was going to check the grounds around the house, he said he heard some woman speaking to him."

"My God," Alby whispered to himself.

"Seriously," MJ responded. "Scary, isn't it?"

"Of course it is! What was she saying?"

It took some time for MJ to reply. The idea was still intensely troubling to her, and every time she imagined it, she would tremble.

"The voice was a haggish woman's," she responded. "And she apparently promised she was coming to get us—me—I'm not sure. But I am sure that Bernard heard it, and that is what caused him to install this alarm."

It became so clear to Alby that Bernard had indeed heard someone—whomever it was, the woman whom Alby entrusted for help, or some stranger who was indeed scoping the house for theft. It didn't matter any longer. It finally made no difference to Alby. Because of this unpretentious yet daunting story, Alby knew exactly why Bernard must be nervous. The realization was nothing short of amazing. Alby had finally deciphered the code that was so difficult to grasp. It was the vision he had been longing to see now for months. The image was in its essence as pure as it could possibly be, and Alby almost wept from the fulfillment he felt as a result. The truth of the idea was a horrifying one, but one that he knew he needed to relay to MJ, sooner rather than later, before it was too late. To do so once again required a courage that he, himself, did not believe existed within his being.

Alby knew that MJ was waiting for a response—some type of reaction to the memory she just entrusted to him. He instead said nothing, acted in no unnecessarily peculiar way to cause MJ any angst. He managed to find the necessary fortitude to finally peer out the window from where he sat across the room. There was no one there, only MJ's reflection in the bed.

"MJ," he began softly. "I believe it is time to share some information with you."

"You are always sharing with me, Alby."

"This will be different, and please assure me that you will be you're your best to stay strong," Alby implored.

"You're scaring me, Alby," MJ nervously stated. "What are you talking about?"

"There is no need to be scared, sweetheart," Alby said confidently in such a reassuring manner that he knew MJ was immediately comforted. "As a matter of fact, if I do not share this with you, you will be in a situation that causes you more fear."

MJ couldn't explain the tears that Alby saw form from her eyes. For some reason, MJ was overwhelmed, and the feeling was mutual.

"Before I begin, I'll need you to remain calm, because I'll need to introduce you to someone."

"I don't understand this! You are going to introduce me to whom?" MJ asked completely confused. "What are you talking about? Who are you going to introduce me to? You don't even introduce me to any of the guys you date!"

"Stay calm, MJ," Alby recommended with considerable reassurance. "I must go find her first, but it is time the two of you met."

He could only imagine the ideas that must have been forcing themselves to the surface of MJ's thoughts, and he had no desire to delay the much-needed conversation any further. It was as if his memories too were being rekindled. And now that they suddenly were, his intentions were to provide MJ with the information that was necessary to help her escape.

"I am so confused, Alby," she cried. MJ couldn't contain the emotions that burned inside her, surely leaving a scarring imprint. Sadness is what she felt—pure sadness without any fear or distrust for the very first time in such a long period of a sheer invalid state. The intense energy of eagerness that existed from not knowing what Alby was about to share with her was as real as the sorrow that was overcoming her like the drowning waters that formed the Mori Point coastal dream.

"Alby," MJ whimpered holding back the choke of tears. "Who is it that you want me to meet?"

"It is time that I go find Catherine," he replied.

CHAPTER THIRTY

Alby felt as if a bomb had finally been detonated. To be able to share what he did with MJ was such a relief. It was true that MJ didn't take the news very well, not well at all as a matter of fact, and his belief was that she would need time to absorb it before she recognized it to be true. If only he were able to find Catherine—the woman he had termed as the 'neighbor'—as he suggested he'd do, before branding the information into MJ's mind, he was sure that her acceptance of the situation would be quite different. To his dismay though, Catherine was nowhere to be found, despite the fact that he searched for her outside as long as he could. Calling to Catherine was in itself somewhat intense and chilling, and he knew he needed to act quickly before Bernard came home.

There were three considerations that entered Alby's thoughts at that moment.

First, it was quite possible that he ceased to have MJ's trust any further. She likely considered him to be insane and was possibly going to ask him to leave immediately once he returned from searching for Catherine, showing up empty handed of course.

Second, he imagined that Bernard was headed home at any moment, swerving through the rain, especially since he had just recently installed an alarm system to care for MJ while he was gone. *Why*, Alby thought, *why did he not simply ask me to stay with her—now more than ever?* Whatever the possible answer to that specific question might be, Alby knew that he needed to leave the scene rather soon.

Third, he could imagine this woman, for whom he made her acquaintance some time ago—in all actuality was Catherine after all. He pictured that she assumed him to be the weak person he had previously imagined himself to be. He imagined Catherine mocking him, suggesting he tried to take matters into his own hands without consulting her help any further. And for this, he thought that Catherine would likely be incredibly angry with him.

When he returned, he found MJ sleeping. She seemed worn and deplete of any youth. It was obvious to him that the shock he shared with her, in addition to suggesting he would introduce her to Bernard's 'dead wife', had caused her to faint. *This is what she needs*, Alby thought. *She needs to reset her thoughts and when she wakes, she needs to think clearly about what I disclosed. It's better for me to leave now when the time is right. It is all going to soon make sense.*

CHAPTER THIRTY-ONE

Alby: This is how I remember it, Doctor. I was not there, but when I regrouped with MJ after she was finally saved, she described the scene as such, which allows me to relay it to you to the best of my memory.

MJ heard them once again. She wasn't solely frightened by the sounds she heard, but she was beginning to become indignant as well. She faintly remembered a strange dream, much like a dramatic film where the main character, Alby, suggested that some mischievous woman, Catherine (previously thought to be dead) was possibly alive, or maybe not. She was so confused, especially when thinking about the other elements to the dream, which were clouded by a personal miasma drifting around in her mind. And like a sturdy smack to her face, she realized it wasn't a dream at all.

Then they reappeared.

Footsteps.

Silence.

Footsteps again.

Silence followed.

MJ immediately transformed herself from feeling perplexed to having a realistic detection of peril.

"Bernard?" MJ called out. "What are you doing, Bernard?"

She continued to call out, impatiently questioning Bernard—or at least whom she anticipated was Bernard. She refused to believe otherwise, and thus persisted on calling his attention.

"Please come to the bedroom right away," MJ continued. "I'm freezing and my head is beginning to hurt! I'm getting myself nervous for no reason other than silly little thoughts."

The sound of footsteps once again ceased to exist.

"Can you check the generator, Bernard? I can't see a thing."

The setting: darkness and fog. The two were becoming indecipherable to MJ, and strangely symbiotic with her experiences. Frankly she was enervated by the setting, and finally eager to move forward leaving this haze behind for good. For MJ was finally seeing the shocking reality that she had been held prisoner in a puritan form of dollhouse hell. More importantly though was an even more disturbing and quite horrific fact. She had held herself prisoner in her own mind, all the while allowing the fog to cloud her judgment and perceptions.

At once, the sound of footsteps could be heard again, this time at a quicker pace. They sounded lighter than a man's footsteps, causing MJ's emotions to stir quite suddenly. Things did not seem right. And with this, MJ felt nauseous.

She thought to herself, *could it be that I wasn't dreaming at all? Am I going crazy? I can't handle this! I don't have the strength to handle this! Is it her? Is it Catherine inside the house, readying to kill me? Has Alby actually found her as he suggested he needed to do?*

While the evidence that Alby provided her was quite sound, MJ still resisted as long as she could, hoping she could find a different solution. Once more, MJ pleaded, hoping that what she remembered from the dream was not correct.

"Bernard!"

The footsteps quickened further, and the closer they came to her room, the louder they became.

"Please, Jesus! Please let me die. I can't live like this any further!"

Outside, each time lightning struck, she could see her surroundings for several seconds at a time. She prayed for lightning to collide with something close by, just to be able to see through the coincidental power failure that she was experiencing. But the lightning only provided spurts of light. She wanted to scream *show yourself* but she was too petrified—physically and mentally—to do so.

And then it came, what she had hoped would happen—a flash of light so rapid, so deep-seated, it was the antidote that allowed the walls to absorb any existing light left by the lightning's remnants. Regrettably her instant reaction rendered her terrified, helpless, and craving sudden death. She almost fainted at the sight of what she saw—a water-doused, drooling female face within inches from hers. She could feel water dripping on her neck, and the stranger's breath was foul and hot, trouncing MJ's intently shocked, icy skin. And then the room darkened, black again, as if the lightning never existed. MJ did more than scream. She wailed so loudly, her throat almost burst.

"HELP ME! OH GOD! BERNARD! *(How could you do this to me?)* HELP ME!"

She could do nothing to shield herself. If she hadn't truly been paralyzed, as Alby strongly suggested, surely the fear would have immobilized her. The worst part was that she lost all serenity and instinct. The shock of the situation was enough to make her forget that simple fucking password to alert the voice-controlled security. She continued to lay completely still and scream until she began to choke. She could feel tears streaming down her face, and once again, she believed she was drowning. Were hear dreams prophetic? Could she have possibly been symbolically foreseeing her demise? Only then did the sound of a horrific, whispery, and unsteady voice break her sobs.

"I told you," Catherine said, now completely concealed by the obscurity of the room's powerless blackness. "I told you I would come to get you."

"Who are you?" MJ screamed. "Is it you? Are you Catherine for real?"

MJ felt a forceful jerk on the bed, and a yank on her duvet. It seemed like minutes had passed by, and with each heaving touch against her, her body substantially ached in a way that she had not felt before. Suddenly, she was completely uncovered—sheets and the comfort of her heavy blanket were now on the floor beside the bed. As she lay there, completely without any barrier between her body and the night air, the room's draftiness pierced her at such incredible intensity. Then came several flashes of storm-fueled light. Though, she did not see the stranger anywhere close by—and she knew she was close—she was grotesquely mystified by something that did catch her vision. If she hadn't seen it with her own eyes, she wouldn't have believed the utter fact that she was strapped into the bed. Across her body in several different places, she could see the shackles. Looped around each wrist and ankle were small belts, wound to their tightest limits. Crosswise her breasts, her abdomen, and her legs were ropes digging into her skin. The sight of it made her body burn. She could see the deep grooves within her flesh, and before the room went dark, she thought she could also see blood at an almost concentrated purple.

"What did you do to me?" She screamed.

At one time, she would have thought to continue screaming for Bernard to help her. Instead, she was horrified at the reality of the situation. She now knew it was Bernard who had done this to her, strapped her in bed. And what simply amazed her was the fact that each time she shook her body to loosen the grip of her torturous confinement, it was the pressure she was creating that made the constant tugs she felt. She wasn't paralyzed as she had thought after all.

"Pacifica!" She shouted. "PACIFICA!"

At once, a siren—the superlative sound of it—rang throughout the room. Red lights flashed every other second, and she knew they came from the system Bernard installed above her bed just that afternoon.

"Pacifica! Pacifica! Pacifica!" She continued to scream. Surely this would scare Catherine away, but more importantly, it would bring Bernard home. She needed to face him; and it would either be his or her demise. *One of us is now unlikely to leave the house alive,* she thought.

"Get away!" She cried. "Leave me the fuck alone!"

MJ thought to herself, *I've got bigger fucking fish to fry. Fuck you Bernard! I am going to fucking escape and I am going to fucking get my revenge on you, sick fuck!*

And then again the voice, "Move. Move now."

"Move!" The voice screamed. It was appalling and vicious.

"Move or you're dead! DEAD!"

Precipitously, MJ found herself on the ground. She was in pain, and the weight of the overturned bed on top of her legs was numbing to the core, yet it seemed to be screening her, protecting her from Catherine. She was no longer afraid of her as she once had been before. Candidly thinking, MJ no longer cared whether or not Catherine was alive or dead. Ghost or not, the bitch was simply making the situation even stranger than it already was. What Alby had suggested to her was clearly playing out to be true. If Alby was right, Catherine was actually protecting her. Still, she couldn't help but think that there was indeed something dangerous about this woman. She still didn't understand everything she had been told, but she was willing to discover what she could to help herself out of this situation. Through the flashes of red, she could see the horrid scene of what looked very much like a half-dead, rancorous woman pulling the bed—and the truth of the matter was that MJ was no longer bound to it.

I will not let Bernard find me dead, she continued to think to herself. *He needs to now deal with me! I must move now!* Methodically, she began to crawl across the floor, dragging her seemingly dead legs behind her, scratching against the grain in the wooden floor. As she did this, she realized she lost a fingernail in the process. The blood oozed from her finger, and her body throbbed with pain. *Keep moving,* she urged herself. *Don't stop!* She could hear footsteps coming slowly behind her. The monstrous invader's breath was wheezing, and MJ knew if she didn't move faster, she'd be dead—not in the least by Catherine, but instead by who she thought was her loving husband.

MJ reached the bedroom closet. Indisputably, if she could trap herself inside (she knew it locked from the inside) this would give Bernard enough time to get home to find her ready to defend herself, ready to pounce. With all of the might she had inside her, she scuttled up the door, lunging her body in the direction of the doorknob. It was painful to do so, but she turned it and pulled it open. It may have been a miracle, or possibly the power of adrenalin, but her mind forced her legs to move, and without hesitation, MJ stumbled into the closet, just as Catherine reached her.

I'm sorry, she thought. *Whether you are here to help me or not, you are not going to get in the way of me getting my retaliation. Go play vigilante with someone else, please.*

The pounding and screaming on the other side of her protective surroundings was deafening. At moments MJ wanted to shield her ears from the horrid sounds. It was only at one brief interlude when MJ realized that she, herself, at times was pounding the inside of the door.

Please come home Bernard, she screamed in her head. *I'm ready for you now, and I am going to make you pay for what you put me through.*

The closet was as dark as the room had been during the storm. MJ felt around the walls, the floors, whatever grooves to which her arms could introduce themselves. *A chain hanging from the low ceiling!* Suddenly there was light. The power was back. She could once again hear the music that played before she slept. With the closet now well lit, MJ could see it packed to the brim. It consisted of old, musty clothes—some of them MJ's for sure, in better days now past, and other clothes had to be those belonging to Catherine.

"Come out here!" MJ could hear Catherine scream. "COME OUT! I need to help you!"

The tears began to swell in MJ's eyes again. She was now curled on the floor, covering her face, laying in a fetal position, trying to grasp the reality of the situation. The sustained pounding was vibrating the closet floor. MJ would take short glances of her surroundings, just as quickly covering her face as much as possible. Through the corner of her eye, she saw Catherine's portrait vibrating as well.

The tarp-like sheet that obscured the portrait then fell, like a graceful, slow-motioned ballerina in flight. The creases, piling upon one another on the ground, flapped loudly to seize MJ's concentration. For the first time, MJ was face to face with the portrait. It glared at her unforgivingly. MJ slowly lowered her hand from her face, blinked three times to clear the tears, and slowly repositioned herself in the line of its sight. A traumatizing shockwave overcame her. She reached for her gaping mouth. Not one sound could be originated from her throat, though she tried. *It is impossible*, she thought. *How could this be?* A mix of emotions stirred inside her. She was stunned, terrified, suddenly paralyzed—again—with confusion and anxiety.

And then it came, finally, and had her senses not have kicked in just at the appropriate time, MJ would not have appreciated that it was she, not Catherine who made the horrible and amazing scream at the sight of the unbelievable scene she saw on the portrait.

The portrait was no image of Catherine as MJ had anticipated for so long. In its place was a picture of Bernard and Alby together, and upon the canvas were profound slits and carvings penetrating the image of Alby's face. Clearly, Bernard had hidden the fact that he had defamed his brother's portrait for some reason in such a horrid, grisly way.

"Think about it," Catherine's cantankerous voice called from the other side of MJ's protective closet door. "You found the pictures didn't you? I have been waiting for you to see them!"

Pictures?

MJ scrambled to understand what she had heard. *What pictures? The others are still in the hallway.* She though to herself, *what the hell has my life become? I have been held captive, been chased by ghosts, and I'm now hiding in a closet waiting to use self-defense against Bernard. Normal people do not wander the roads I have traveled. For the rest of my life, whether it ends tonight or years from now, I am going to be dealing with this.*

MJ cried uncontrollably. The consideration was too much to swallow, and she knew that anyone observing her at this moment would agree that life for her truly was depressing.

And then she laughed in ridiculous fashion.

For the rest of my life, she thought again. *I'm going to be strong now for the rest of my life.*

Alby: That is when she found them. The others, I mean.

Dr. Armstrong: You are referring to the pictures? She found the other pictures that were tucked in the crevices of the portrait tears? The ones that Bernard left hidden there, reminders that validated the power he believed he had?

Alby: Well, yes, those too. She did find the remaining pictures. Disgusting, aren't they?

Dr. Armstrong: I have seen them, yes. The police provided me with copies of the originals, images that I could use in MJ's treatment. And yes, the images are sorrowful expressions of human behavior at its worst.

Alby: Human behaviors. I find that statement odd.

Dr. Armstrong: Why is that, Alby?

Alby: There is nothing human about any of this. If there is one thing I have discovered through this entire experience, each one of us are surrounded by demons who yearn to grasp onto what little remains we have of our lives. It goes without saying that MJ has had her demons for far too long during this situation. Bernard, as sick as he is, is surely dissected by demons in every way. I, too, have had mine. I was perfectly fine the way my life was before all this.

Dr. Armstrong: Were you?

Alby: Actually, I was. I wasn't asking to be comforter to someone who needed help. I was fine studying my plants and exploring nature.

Dr. Armstrong: And yet, fate dealt your cards, Alby, and introduced you to someone you were responsible for saving. Sometimes, we do not know why we are *sent* to do the things we manage.

Alby: Insightful.

Dr. Armstrong: Please clarify one thing for me. You said, '*well, yes, those too*' just a moment ago.

Alby: I'm sorry, '*well, yes, those too*'?

Dr. Armstrong: In reference to your suggestion that MJ found '*the others*', I had asked if that was the moment she found the other pictures we were just discussion a moment ago. You said, '*well, yes, those too*'. What exactly did you mean, Alby?

Alby: I meant *the others* who were haunting her as well.

CHAPTER THIRTHY-TWO

Alby: MJ continued to describe the scenario to me in such detail. It was almost difficult for her to get through this part, but I encouraged her to do so.

MJ stared at the pictures she found stuffed behind the eviscerated canvas. This beautiful portrait of brothers who were at once so close was now tethered. Bernard, someone who had let sickness and anger control him, had destroyed every good element that fueled his life. It was not just sad, but it was pathetic as well.

What she saw was so unbelievable, she needed to touch the glossy film as if by doing so, she could prove that the images were not faked. She pinched herself to satisfy any confusion of sleep. And that is when reality set in and the scream that had been effervescing inside the pit of her stomach pushed through her diaphragm and surfaced with such strength that it almost shook the house. The scream was enough to stop Catherine from pounding and cackling as well.

"What is this? What the fuck is this?" MJ screamed. "I can't believe what I am seeing!"

Dr. Armstrong: Alby, please describe for me what MJ saw.

Alby: It is almost difficult for me to vocalize as well.

Dr. Armstrong: It is time for you to do so, Alby.

Alby: MJ saw pictures of Catherine hacked into pieces, by the same once bloodied axe that was lying beside her. It was a grotesque scene for her to view, and she apparently almost vomited at the sight of it. It was then that MJ realized that Catherine had not died in a freak accident on the stairs. At that moment, MJ finally knew Bernard had killed Catherine out of rage. And Bernard had snapped the photographs as mementos of the work he did.

Dr. Armstrong: No, Alby. It wasn't quite at that moment, was it? I know you can articulate this, Alby. You, not just Catherine, are responsible for bringing MJ to safety. You can do this.

Alby: *[With deep breaths]* MJ also found the photographs of my body lacerated, dead, right next to Catherine's.

PART FOUR:

More Matters

"I declare to you that woman must not depend upon the protection of man, but must be taught to protect herself, and there I take my stand."—Susan B. Anthony

CHAPTER THIRTY-THREE

Dr. Armstrong was so proud of his patient. Treatment was progressing nicely. The pace of time was allowing MJ's survival to kick into high gear, and the doctor found the development to be positively sufficient. As he had suggested to the detectives and to Alby himself, Dr. Armstrong had treated similar cases other times. Each of these circumstances had varying degrees of sensitivities and horror stories to accompany the reasons behind them. Often, Dr. Armstrong saw these issues resulting from a patient being held captive, raped—unfortunately at times by a loved one or family member—or being kidnapped by the occult. Each of these, barring the occult—though Bernard's disgusting behavior left the doctor somewhat debating whether or not Bernard was indeed part of one—each had seeded an environment where MJ quite methodically introduced herself to the many people who helped her cope with the terrible actualities she was facing.

While he was certainly his own person, his own personality, with a determined and formed reality of his own, Alby was beginning to shift into a calmer state of mind now having revealed the scene on the photographs. Alby was physically beginning to look more like MJ again, and the patient sitting before Dr. Armstrong was once again tranquil and a bit more awake.

"Welcome back, MJ," the doctor said.

CHAPTER THIRTY-FOUR

"So he mocked her?" Detective Elphorantis suggested.

"Bernard is a sick man, detective," Dr. Armstrong responded. "He absolutely needs help. Help that I cannot provide unfortunately now that I am focused on treating the woman he abducted."

"This is not my area of expertise," Elphorantis adamantly interjected. "I have no problem with therapy and those who perform it, but I am a man of law. Frankly, I don't care if that man gets help or not. He deserves to be locked in prison for life!"

"You might be quite right," the doctor confirmed. "Quite right. But as someone who *does* have expertise in this area, detective, I can tell you that his attorneys are going to try intensely to discover some sort of insanity. I may be called to the stand to provide my professional opinion. And to be honest, I am hard pressed not to ask myself whether or not he too has issues."

"So what happens to her in there?"

"MJ?" Dr. Armstrong replied.

"Yes," Elphorantis confirmed. "What happens to her now?"

"I will work with her to get her to a point where she can accept her situation and learn from it. She'll need to also accept *the others* who have joined her. Some days she is MJ, other days—when MJ needs to be comforted—Alby takes over, though it has been quite some time since he has surfaced. When MJ needs protection, which is most of the time these days, a challenging and forceful figure—Catherine—surfaces. And Alby mentioned there were others inside MJ as well, others who serve different purposes. Others whom I have not yet met."

"You talk about these people as if they are *real people!*"

"Well," Dr. Armstrong softly interrupted. "I am suggesting these are real personalities, separate from MJ's own personality. They cannot exist without MJ, but now neither can MJ exist without them. Their relationships are symbiotic with one another. And this is how it will likely be for the rest of MJ's life."

"I am so confused," Elphorantis proclaimed. "Alby and Catherine were real people. They are dead, killed by Bernard because the two of them were having an affair. Are you suggesting these people came back from the grave and are now possessing MJ?"

Dr. Armstrong stopped short of professionally chuckling, and then considered the action as likely being considered demeaning. He reminded himself that many people, surely the detective included, were not experts in the field of Multiple Personality Disorder.

"Not in the least, detective," he countered. "These personalities exist because of MJ. She created them—created them from the memories that swirled around in her foggy mind. She also created them from the images and thoughts Bernard placed into her head. Therefore, Alby and Catherine—not the physical people who were murdered, but the idea of them—became characters in her own head."

Detective Elphorantis placed his hand on top of his head, rustled his hair a bit, shook his head, and raised his brow. It was obvious to Dr. Armstrong that the detective was having a difficulty understanding the realities of this disorder. At the same time, Dr. Armstrong could see that Elphorantis wanted to truly understand it, with precise, surgeon-like efforts.

"Through the limited time I have spent with MJ since her arrival here," Dr. Armstrong continued, "it has become evident to me that she began creating these personalities after Bernard repeatedly and graphically raped her. According to MJ, often during these times, before she invented Alby, MJ would begin to escape to some type of foggy state. Some sort of migraine usually accompanied this after effect."

"And why was the new Alby gay? Why is Catherine some sort of hag?"

"Alby *IS* gay," Dr. Armstrong corrected. "Catherine *IS* a haggish character you must understand."

"I beg your pardon?" Elphorantis responded.

"Not *was*, detective," Dr. Armstrong clarified. "These personalities exist. They are, not were."

"Well, why are they the way they are?"

"Quite simply because MJ made them that way," Dr. Armstrong continued. "There are various justifications that I could make, but won't, that are the cause for MJ's decisions. However, I would assume that Bernard, in his sick way, could not admit to himself that his younger, frailer, prettier, very heterosexual brother stole his wife from him. I would further assume that as a result, Bernard described his brother to MJ—and anyone else—as gay, someone who wouldn't and couldn't possibly be interested in women. In a way, though there is nothing wrong with being gay, it was Bernard's strange way of punishing his brother."

"And, let me see if I have this right," Elphorantis proudly stated, "MJ therefore imagined the character of Alby as being gay?"

"Quite possibly, detective," Dr. Armstrong replied. He could see that Elphorantis was pleased with himself, and to suggest approval of his realization, Armstrong smiled and provided a "good work, detective."

Elphorantis smiled.

"We are Pacifica's finest," the detective replied jokingly.

"I certainly see that," Dr. Armstrong announced. "Have you been able to determine why MJ envisioned Alby to be a botanist?"

Elphorantis paused, readying himself to respond, but said nothing in the end.

"She was yearning to be free, yearning to be part of the world outside her room. She was desperately trying to survive in her new reality by imagining the nature that was just on the other side of her window, but still too far from her grasp."

"This is amazing," Elphorantis interposed.

"Further," Dr. Armstrong resumed, "I would assume I will discover that Bernard did not have the nicest things to say about Catherine, and MJ was likely perceptive of the way he framed her . . ."

". . . Hence, the hag," Elphorantis interrupted.

"Once again, likely, though I am sure the haggish appearance is a combination of MJ's need to create a frightening character who could protect her at a moment's notice. I mean, who would mess with someone that looked like a ghost or witch, correct?"

Elphorantis continued to stare in amazement, waiting for further information.

"And when Alby, MJ's comforter, was unable to protect MJ the way that she required, he sought out Catherine, the protector, who in addition to the positive reinforcement Alby gave, forced MJ to move and escape."

"This is sick," Elphorantis said quite emphatically.

"Well, detective, I would not necessarily suggest you are wrong. Officially, MJ is sick and she needs treatments. However, she is not psychotic, and she is dealing with the situation actually in the best way for her to cope with it. Some might actually interpret this to be somewhat beautiful."

"Maybe for you fancy city liberals," Elphorantis responded. "Not for me."

Dr. Armstrong motioned toward MJ, who now was lying in bed, peacefully sleeping by a drug-induced therapy-like temporary coma. The image was different than before. Just some short time ago, MJ was living a pure hell from which she was burning, unable to escape. She was now safe, protected by modern medicine, a police force who came to her aid, and professionals who cared for her success.

"It is quite interesting, detective," Dr. Armstrong mentioned. "The scene here is tranquil, isn't it? And yet, being held in your cells at the station just ten-to-fifteen minutes south of here is a man, Bernard, who is experiencing something quite different, I am sure."

Elphorantis said nothing. He thought it better to not get himself, or the legal process in which he proposed he would be fruitful, in any sort of trouble. He had full intentions to ensure that justice was served coldly to Bernard in every way that he deserved, and any further comment he made might put that plan in danger.

"I have another interesting fact to share," Dr. Armstrong suggested. "Bernard met Alby, not the real brother, but the new personality."

"I'm not following you," Elphorantis replied.

"Apparently Bernard had conversations with Alby while MJ was 'hibernating' of sorts. I imagine that his first meeting with Alby was quite unbelievable for him."

"MJ shared this with you?" Elphorantis asked.

Dr. Armstrong nodded in confirmation, but he quickly corrected himself by reinforcing it was indeed Alby who shared the information with him.

"My understanding," Armstrong provided, "Bernard found the situation to be quite shocking at first. I assume that Bernard believed MJ was either playing a joke on him, or tantalizing him in some type of way."

"When did Bernard first, I guess you could say, 'meet' Alby?" Elphorantis asked.

Dr. Armstrong took a moment to gather his thoughts. So much had happened in such a little amount of time.

"I'm not quite sure, detective," he responded. "But you see, the two of our professions are more similar than you probably expect. You investigate the realities of a situation in order to determine the outcome. I somewhat do the reverse. I view the realistic outcomes of an event in order to determine the realities. I will, without any doubt, be identifying the timeline of events that led to the situations we have and will continue to discuss them for what I am sure is to be a long haul."

"Let's just be sure not to take too long with this," Elphorantis was happy to reply. "Similar as we may be or not, I want to get this to trial as correctly and as quickly as possible."

"I believe," Armstrong continued, "No, I am actually quite certain that Bernard started to realize that he was witnessing his conditioning in successful action. I would also assume that he would, at times, become upset if he believed any sign of courage from MJ was a result of Alby or any of the other characters in her head."

Elphorantis continued to stare into space, trying to make sense of the information being served to him. It was a difficult science to follow, especially for someone who spent much of his career avoiding the hoopla of *what-ifs*.

"Let's not forget," Armstrong continued. "Bernard has some experience in the management of the psychosis. His research in neurodegenerative diseases, if I am correct about that, was sometimes interrupted with off-kilter recommendation involving strange plans for research. That is, at least, what was suggested by some of his work colleagues, correct?"

"Yes," Elphorantis responded. "We interviewed a woman named Shoshanna. She suggested just that very thing actually. We're expecting to interview a few more people he worked with, as soon as we can bring them into the station."

"I would therefore presuppose that Bernard used this new reality to his advantage. It was his way to ensure additional control over this woman he abducted. She was now speaking with a new *friend* and would likely make no attempt to escape."

Dr. Armstrong gathered additional thoughts and tried to arrange them in a fashion that was surely organized in a way that would assist the detective with what he needed to move the issue forward. He was certainly glad that he was not a detective. He'd much rather manage the side effects of medical sickness, not the legalities of what they caused.

"Alby told me an interesting part of the story a bit ago," Armstrong continued. "He had informed me that at one moment, he and MJ were having a discussion."

"Now, how the hell does something like that happen?" Elphorantis interrupted.

"You mean," Armstrong responded, "How does one carry on a conversation with oneself?"

"Exactly."

"Well, with all due respect, detective," the doctor continued, "I don't believe I need to detail the fact that many people, either with a Multiple Personalities Disorder or without it, often have conversations with themselves."

"Fair assessment, Doctor. Please continue."

"Actually, it is more likely that one personality will take charge of the vessel, if you will," Armstrong reassured the detective.

"Again, I'm not quite sure I am following you."

"Often if one of my patient's multiple personalities decides to 'take over' for whatever the specific reason might be, typically the personality expects to move the host aside. The host, my patient, will then lie dormant until the personality is willing and ready to give up the control of that situation. But it has happened, and more often than I had expected in the past, that personalities can confer with their host, and vice versa as well."

"I appreciate the explanation," Elphorantis assured. "This is not the typical situation I have had to encounter, at least not at the Pacifica Police Department."

"I understand," Armstrong responded. "May I proceed?"

"Please do."

"I don't need you to speak for me to Bernard!" the doctor stated. "That is what MJ said to Alby in one of their heated moments. She didn't want Alby to take over, I am assuming. She continued by telling Alby, *'I can handle having a conversation with him. I'm a big, girl.'* Quite fascinating that she was already beginning to project authority as host. And it is likely that she still was unaware that Alby was not a physical person yet."

CHAPTER THIRTY-FIVE

In her sleep-induced, temporary coma, MJ again dreamt of walking on the beach. Passing the same flock of seagulls she had once seen before, she felt comforted and free. The waves of water that began to gently wash her feet from the rising tide no longer seemed to cause her any apprehension. If she felt any angst at all, it was that she could not seem to find her friend Alby. With this, though reassured by her surroundings, she felt a deep sense of bereavement and confusion as to why her friend had not been by to see her recently.

MJ stared at the seagulls, feasting on whatever it was that they found on the beach. She noticed how the mother birds seemed to be nestling their young. MJ had an unfathomable appreciation for this. Protection. Protection is what she suddenly felt. There was no fog, no mysterious coolness surrounding her, only sunlight warmly kissing her skin and beckoning to her. MJ took a moment to stew in the temperateness. She closed her eyes and imagined things so clearly.

MJ thought of the time Bernard, almost shamefully and in a demeaning way, suggested that they call Alby to stay with her when she was getting nervous about staying on her own. She had not seen, because at that time she had no desire to, that Bernard was mocking this personality she created. And disgustingly, Bernard was reveling in the fact that his experimentations on her had worked.

Items were beginning to make sense to her in a way that she had never thought they would. She continued to compose her thoughts like the conductor of an orchestra, swaying emotion to the side while bringing out the percussions of reality. She thought back to Bernard telling her how his colleagues, Marcus and the others, would often ask for clarification when he would slip and mention anything about a 'sick wife'. To them, his only wife had already died, and they must have been concerned for their safety—for it must have been true that rumors were eddying around the idea that maybe, quite possibly, Bernard was somehow responsible for the unfortunate mishap of Catherine's demise.

The sun was shining brighter than MJ had witnessed—or felt—in quite a long time. She was fascinated by its intensity and the clarity of the environment. The smells were pleasant. They reminded her of times, before her mother abandoned her, that she would go to the beach with her father. Her father—it had been so long since she thought about him. *Dad*, she softly thought. *Dad, whatever happened to you?* Within her dream, MJ began to delicately cry. She knew it was likely that her father, like her mother, was a junky and unfit to raise a child. But she began to remember that he told her stories about princesses and giants, monsters and goblins, and heroes—heroes that would somehow swoop into a treacherous moment of every story and save the day. Her father also told her stories about kids who very much loved their parents, but were likely some day to be rejected, and when in fact they finally were—due to a storm at sea—they had to rely on themselves to survive. At that moment, MJ knew her father was trying to prepare her for a life on her own.

MJ found it interesting that, when she first met Bernard, she had sought so long to escape the city surroundings to find a place that would be peaceful—an escape of sorts. Was she escaping from the pain of her childhood memories? Was she escaping from the stress of her new life? She was smart, but she was working as a stripper, and the thought disgusted her. She preferred not to be touched, and she desired not to be surrounded by nonsense. Maybe this was why she had been so quickly attracted to Bernard. Maybe, because of his own demons, he sought the same and found it in Pacifica.

MJ thought back to the night when she saved herself from the clutches of the mechanical bed that kept her prisoner. As she swayed too and fro she remembered the pain she endured as the straps first tightened and then finally snapped. All the while she pictured her newfound friend, Catherine, guiding her, providing her courage to take the steps she had thought about once doing when she first woke to find herself being held prisoner in Bernard's house. She also felt pride in the fact that before leaving the house that evening, prior to Bernard's arrival, that she pooled the blood leaking from her damaged finger to craft a note to him on the closet door: *I'm back, I've been watching, I have her.*

Her greatest accomplishment yet was the fact that she grabbed the pole once used for her intravenous drip. She dragged it behind her, treading through the mud outside, both she and the dragged pole leaving footprints up to the area where she finally attacked Bernard when his back was turned to her. It was then that Catherine took over.

Her thoughts shifted toward Alby. MJ realized that Dr. Armstrong must have first been confused when Alby suggested he physically sought out Catherine. She imagined Dr. Armstrong thinking how he would have been able to do so while MJ was strapped to the bed. It must have been reassuring for Dr. Armstrong to finally determine that Alby and Catherine would meet in an outside, unknown, misty and somewhat mysterious place shaped within the boundaries of MJ's psyche. What seemed rather funny to MJ was that Alby despised the fog that she seemed to love. And this now made sense. To her, fog was the start of the takeover of her personalities—a transition time between MJ as host and another personality being forced to act.

The sun continued to beam. The seagulls began to fly from their prey, and the mothers seemed to be encouraging their young to finish their feast and now fly on their own. The vision was an interesting one. It was a representation for life itself. MJ thought how odd it was that we human beings are born to enter an unplanned, incalculable system of events. We are merely raised to depend upon ourselves and hope for the best. Is that for what she had in store? Was she now hoping for the best?

CHAPTER THIRTY-SIX

MJ woke, groggy, feeling feeble and used. She knew where she was, and she also recognized that the people who surrounded her were there to provide security and assistance. Dr. Armstrong was close by, and nurses and technicians swirled about her bed, completing the obvious necessary paperwork any patient would expect, wiping her mouth, asking if she needed assistance, changing her drugs, and such.

There would be no need to call Catherine to help her manage the situation. As MJ had learned over the matter of the past several days, Catherine was a force to be reckoned with. Bluntly, Catherine was a bitch. Not the type of bitch that the ignorant man uses as a way of describing a powerful woman. She was a true bitch through and through, strong and powerful, but probably a bit too insolent for MJ's liking. Even amongst memories of the real Churchill, and the type of activity within which MJ would partake there, Catherine's behavior was still a bit more unrefined when compared to MJ's. And MJ was proud of herself for at least never having lost the manners she gained from her life experience.

Recently, MJ had what seemed like visions maturing into place. These images in her head were apparent recollections from her past, both distant and recent. She preferred not to have revelations from either time period, but she also knew, thanks to Dr. Armstrong's recent help, that in order for her to heal, exploring her thoughts was part of that process.

She remembered the night that Bernard claimed to have heard someone speaking aloud, someone suggesting that she was going to '*come soon*'. Three things at that moment raced through her mind.

1. Catherine had made herself known to him. Without MJ even knowing it, this Catherine personality that lived inside MJ had

2. indeed projected her voice quite strongly so that Bernard knew she'd be after him soon.
3. MJ no longer viewed Bernard as the intelligent man she was fortunate to have in her life. *What a moron he is*, she thought to herself. *What an idiot to not even realize the voice was coming from my body. I was lying right beside him.*
4. And with that said, the final thought that she had was one that disgusted her. The fact that she had all too often laid with him, as lovers do, was making her want to vomit profusely.

MJ was told that it was ok to feel anger toward Bernard. Dr. Armstrong was hopeful that eventually, when both he and MJ agreed it was appropriate to flush some negativity from her system, that MJ's anger would lessen. The energy that accompanied these feelings of hers required an exertion that could clearly detonate the next atomic missile if necessary.

"That is not the type of tension you need built-up inside of you," MJ remembered Dr. Armstrong expressing. She found his next statement more interesting. *"The tension is not good for any of you in there."*

For some reason, she knew this to be true; and Dr. Armstrong's recognition of the other characters that resided inside her was comforting to say the least. She remembered coming to the realization, as she huddled herself into the security of the bedroom closet that squally and tempestuous evening, waiting to escape after getting some type of revenge on Bernard, that she would be hurting for the rest of her life. She also remembered that she grasped the truth of her particular gift. MJ had others surrounding her, inside her, speaking to her. Multiple personalities? Possibly. She preferred to think of them as souls from time past, guardian angels if you would. And they would be with her for the rest of her life.

She may not have been the most educated person on the planet, though she was smart, she read profusely, and she had an incredible command of her language. She may not have been the ballerina she was led to believe she was, but she was talented. And thanks to Bernard, she may have confused her pimp and stripping den mother for her physical family.

She knew full well that these other personalities or beings would never leave her. Now she needed to deal with a new reality. MJ needed to determine whether that was something good or bad for her to endure. At that moment, MJ reminisced about her time with Alby. It has been some time since he had visited her. Dr. Armstrong expressed his gratitude to

MJ for having introduced them. This obviously was evidence that Alby had been around, to the hospital, checking on her and speaking on her behalf. He had yet to make an appearance to MJ though. And she missed him.

Thinking to herself, MJ realized, *I would have never had the courage to escape if Alby hadn't planted the seed in my head.*

It was recently that MJ felt comfortable expressing this to Dr. Armstrong. At no time did the doctor ever demonstrate disappointment or dissatisfaction with MJ's discussions. It was true that he accepted the realities of these 'guardian angels' as a good thing for MJ to endure. He did, however, start to gently encourage MJ to think about her escape a different way.

"MJ," he began softly. "Alby and Catherine were indeed quite instrumental in your making it to the hospital. But, I want you to consider the story of the *Happy House of Saddened Gulls* that Alby told you."

MJ paused for a moment and shifted her body toward the doctor. She was still learning to reuse her muscles. The mobility she actually had, despite her being repeatedly told she was paralyzed, was still foreign to her. She enjoyed the ability to shuffle and shift, but she also considered the strange pain she felt every time she did.

"That story made such an impression on you, didn't it?" Dr. Armstrong asked. Sadly, MJ nodded her head and uttered a gentle, whimpering "yes."

"The story came from somewhere, MJ, deep in the recess of your mind."

It wasn't until this moment that MJ had apprehended the veracity of the situation. Alby was real to her, but not real in the sense of the external, physically present world. There was no Alby to physically collect memories to dictate a story like this. Somehow, yet not quite understood, the story came from something that MJ experienced. Alby, upon voyaging through MJ's mind, stopped at this memoir, something in which he saw as an interesting and a relevant reminder for MJ to consider. What this was exactly was unknown to her. *Maybe,* she thought, *maybe she would never know the reason for it.* And then she remembered. *My father told me this story long ago!*

And then came the question she expected.

"MJ," Dr. Armstrong stated firmly. "Do you know where you learned that story?"

"I'm afraid you are about to tell me."

"Nothing of the sort," he replied. "I don't know where you learned about the story. That is something I am hoping we can discover together. It did however, I believe, become the catalyst for helping you make the connections about those who guide you, and the need for you to find a happier place to escape to."

MJ liked this.

Pleasure.

Could it be that she was actually feeling something pleasant? Something, that is, that was true and unconditioned was now finally making her thankful.

Dr. Armstrong could see that MJ was becoming more confident. He, himself, was growing in conviction as well. His faith was that she would be accepting of her new reality and would find peace with her life.

MJ explored deep into Dr. Armstrong's eyes and placed herself in a position where she philosophized about what he might be discerning. Comparatively she felt ashamed for intruding upon his thoughts. The other part of her knew that she was only making assumptions, and thus the onus she placed on herself was really unnecessary. She pictured, clearly, that Dr. Armstrong had high goals. *This case is exactly what I am going to use for my next publication,* she pictured him thinking. *This is the type of work that will help me project some authority and expertise in the study of multiple personalities. I am going to show the world that, while not curable, this is a disorder with which one can comfortably live. Surviving a harsh abduction has been done in the past. But now, I am going to be able to write the manual for how to actually do it. And MJ is going to help me. I am going to provide assistance to so many clinicians out there who need a guide in dealing with such a trauma.*

Somehow MJ knew Dr. Armstrong was thinking this way.

It was during this time with MJ that Dr. Armstrong realized the power of the *Happy House of Saddened Gulls,* and he knew quite well that deep in the recess of MJ's mind, she created a pathway to explore the meaning of the parable. The mind truly was a commanding and pungent instrument, and Dr. Armstrong honored his profession by making the instrument the most wondrous one to study. *If only,* he thought to himself, *Bernard had used his psychological skills and abilities to provide positive outcomes rather than disgusting experimentations.*

Instantly, upon judging Bernard, Dr. Armstrong was filled with an emotion he often did not feel as a medical doctor and psychiatrist. Guilt.

CHAPTER THIRTY-SEVEN

Alby: Well, you have been extremely patient. I'm sure you are trying to think through the possibilities for the story's conclusion. I think now is the time to tell you the ending of the Happy House of Saddened Gulls, MJ.

MJ remembered the conversation as if it were yesterday. Alby had mentioned that there was something he needed to tell her. His demeanor was much different than she had ever witnessed before. He seemed to be at peace with some clarity, yet sad at the same time. She saw loss in his face, and strangely was feeling the same type of loss as he spoke. She knew the information he was about to share was not something that would be easy to hear. He had just moments ago urgently stated that everything made sense to him. He was describing himself as 'stupid' and 'oblivious', and he continued to express disappointment in the fact that he hadn't seen it all before. MJ was confused and scared. She told him as much. If it were true that the information was going to be difficult to digest, then MJ welcomed hearing the end of the Gull story for now.

"Well," MJ implored. "Get on with it then."

Alby closed his eyes and breathed in the air surrounding them. It was serene, and he knew soon that MJ would be safe when his plan worked.

"Before the story ends, one of the issues I hadn't yet mentioned was the issue with the wishes."

"The wishes?" MJ questioned.

"Yes," Alby replied. "When the children were a bit younger, before living at sea was unfolded within their proverbial deck of cards, each of them secretly wished about the life they had expected for themselves. Quite a mature thing to consider when you are a child."

"I'm not too sure about that," MJ insisted. "Children wish all the time."

"Yes, for princes and money and jewels and fame—for material things, often not too much different than the wish lists of adults. The Gull children wished for their lives to be better in ways that were deeply developed and ripe."

MJ considered the response and was intrigued to learn more.

"Sylvester wished for nothing except to please his parents. He reflected on his life and his interactions with not just family, but town's folk, and he knew that he was not the manly type of boy that his father had expected. *If only,* Sylvester thought, *I could be put into a perilous situation where I could prove my worth.*"

"How sad," MJ responded. "How profoundly sad for a child to think this way."

"Daphnis had a wish that was slightly different," Alby continued. "Instead, he wished that his parents would learn to live on their own, learn to be happy with one another so that he could explore life the way he felt was natural for him to do so. Daphnis felt pressured to remain with his family, always. He knew quite well that the life he was currently living, and expected to live in the near future, was not going to allow him to be on his own."

MJ continued to listen intently. She believed she was starting to see where the wishing journey line was heading, and she felt moved for the children as if they were her own.

"Holly obviously wished for love," Alby continued.

"That's what I assumed," MJ responded.

"Well, don't assume what I mean by wanting the love of her parents or of the boys in her town," Alby interjected. "Holly's wish was more about loving herself. She stared at herself in the mirror one day, partially blinded by the reflecting light of the intruding sun that harshly was bouncing off the glass from her window, and she cried. She cried for an hour or so. And she wished that she could be brave enough to love herself."

"If you are intending to depress me, Alby, you are doing a good job."

It was as if Alby ignored the statement. He continued developing the story as he went, in methodical fashion, approaching the point where he once left off.

"So, as Piper struggled with the voices in her head—one suggesting to end it all overboard, and the other telling her to be brave—she began to head below deck."

"Wait a minute!" MJ screamed aloud. "What about Piper's wish? You forgot to mention what Piper had wished for!"

"Actually, I didn't." Alby gently laughed. "Piper had no wish. She couldn't wish for anything more than what she had already been given."

"I'm totally confused."

"Let me proceed," Alby implored. "I promise you that there is an end."

MJ blinked in approval, and Alby continued.

"As Piper walked below deck, she paused with dedicated thought upon each slow step she took. She deliberated on the details of each of her siblings' wishes. It seemed to her that each of the wishes had indeed been granted. The thought, once fully realized, was a chilling tale of misfortune and despair. For in fact, Sylvester did get his wish. He was placed into peril and reacted terribly when faced with the notion of handling a dangerous situation."

"Well, he simply reacted in a way that was natural to him," MJ retorted. "There is nothing so terrible about that."

"Precisely," Alby responded. "That is the point. He tried to escape his nature, but it came back to him when faced with the means to act."

"I'm still not sure if I get the message you are trying to give me here."

"Let's continue then," Alby replied. "Daphnis also got his wish. His parents went away, as he had hoped."

"Not the way he had intended," MJ interrupted.

"That doesn't matter," Alby laughed. "His wish was for them to depart and they did. And he is now faced with the consequences of that wish, and he is now expected to live the life he had intended for himself."

MJ stared at Alby.

"What?" Alby asked.

"You're an ass hole."

"Hey, don't blame me, dearest," Alby stated. "It's not my story."

"So what then come's of Holly's wish for self-love?"

"She is now alone. She is abandoned by her parents and unable to depend on them or the boys in town. She is faced with the ultimate reality that if she does not love herself soon, she will be left completely alone."

"And Piper?" MJ asked.

"When she reached the bottom step, she spanned the room with her eyes. And she saw nothing," Alby responded.

"What do you mean by *nothing*?"

"There was no one below deck—no Sylvester, no Daphnis, no Holly. There were no extra bunks beyond hers, no belongings or sentimental memories other than her own."

"What happened to everyone?" MJ queried, expecting an immediate response.

"For a brief moment," Alby continued, "Piper thought there was a possibility that her siblings had finally had enough—maybe tempted by the same voices that she struggled with as well. It was her instantaneous expectation that her siblings submitted themselves to the ultimate end—that they jumped overboard and drowned themselves in the sea. But this, as she soon discovered, was not the case whatsoever."

Alby hesitated momentarily to gather his thoughts and compose them correctly in a fashion to present the ending effectively.

"And?" MJ commanded.

"The reason why Piper never had a wish of her own was because Piper was the result of all of the wishes combined."

"What, Piper was not real?" MJ asked.

"On the contrary," Alby retorted. "She was quite real. She was indeed the Gull child. There was only ever one child to begin with."

"What?"

"Sylvester was born and, for whatever reason, was a major disappointment to his stern father and his doting mother. The result of constantly denying him affection led Sylvester to acting in ways that made him misunderstood by the town's folk. They too put him beneath their interests, ridiculed him, and made him feel anxious. While individuals are the only ones who can control how others make them feel, Sylvester was simply a child at that time. He therefore forced himself to change, became more adventurous, more of a loner, more like a rebelling youth."

"Like the way that Daphnis acted," MJ responded.

"Correct. But when he matured a bit, he created a persona that was natural to him, and he began to act on his impulses, like anyone of us would do as we grow. He may have been misunderstood, but to him it was natural to be in love with that town's boy, Duke. And for Duke, whether it was nature or curiosity, it doesn't matter. He replied in kind."

"And the two continued to see each other until they were caught by a stern and disappointing Gull father, I assume!" MJ blurted out.

"Precisely."

"Piper, the *perfect* child that the Gull parents had always expected, was obedient, decisive, responsive, and—to be honest—boring. Is it that the parents were only satisfied once they re-groomed their child to be a more respectful android, void of any natural urges? And then they took their child away from the town—to sea—when nature caught them?"

"You are brilliant, MJ," Alby replied.

MJ smiled. Details of this formula were beginning to make sense in so many ways. She almost felt a connection to the characters, even more so now.

"The one thing I do not understand," MJ began. "—Sylvester became a girl—Piper?"

Alby laughed a bit. "No my dear. The sex of the child does not matter. The story is about the stages of growth, and our urge to please those whom we love—those who are supposed to love us as well. We are born ourselves and are either a gratification or a letdown. We grow in response to this, and sometimes rebel. We then mature and respond to our own love. Ultimately, we are led back to care for those who raised us. If we have not come to terms with ourselves, not become happy with who we are, then we are faced with becoming androids—as you said."

"Very interesting," MJ responded. "Very strange, but very interesting."

"You could also say that each character represented a different stage in the child's life, a different personality if you will, not necessarily a physically different person."

MJ one again smiled. Slowly, more tears began to form in the crevices of her eyes. She desperately tried to blink them away as they flooded her vision quicker than she anticipated. Alby looked at her compassionately. He knew that factors were beginning to manifest themselves for MJ in the ways they had for him some moments earlier.

"I think I know what you are about to tell me," she said.

He replied, "I thought as much."

CHAPTER THIRTY-EIGHT

"It's time to leave us, MJ."

The voice from the doorway was distinctly different. Empathetic was not how MJ would describe it, not in the least. It was, as an alternative reflection, absolute and methodical, disciplined and to the point.

To MJ, the pronouncement was bamboozling. She raised her body only to see a stout and self-assured woman standing, framed within the distant doorway, just as if she was one of Bernard's old hallway portraits. She was dressed in a grey suit, fitted perfectly to the cherubic bulges that protruded from her frame. Her hair, jet-black and sleek, was pulled tightly back, pinned up and swirled into some interestingly arranged bun that was plopped on the surface of her skull. Surely this woman was some sort of socially mandated caregiver. Immediately MJ appreciated the fact that she would be enduring some assistance and purview for a considerable period to time. While she welcomed the help the system was willing to provide, receiving it made her feel somewhat awkward and remorseful.

"Leave?" MJ questioned. "I wasn't yet aware that it was time for me to go?"

"I see. You don't want to leave us?" The woman questioned. "How adorable, my dear! Well the staff certainly enjoyed having you here, but all things come to an end eventually. It is now that time for you, my dear. It is time to check yourself out of the hospital's care. I'm sure there may be a request to visit Dr. Armstrong on a regular basis from this point forward, but it won't be necessary for you to be held under observation here."

"I'm happy to leave, but to be honest, I am a bit scared as well," MJ replied. "It's been some time since I was out in the public, you see, and . . ."

"I know all about your story, dear," the woman harshly interrupted.

MJ knew the woman likely did not mean to be rude, but her forceful behavior of interrupting such a delicate topic was tactless.

"I was simply going to add that Dr. Armstrong had not said anything to me about checking-out. I assumed he would have mentioned it."

"No, dear, that's my job. Typically it is always someone in my position's responsibility to relay such news," the woman retorted. "My name is Clara Millstone. I'll be guiding you through the departure process."

"Departure process?" MJ asked in a completely bewildered fashion.

"Yes, my dear. That is what we call it. We'll review a few items about exiting the hospital, and then we'll discuss your next steps for making the necessary arrangements to live effectively in your society."

"Wait, you mean I am to leave right now?" MJ asked.

"That is correct, once we will have finished our discussion," Ms. Clara Millstone replied.

"Dr. Armstrong, will he come to give me further instructions as well?"

Clara bit her lip. Her patience was clearly wearing thin.

"Dear, Dr. Armstrong does not have his rounds today," Clara responded. "He will be contacting you once you have settled yourself back where you belong. It will be his responsibility to check on you, you understand. It will be my responsibility to ensure you are doing what you need to do. I will be the one providing you with the support that is necessary for you to continue."

"My apologies, Ms. Millstone," MJ responded. "It is just confusing to me. I was recently in a session with Dr. Armstrong, and he hadn't indicated that we were nearing a time for me to depart."

"I am happy to call him for you, dear," Clara interjected. "However I must warn you that he is quite a busy man. Recently he has been insinuating the need to publish some work. I think you may be one of the subjects that he wishes to highlight actually. What fun."

With each passing minute, MJ realized that she did not like Ms. Clara Millstone. She wished Catherine would float back and lecture her about couth and demeanor. MJ truly wondered if Clara knew that MJ had just been through a very traumatic experience—a victim of kidnap, rape, consistent abuse and conditioning, and now dealing with people living inside her head? *Have some sympathy you crud,* MJ thought. Truth told though, if what Clara expressed just then was true, MJ was disturbed. MJ didn't appreciate being the topic of Dr. Armstrong's publication. It was not appropriate, in her mind, to have her life on display for everyone to ridicule and dissect. *Why would Dr. Armstrong think it ok to broadcast details about my horrible experience to the rest of the world? I'll never be able to face anyone again!*

As Clara continued to explain the discharging requirements, MJ couldn't help but continue to disregard her words. Here, Clara was robotically discussing information that MJ obviously believed not to be relevant to her. MJ stared blankly toward Clara, gently sneering as she picture turning the knob of a radio down bit by bit. MJ also took an opportunity to view the scene outside the window, just to Clara's back. There she also continued to stare at the fog forming over the Cole Valley section of the city, directly underneath her hospital window. Seeing it was once again a beautiful experience. The mist swirled in so hurriedly, and it carried with it a smooth and gentle serenity. It engulfed the area like a winter's blanket that yearned to secure her. Its consistency was not like the kind she often witnessed in Pacifica. That was lighter, like cotton. This was flatter, like silk. And while it was magnificent, it became unnerving after some time. Its slender disposition and its serpent-like movement began to make her slowly feel uneasy.

"MJ," Clara's voice interrupted once again. "I may be wrong to assume this, but it seems you have not paid any attention to anything I have just instructed you to do."

To Clara's bewilderment, and quite frankly to MJ's as well, MJ was able to rather poetically recite back the information that Clara had shared just moments ago. It was as if MJ, not fully realizing it, had been listening to Clara all this time, despite her focus on something other than the conversation.

"Why, yes," Clara said in a not so reassuring manner. "Yes, that is correct. That is exactly what I just said. Impressive, my dear. And with that, I would assume you are ready to get dressed then?"

MJ concurred and slowly shifted herself from her bed. For some time, MJ thought, *I have been literally and figuratively chained to a bed for so long. It almost seems inappropriate to stand and walk about. Am I really ready for this? Am I really ready to be discharged and live on my own?*

She was then reminded of her new reality. MJ was indeed not alone, not in the least. Somehow, sometime, somewhere Alby would resurface, and surely so would Catherine at some point. And as much as she preferred to see Alby, should Catherine come first, that would suit MJ just fine. She intended to thank her for saving her life. Catherine too, according to MJ and Dr. Armstrong, was equally responsible for helping her to abscond danger.

As MJ moved toward the drawer that housed her hospital-donated clothing, she glanced back at Ms. Clara Millstone, who stood there in steadfast fashion.

"Excuse me," MJ began, "I am guessing that you are going to give me some privacy?"

Clara, a bit shocked by the speculation, responded, "Oh yes, dear, of course. My apologies. I'll just wait in the hallway. Just call for me when you are finished."

MJ once again nodded, but her smirk demonstrated a taste of continued dissatisfaction for Ms. Millstone. Whereas Dr. Armstrong was considerate, passionate, even caring, Clara Millstone was rude and devoted only to the business of medicine. *Maybe,* she thought to herself, *this is how caseworkers need to behave? It must be difficult to manage the load of patients with such serious issues facing them.*

Dressing in the garb laid before her, MJ did something she hadn't done in a while. She thought of her mother—not the Wendy-mother who was created by Bernard, but her real mother, the one who mentally and then physically abandoned her so long ago. The neglect and utter relinquishment of parental accountability disturbed her even more now. She thought about the Gulls, and the wishes each were eventually granted. She carefully measured the happiness they initially sensed and the eventual sadness that led to the fall of the house. It all seemed to be fueled from an early stimulus—a catalyst that drove the hunger for each of their desires.

Was this something she was experiencing? Did her real mother's carelessness force her to grow too quickly, unintentionally robbing her from her childhood? She was ultimately granted her wish to meet someone—to feel the type of love she had hoped for someday. But she hated Bernard for allowing her to feel that spark of hope and joy, only for it to be shattered by cruelty. She could imagine Alby telling her to focus not on the cruelty, but on the positive aspect of the situation. In reality, he'd surely relay, MJ obtained acceptance and care from her new family—from him, Catherine, and the others. This thought bizarrely comforted her until she remembered Alby was nowhere to be found or felt. She wished he would return, and the pain that resulted from this thought certainly surfaced itself majestically.

"You look troubled, dear," Clara's voice called from the entrance to the room.

MJ quickly turned in a motion that over-stimulated the muscles within her back and neck. This caused her to quickly scream from pain.

"I thought you told me to call for you when I was done?" MJ yelled impatiently. This Clara Millstone was really annoying her.

"You were taking a considerable amount of time, dear. I thought perhaps you needed some assistance. It seems I was correct."

"No, Ms. Millstone . . ."

"Clara," she corrected.

"No, Clara. I'm actually fine, thank you," MJ responded harshly. She didn't mean to be rude, yet Clara's attempt at showing concern for her was a failure at best.

"Is there anyone here with us?"

"Do you see anyone?" MJ snarled.

"The question is, do you, dear?" Clara answered.

"I see," MJ embarrassingly stated, pausing for a brief moment. "You needn't worry about me going crazy on you, Ms. Millstone. You needn't worry about whether or not I am hearing voices in your presence. I am getting this under control, thank you very much. And by the way, I reject the notion of asking me that, Ms. Millstone."

"Clara," she once again corrected.

"Yes, Clara."

"Dear," Clara said carefully. "I obviously know a lot about your case. Whether you want it or not, I am here with you. There is no reason to reject the offer or argue the situation any further. I can see that something is disturbing you. Won't you allow me to help you?"

"You won't understand," MJ answered.

"Not fully, probably not like you understand it," Clara stated in agreement. "But I do understand the scenario you went through, and I'd like to listen and offer help where I am able to do so."

MJ surprisingly appreciated the essence of this response. At least Clara was not pretending to fully comprehend the state in which MJ found herself, and she was transparent in that regard. MJ respected the sincerity in Clara's candor. It was a courage that MJ wished she possessed. And as a result, MJ opened herself to Clara a bit further.

"I was thinking of Alby," MJ stated.

Clara just looked at her, but not judgmentally. It was a stare that demonstrated an effort to understand that which shrouded MJ.

"I was wondering if I would ever see him again."

"You don't feel anything?" Clara questioned.

"Not at all. I do feel some presences surrounding me, even specifically at times I believe Catherine is lurking about in my head, but I do not feel him. And I miss him."

"I'm sure you do dear. Alby is part of your life now. He will be part of your life forever it seems. I'm sure he will, at some point, resurface or attempt to resurface again, though I cannot determine whether or not that is a good thing."

"Dr. Armstrong believes it is good for all of the people in my head to be with me, physically and mentally," MJ responded.

"Can I tell you a secret, dear? Just between us gals?"

Now it was MJ who discovered she was gazing intensely. With her eyes, she motioned for Clara to continue.

"Dr. Armstrong seems to be in this for himself," Clara stated in a convincing manner. "I believe you are the case that will make him rich and famous. I'm just . . . well, my apologies, dear . . . I really . . . I shouldn't continue."

"No, please do!" MJ insisted. "What exactly are you suggesting, Clara?"

Clara walked toward the mirror and took a moment to straighten her clothing and gradually coif her hair before answering.

"I'm just concerned that you may be being used again."

MJ said nothing, but simply stared at herself in the mirror as well.

"And, I think you know this, dear. I think you feel it too."

Still, not one word was uttered from MJ's lips.

"Now," Clara said. "I think you are truly ready for the departure process. As such, mind if I tell you another secret, dear?"

CHAPTER THIRTY-NINE

MJ was already gone by the time Dr. Armstrong entered the room the following morning. Nothing, apart from her absence, seemed to be visually disturbing him. No evidence of struggle. Nothing was overturned. None of the room's contents seemed to be disheveled. He was still gravely concerned for MJ's safety. Equally, Dr. Armstrong was unsettled by the inept service that clearly was responsible for letting a significantly traumatized patient leave without warning him.

"You said that she hasn't been here since late last night?" Dr. Armstrong questioned the nurse who stood silently by his side. A certain tone of irritation trumpeted itself along with the words it rested itself upon.

"That is correct, doctor," the nurse, Jeffrey Thomason, replied.

"And nothing further has been discovered," Dr. Armstrong continued, this time in the direction of Barbara Tolson, the hospital security guard on duty.

"No sir. We have already alerted the San Francisco authorities surrounding the hospital as well as those in Pacifica in case the patient heads back there for some reason.

"I'm not quite sure she'll have an interest in going back that way," Dr. Armstrong replied, to some extent polishing away any indication that the security details were on target for finding her. "Thank you for the update, but where was the security-designate last night when MJ left the premises?"

"Sir, I am not the one who was on duty last night. We're bringing in our security chief to address further questions about this," Barbara Tolson responded. "I don't want to misrepresent the situation. I started duty early this morning and discovered this news as soon as you heard it."

"I can appreciate that," Armstrong interjected. "But someone majorly screwed up here, Officer Tolson. It is not ok that my patient is taken from the hospital by someone without my authority."

"But doctor," Nurse Thomason calmly exclaimed. "Your patient checked herself from the hospital's supervision. She signed the self-release form herself, dated last evening at 11:07 PM Pacific Time. Here is the information."

Thomason motioned toward the paper he held, and handed it to Armstrong in a prompt fashion. The doctor intimidated him somewhat, as Thomason knew that Armstrong was livid about the entire situation. At the same time, Thomason had great respect for this highly complex and patient-focused man of science. Armstrong, in many ways, was Jeffrey Thomason's idol.

Dr. Armstrong eyed the report log up and down, turning it over once, and then back again, analyzing the details of the information provided on its surface.

"I just cannot imagine it," he said to himself, revealing a hint of struggle. "I cannot imagine that MJ would have wanted to leave at this time. She seemed to be progressing adequately with the care we were providing her. This is confusing and alarming to me."

"We will find her, sir," Barbara Tolson said. "Like I said, we're working with some very active authorities."

Dr. Armstrong handed the paper back to the nurse, who took it without hesitation.

"I assume Detective Elphorantis is aware of the situation?" Armstrong directed toward Tolson, still eyeing the paper he handed to Thomason.

"He was first to receive the information, according to the details that were shared with me," Tolson replied.

"Thank you, Officer. Please keep me updated."

Tolson jerked her head into a somewhat forced nod, and exited the room quietly. Dr. Armstrong wasn't quite sure whether or not he actually heard her say "dick" as she left the room, though he didn't care. As far as he was concerned, this security service was a pathetic example of heedlessness and imprudence if he ever saw either in action.

"Doctor," Thomason called. "You had mentioned that MJ would likely not go back to Pacifica?"

"That's correct, Jeffrey. Is there some reason you are asking this?"

"Well, I have spent a considerable amount of time with her, to help manage the medication intake and her nightly care. Forgive me if I am not going to make sense in a moment. I've worked the past 48-hour shift straight without many breaks, especially in light of this issue."

"Please continue," Armstrong requested.

"Some of the nursing staff members, me included, who have been monitoring the Kaplan-Meier survival and prognosis study—in which MJ is part of—have noticed some things about her that would lead me to believe that she might actually try to go back to Pacifica."

"Wait, what survival study?"

"The hospital is undergoing reaccreditation and nursing achievement status, and we need to demonstrate that we've done some measurements on how quickly and effectively patients are reacting to their medications. I am handling the psychiatric and neuroscience portions of the study," Thomason stated with a proud smile.

Armstrong did not react. He impatiently waited for the conversation to continue.

"Anyway," Thomason interjected into the silence, "I have witnessed MJ being a bit more—I shall say *aggressive* lately. I'm concerned that she may be seeking revenge."

"Why am I not aware of this?" Armstrong insisted harshly. "I'm fully aware of the issues that are causing her to struggle with her anger, but why am I not having these types of conversation with you and the rest of the nursing staff more often?"

"Doctor, we highlight all of these observations consistently."

"Not with me!" Armstrong retorted.

"Electronic Health Records, doctor."

"Never mind," Armstrong replied. "What types of revenge are you concerned about? The man who captured her is with the authorities, locked away in a cell until his trial. She knows this. MJ would be unable to do anything to retaliate against him."

"I'm not quite sure that she is aiming to get her revenge on Mr. Matters," Thomason clarified. "And, I'm not quite sure exactly what has made her more aggressive, or where this energy seems to be appearing from."

"What are you referring to?"

"We know we are addressing MJ—in other words, we know we are not speaking to Alby or Catherine, especially when she begins to talk about '*searching for answers*,'" he continued. "But, in a way, it seems as if someone else is speaking for her. The words don't sound natural as she says them."

Armstrong, taking a momentary suspension from being the medical center's mishap micromanager began thinking again like the skilled psychiatrist for which he was truly.

"Look, nurse, Electronic Health Records or not, if you are implying that another personality yet unknown to us had surfaced, that requires a direct conversation with me."

"Yes, doctor. It was merely a thought, not a diagnosis obviously."

Armstrong ran the list aloud once again. "Alby is the comforter—the personality that helps MJ cope with the challenging specifics that have surrounded her for so long. Catherine is the protector—the personality that enters to guard and defend her when MJ, Alby, or any others seem to be too weak. If what you are inferring is true, we better find MJ rather quickly."

"May I ask what you are thinking, Doctor?" Thomason queried. "I know that we must find her immediately to continue her care, but now you seem to have an even more heightened level of concern than you had before."

"If a personality has just presented himself or herself as the aggressive personality—the one who is taking over to enact revenge on someone from MJ's past—I fear this will push MJ over the cliff, metaphorically speaking. I believe once an aggressor appears, it will be very difficult to get the host back."

"MJ, or whomever it was that was speaking for her, was constantly repeating something about seagulls," Thomason interjected. "She was saying something about a shipwreck or a storm—something about finding the children."

Armstrong paused. "She was referring to that story about Happy or Sad Gulls," he said. "I'm not sure which of them were happy and which were sad, honestly. If she is referring back to the story, maybe we are not talking about another personality at all."

At that moment, two others entered the room—Detective Elphorantis and Head Nurse Evelyn Rutgers.

"Doctor," Elphorantis stated firmly as he entered.

"Detective, Evelyn," Armstrong replied.

"Seems as if we have a concerning matter on our hands," Elphorantis resumed.

"To say the least," the Head Nurse validated.

"Do we have any leads yet?" Armstrong asked.

"We're taking precautionary measures. Head Nurse Rutgers provided me with something she found," Elphorantis said, motioning toward Evelyn, guaranteeing her it was sufficient to share the information with Dr. Armstrong.

Evelyn walked toward him, holding a piece of paper, slightly crumpled, with familiar and neatly decipherable penmanship upon it. It was addressed to Dr. Armstrong.

"What goes on at this medical center?" Armstrong insisted. "I am MJ's physician. I should be made aware of these things immediately when discovered."

"It's in the Electronic Health Records, Doctor," the Head Nurse responded.

"Oh, damn the records," Armstrong retorted.

"I provided a copy to our security chief, I also summarized the letter for those '*damn*' electronic records," she responded sarcastically. "But I kept the original and provided it to the detective. I do not think our medical center security is prepared to handle matters like these. It is best left to the professionals."

Dr. Armstrong began to appreciate Head Nurse Evelyn Rutgers. He finally witnessed someone taking authoritative action in a way that he had expected.

"Thank you, Evelyn. Seriously, thank you," he said. He motioned his next question toward the detective. "May I keep this to analyze the content?"

"I'm afraid it is evidence," Elphorantis responded. "But obviously, we bring this to you as we need your assistance in finding MJ. Who is Clara Millstone?"

"Clara Millstone?" Armstrong responded.

"The letter is signed by a Ms. Clara Millstone," Evelyn interposed.

"Thank you, Head Nurse," Elphorantis again said emphatically, and looking toward Dr. Armstrong he continued, "I can take it from here. Are you aware of anyone named Clara Millstone who works at the medical center? Is she a case worker or Social Worker?"

"I don't recognize the name—she could be," Armstrong answered. "I don't interact with everyone on staff. We have quite a large group of interdisciplinary professionals who work with our patients. The letter is clearly MJ's penmanship."

"Forced to write it, perhaps?" Elphorantis asked.

Armstrong looked up at Jeffrey Thomason and gently smiled. "My good man, it seems as if you were correct."

Thomason, with a face that almost flushed by his hero's recognition bestowed upon him, nodded in agreement.

"Detective, unfortunately I do believe she was forced to write this letter."

"Someone kidnapped her? This Clara Millstone—could she have been the person spying on MJ all along? Is there a connection here?"

"I think," Armstrong continued, "MJ was indeed kidnapped, but not by someone physical. I believe she was kidnapped by a personality who is quite effectively taking over her host responsibilities. And if I were a betting man, I don't think she is heading to Pacifica. I believe that my patient—the one who dreamt of drowning, the one who was at one time terrified of water, the one who has relied on her personalities to guide her through difficult choices—I believe this woman is sea bound."

"Sea bound?" Elphorantis questioned with evasiveness.

"Yes, sir," MJ's doctor replied. "It is my only hope that this Clara Millstone will be a voice of reason instead of the voice of illogicality. I hope that the revenge she is planning to seek is not on MJ; and if it is, I further hope that MJ chooses the rational outcome and is not pressed to end everything overboard."

CHAPTER FORTY

To Dr. Marco Armstrong:

We have come to the ultimate decision that MJ 'Matters' will no longer need to be under your care. We appreciate all efforts you have made to help her heal. And we have decided we ~~like~~ liked you. But it was my assumption that you intended to selfishly position MJ as the next subject of your publications. We believe that MJ has been exposed to enough experimentation recently; and when I presented this information to her, MJ agreed. Therefore, at this time we have together determined that we who support her at every waking moment are better equipped to handle MJ's health. We know what progress you have made with her, and we will continue to work toward an outcome that is best for her security.

MJ has certain issues that she must address. These issues will require the most delicate means of strategic insight surrounding matters of reprisal that will only be possible so long as MJ is solely focused on planning for it. For this reason, she cannot be easily distracted by further sessions, pill schedules, and substandard meals. She wants you to know she hates the hospital Jell-O, by the way.

We ask that you not search for her. She is with the Gulls, and much like their chronicle, they traveled far and wide, away from their physical surroundings in order to face their fears. They were, however, unable to be found because, despite all evidence that pointed to the impossibility, the children remained at sea to maintain the search for their parents—either for a happy reunion or to seek a vengeance for forsaking them. (I hope it is for vengeance, to be honest with you.) As such, efforts to search for her, as she wanders with them, would be wasted. ~~We are~~ I am with her. She will be guided well. Head Nurse Rutgers can take the planned daily briefings and MJ's pills, and the Jell-O that was prepared for her, and along with your *publications, shove them up her ass. And if there are any items left over, please feel free to pile them neatly into Bernard's ass as well. Of course, I write this with the utmost respect.*

If I believe it to be necessary, I will contact you. Though, I do not anticipate that you will receive further communication from me, at least at any time soon. With that said, I wish you well.

*Respectfully yours,
Miss Clara Millstone and the Gull Children*

ACKNOWLEDGMENTS

As early as I can remember, I always did certain things the defined my childhood. Along with my siblings, I created *Saturday Morning Games*, to the certain annoyance of my parents, when we woke incredibly early to start a Saturday filled with wild outside activities. Additionally, I often collected my sisters' dolls and stuffed animals, lining them up to be part of my class where I imagined myself as teacher, providing the lessons I thought were better taught by me than my own real teachers (I clearly was fooling myself. My teachers were indeed excellent for the most part.) Last, but not least, I always wrote stories. Some were one page long, others were twenty pages in length. Regardless, I had ideas formed from experiences, crafted in a way that I hoped would not only be interesting but entertaining to those who read them.

I continued to develop this passion in a way that was always personally rewarding to me. With that said though, I was beginning to think that my passion was one I'd only share with family and friends, but probably never through a publication for the general masses. Instead, I was quite satisfied with quenching my other thirsts—building and maintaining a good career in learning leadership, medical education, biostatistics and epidemiology.

Then, over the last couple years prior to the completion of this novel, I met MJ Matters, Bernard Matters, Alby Matters, and those vexatious Gull children, or maybe they met me. At least the idea of them formed over the course of time. With this, I knew it was ripe for me to again explore the opportunity writing a work of fiction that would make me proud. I encouraged myself to think positively about this novel's final outcomes, and I envisioned the possibilities. I believed if I could visualize its merit I might achieve a successful result. This is advice I have gained by having had successful interactions with various personal stakeholders over the past years, most specifically due to those teammates of mine with whom I currently work. I also applaud and thank those colleagues in the Continuing Medical Education industry who have often encouraged me to engage with them in considerable dialogue which ultimately provide me with the boundless ends to creativity.

Therefore, I acknowledge many for the completion of this work. They know who they are, and I am eternally grateful for the impact they have made on my life. Specifically though, I must thank my parents, Joseph and Bernadette. My father—an author and psychologist, and my mother—everything else—inspire me more than I give them the credit. I also thank my sister, Jacqueline Ruggiero. Her skillful art as an actor, playwright, novelist, mother, and caring sister was a major source of editorial inspiration and help in crafting this story in the most appropriate way. Further, I would like to thank some of my test readers: Yonaira Rodriguez, Anthony Lupian, Daniel Sullivan, and Steve Herrick, friends and colleagues who reacted honestly and openly. I also abundantly value the support that Nancy Paynter, Karen Thomas, and Janet Moga, friends and colleagues, has always provided to me whenever I wished to act on any idea I believed was innovative.

I thank my siblings, the Ruggiero Children, their partners, and my in-laws, the Gilmores and their partners.

Last but not least, I'm honored to thank my own partner, Ralph Gilmore. It is because of him that I strive to be better than what I am. He is, in every way, my balance and motivation. And, to my satisfaction and fortune, he is real—not just another one of MJ's personalities. Thank goodness.

ABOUT THE AUTHOR

John Ruggiero, a recognized leader in instruction and learning, has led educational design and outcomes assessment within multiple types of organizations. Over the past fifteen years, John has invested work in educational leadership, having first served as an administrator at a college preparatory, building post-educational and continuing educational dialogue within the community through a social *Community-as-Laboratory* approach. Since that time, John has merged his background in educational leadership with his other expertise in epidemiology and biostatistical research by specifically focusing on medical education and its impact on clinician behaviors and overall improved patient care.

Years ago, John's mother and father were both diagnosed with different forms of cancer. In order to stay positive and encouraged, he and his family members did everything possible to make life worth living by vacationing, gathering, and even often creating and telling stories to one another. Years progressed, and beyond the misfortunes of cancers, and after watching several members of his family suffer from dementia and Alzheimer's disease, two years ago he joined a fiction-based reading/writing association to stay grounded, positive, and to exercise his creativity. Doing so reminded him of his early passion for writing fiction. Upon completing a shorter version of *Isolated Matters* as an assignment from this group, John was encouraged to seek every possible avenue to get this story published. He is energized by the possibility of hopefully having others enjoy his completed efforts.

John earned a Bachelor of Arts in Social Research & Statistics from The Catholic University of America in Washington, DC, and a Master of Public Administration in Pubic Health, Biostatistics & Epidemiological

Research, and a Doctorate in Philosophy in Educational Leadership from Arizona State University and Madison University.

Currently, John and his partner share their time on two coasts. They live a considerable amount of the year in the San Francisco Bay Area. Additionally, they spend a portion of their time traveling back to the Philadelphia metropolitan area—their original hometown—to be with extended family.

John will be providing a considerable portion of the proceeds from this and future works to charitable healthcare organizations focused on furthering cancer and mental research, something for which he feels is not only his duty, but also his pleasure to do so. He asks all those who consider purchasing this or future stories to help him with this cause.

Edwards Brothers Malloy
Thorofare, NJ USA
February 25, 2014